Apricity

A NOVEL

MELODY KELLY

APRICITY-

> *the warmth of the sun in winter (Oxford English Dictionary)*

This book is dedicated to my mom, a true book worm, who inspired my love of stories, especially love stories.

CHAPTER 1

CORA

"Make it stop," Cora Lane whispered into her dark bedroom as she heard an engine revving loudly outside. "Too early."

Wrapping her pillow around her ears, she rolled over away from the sound, sleep tugging her back under. She roused again as Atticus rushed out of the room, barking madly.

"It's okay, baby. I'm coming," she said, as she stumbled from the bed, her plaid flannel pajamas twisted, her hair a wild mess around her face, wiping sleep from her eyes.

Atticus was in full protection mode now, growling and barking sharply at the window as Cora entered the living room.

"Come on, buddy. It's okay. I'm sure it's okay," she said, stopping at the window, stroking her anxious pup.

Squinting hard out the upstairs window down to her snow-covered front yard, she saw what had caused the ruckus. Someone was plowing her long, winding gravel driveway, the sound of the plow and the occasional accidental spray of rocks making quite a bit of noise in the quiet of predawn.

There were only two other houses on this street. One was at the bottom of the road near the highway, and she'd only met that family once. So, they didn't seem likely as her current good Samaritans. The only other house was the long abandoned one at the top of the road that was recently bought by a developer, an unlikely helper in this situation.

So, who was doing the good deed? She had lived in the house for a decade, and not once in that time had anyone else ever plowed her driveway except Jeff, and with a pang in her heart, she knew it wasn't him, wouldn't ever be him again.

Heading downstairs, she grabbed her winter coat not bothering to zip it, shoved her feet into her snow boots, and opened the front door.

"Stay," she said to Atticus as he whined at the door. "I'll be right back."

The German Shepherd whined again.

"I don't think anyone who plows our driveway is looking to hurt me. I'll be fine."

She stepped outside and rushed down the path, eager to get to the stranger and the plow. But the mystery person was driving away. This made her reckless, and she moved faster, heedless of the weather. Suddenly, she felt the slick of an ice patch under her boot and slipped, falling hard into the fresh snow. Luckily, she didn't hit her head. The snow was a cushion, but it hurt just the same. Taking a quick inventory of her body and determining it was safe to stand, she tried to get up.

"Stop. Don't move," a voice said.

Cora stilled and blinked up at the stranger. There in the falling snow, she saw a huge hulk of a man, dressed in jeans and a heavy coat, a toboggan on his head, snow covering his clothes. He looked big and stern, and from her position on the ground, just a little bit scary. She tried again to stand.

"I said don't move. You might be injured."

The stranger dropped to his knees beside her, and she tried to scoot away from him.

"I won't hurt you. I promise," he said, but there was kindness in his voice this time, as if he'd just now realized she might be afraid.

"Who are you?" Cora asked, voice strong even as she began to feel a sharp pain in her back.

"I'm your new neighbor, Cole Houston. I bought the old place up the road."

"I'm Cora Lane," she replied, and this time the pain made her wince.

"Okay, enough chit chat. I saw that face. You're cold and hurting. We need to check you out and get you out of this weather. Will you let me help you?"

Cora nodded. Cole pulled off his gloves and lifted his big hand. With a gentleness that surprised her, he slid his hand over her head, checking for cuts, bumps, or tender spots.

"I didn't hit my head."

"Just checking," he replied. "What made you wince then?"

"My back. I landed flat on my back, and I think I may have bruised it."

Cora had managed to rise up to her elbows while trying to get up, and now she felt Cole rub his hand gently down her back. She flinched as he reached the middle.

"Right there," she told him.

"Can you wiggle your toes and move your legs?"

"Yes."

"Okay, let's try to get you standing," he said as he stood up and held out his hands to her.

She reached up slowly and put her hands in his. It was like sliding cold fingers into a warm glove, the heat and comfort an immediate relief. She heard Cole let out a short huff of breath.

"I'm sorry. My hands are cold," Cora said as he lifted her out of the snow.

"It's fine."

When Cora was fully standing, he brushed the snow from her.

"What were you thinking, rushing out here in your pajamas, no gloves, no hat, and your coat not zipped?" he asked with a hint of anger and a whole lot of judgment.

"Excuse me. I woke up to noise in my driveway, my dog barking up a storm, and you want to know why I rushed out?" Cora replied sharply. "I was keeping an eye on my own property. I can make it from here. Thank you for your help, Mr. Houston, but I can plow my own driveway."

"Dammit," he muttered as if scolding himself. "I didn't mean to offend you. I was just," Cole replied, but before he could finish Cora put her hand up.

"Goodbye Mr. Houston," she said firmly.

"Wait, let me at least help you to the door," he said, rushing to take her elbow as she turned to walk back to the house.

Cora shrugged him off, feeling pain shoot up her spine, and walked straight to her door and into the house without looking back. She locked the door behind her and sat down on the stairs. Atticus came immediately to her side, nuzzling her hands and licking her face. Head in her hands, Cora started crying. She was embarrassed, cold, wet, and in pain. It was only dawn, and already the day was off to quite a start.

Much later, after a hot shower and a couple of pain relief tablets, her back felt better. She was moving slower than normal, but she managed to walk down to the barn to look after her small brood of chickens, goats, and one cantankerous donkey. Cora felt a bit bad about the altercation with Cole Houston. He'd only been trying to help, even if his manner was rude. And she, who taught her second graders every day to be kind helpers, should have at least said a more sincere *thank you.*

"Oh, Atty, I think I'm going to have to talk to Mr. Houston."

She said this as she walked around the kitchen, collecting her coffee and her lunch bag. She then moved to the entryway to make sure her school bag was ready. Grabbing Atty's therapy dog harness and leash, she made quick work of getting him ready for his day at school as well. Snow rarely cancelled school in the Hudson Valley. They just moved it over and went about their business.

Once outside, Cora saw immediately that her new neighbor had also cleared off her car and left her windshield wipers standing straight up to keep from being buried under any more snow. She'd missed those details in the predawn gloom. A thank you was definitely in order and maybe some cookies to sweeten the words.

She got the car heating up while Atty took a potty break. Hearing a sharp alert bark, she looked up to find Cole Houston in a large black truck driving up her perfectly clear driveway. She called Atticus to her side and walked toward the truck, leash in hand, but Cole was already walking toward her.

"What are you doing up and about? You should be resting your back," he said with a frown.

"It's fine. Nothing a little Tylenol won't fix. Besides, I've got to get to school."

Though his tone and frown didn't sit well with her, she pasted a friendly smile on her face and held out her hand. He just stared at it.

"I think we need to start over. Thank you very much for your help this morning. You were clearly just being a good neighbor. I'm Cora Lane, and it's nice to meet you."

Slowly, Cole took her hand in his, and she felt the same warmth radiate through her that she'd felt earlier this morning. Her brain fritzed a little at the contact. For the first time, her surly new neighbor smiled.

"Cole Houston," he said with a nod of his head. "And it's a pleasure to meet you as well. I'm sorry I scared you this morning. Let's be real. You're hurt because of me, because I caught you off guard."

For a few seconds they just stared at one another. He was gruff, she thought, but goodness, he was handsome. She was thankful when Cole broke the silence.

"Who do we have here?" he asked, kneeling down. "I've never known a dog to sit so still when meeting someone new. I heard him barking at me this morning. Didn't think he saw me as a friend."

Atticus stood completely still as Cole stroked his head and back.

Cora laughed and said, "This morning he was working the guard dog shift. Right now, he has his therapy harness on, and he's all business. The minute I put it on him, he becomes a gentle giant ready to make some kiddos feel good. He won't break unless I give him the signal."

"He's a good dog," Cole said, standing back up.

"He's my best friend," Cora replied simply. "Well, I really need to get to school. Thanks again."

"You're sure your back is okay? It has to be bruised."

"I'm fine. Have a good day, Mr. Houston."

She turned back to her car. She couldn't stand around and stare at this man all day.

"It's Cole," he called, just as she reached her car. "Call me Cole. You have a good day too."

In the car, she settled herself and Atty, her heart beating fast and her thoughts a jumble.

CHAPTER 2

COLE

"Well, that went well," Cole murmured to himself as he pulled out of her driveway and headed to the main road below.

He should have known a single woman in an isolated place would be suspicious of a stranger in her driveway, no matter what helpful chore he was doing. He'd just been hell-bent on helping her, and he didn't really know why. Months ago when he first drove up the road to see the property he now owned, he noticed her house. On other visits, he caught a glimpse of her or her dog but never anyone else. This morning while clearing his own driveway, he saw hers still blanketed in white, her car almost invisible. His response had been automatic.

He was just being a good neighbor. Most people in town still expected him to clear all the land he'd bought, knock down the grand old house, and put up a fast row of fancy homes. That had, in fact, been his original plan but not anymore. Now he was staying, so clearing his neighbor's snow simply seemed like a nice way to make a good impression.

He hadn't counted on scaring her, causing her to fall, or offending her by trying to boss her around. And more than anything, he hadn't expected his reaction to her. He felt something when he looked at her, something unfamiliar and unsettling. She was a beautiful woman for sure, but it wasn't mere attraction that made his heart stutter in his chest.

There was a connection there, some spark between them, that only grew when he felt her hand in his as he helped her off the ground. Feeling completely off kilter with the whole situation, he'd been harsh with her, bossy and rude. Cole wished now he'd stuck to plowing his own driveway.

He needed to get on with his day. He'd arrived yesterday morning, signed the closing paperwork, and gotten the keys. Though he'd been in town several times over the last few months, this was his first morning as a resident. First on his schedule was finding another place to stay. One night in his huge fixer upper, and he needed it to be the last. He might be tough, but even he needed a working furnace, some appliances, and more than an air mattress. He was cold, and his back hurt.

Cole never intended to keep the house. He was a builder and a developer. He bought land, and he built houses. But lately, he'd been bored, uninspired. It felt like he was living the same day over and over again. A rough start in life had created a longing for control and routine that he'd successfully filled. Yet, no matter how many shiny, new houses he built, Cole knew he would never be able to make up for the home his younger self had craved.

When Gavin called with the opportunity to develop some land in New York, Cole jumped at the chance. Diving head first into a new and very different kind of project seemed like the perfect way to shake off the boredom he was feeling. From the moment he set foot on the land and saw the house, he'd known he was in trouble. It was a beautiful piece of property, the landscape so different from what he was used to, the peace it afforded intoxicating. It sparked an excitement in him he hadn't felt in a long time, maybe ever, and it had nothing to do with changing it.

For a while, Cole stuck to the original plan, talking to Gavin about the development of five large homes, clearing acres of forest, and rerouting a nearby stream that was important to the town for both ecological and historical reasons. But the more they talked, the less interested Cole was in that plan. The land and the house that stood on it called to him in ways he didn't understand. In a rare, impulsive moment, he called off the project and decided to restore the house himself. He wasn't sure he would stay, but he knew he couldn't change the unspoiled beauty of what he'd found there.

Now he was living in a crumbling, old relic that felt like an icebox and looked like a demolition site. He didn't know what was happening to him, but he didn't seem to be able to stop it. He'd traded a comfortable, orderly life for this, and he wasn't sure it was a good idea. But for the first time in a long while, he certainly wasn't bored.

So, first breakfast, and then a new place to stay while he brought the house back to life. Cole made his way to the quaint main street of the small Hudson Valley town of Longview. He'd driven through town a few times over the last few months, usually on his way to a town hall meeting, but never really paid attention. Now that he planned to stay, at least as long as it took to restore the house, that would have to change.

He stopped at the first restaurant he found. It was a small café tucked in between a barbershop and an old-fashioned drugstore. Normally, he was a drive-through breakfast kind of guy, not one to take the time to sit at a table and savor the meal. He liked an Egg McMuffin and a hashbrown eaten while driving and washed down with the hottest black coffee he could find.

Today, he was going to give On the House his business because he was hungry, and it was the first thing he found. Also, he actually needed to engage in conversation if he was going to find a good local place to stay that wasn't a chain hotel twenty miles away. He was looking for some recommendations for a crew to help him get started on his house as well.

He cringed as he approached the bustling little café. Here were two things he didn't enjoy, people and cutesy, trendy places that used words like artisanal and farm-to-table to describe the same crap he could get somewhere else cheaper. It was just a breakfast sandwich. He didn't need to know the biography of the damn chicken to enjoy the eggs. He stopped at the door and steeled himself for the sensory onslaught he knew was coming and then stepped inside.

To his surprise, it wasn't that bad. Sure, there were handcrafted lattes listed on the chalkboard menu above the counter, and he was pretty sure he heard a young woman ask for local honey in her smoothie, but the overall feeling was comfortable. The aroma was intoxicating, that heavenly scent of pancakes, eggs, and bacon all cooking on the same sizzling griddle. Cole loved no other meal with the passion he saved for breakfast, and he was happy to stay just for the smell of the place.

He waited at the counter to place his order, a sausage, egg, and cheese breakfast sandwich on an everything bagel with a large black coffee and a warm cinnamon roll to top it all off. With his coffee in hand, he found a small table at the back and settled in to wait on his food. No one looked at him or seemed to pay him a bit of attention. This was New York, not Texas where he was born and still called home. People up here minded their business and let you mind yours.

He knew some of them must recognize him. More than a few locals had attended the town meetings when his proposed development of the old Westfield estate and grounds, some thirty plus acres of land situated at the foot of Black Stone Mountain, had been up for discussion. It was prime property and somewhat renowned in these parts. Lots of people were curious.

Some were just nosy, but quite a few had significant questions. Issues of conservation, ecological ethics, and water quality were all topics that came up often. Cole understood their concerns and addressed each one of them, but inside he couldn't imagine actually doing the project he planned. It had taken time to decide what he actually wanted to do instead.

It was on one of his visits that he'd first seen Cora. She was just a wisp of a woman but strong as an ox, digging a sizeable hole in which she was about to plant a huge tree that sat wrapped in burlap nearby. She was dressed in a tank top and running shorts with a baseball cap on her head. All he could see was long tan legs, a ponytail sticking out the back of the cap, and toned arms slicing through the rocky ground with ease.

It was an attractive image, but there was something else. Cole didn't stop or even slow down. He didn't want to alarm her. Yet, he'd never wanted to stop and stare in his life like he wanted to then. There was a peace, an air of competence and capability that hung around her.

He wanted to watch her like one would look at a painting in a museum, but a huge, intimidating German Shepherd was jogging toward the edge of her yard, letting out short warning barks at Cole. He saw her raise her head and call off the dog. She looked at his truck for a moment and then went back to her work. Cole continued driving.

"Here you go," he heard a voice say, breaking him out of his thoughts. A red-headed woman with a nametag that read *Marge* put his plate down in front of him. "I'll get you some more coffee. You need anything else?" she asked, smacking her gum, her hands on her hips.

"Thank you, and yes, I actually do. I'm new in town, and I'm looking for a local place to stay long-term while I fix up my house. Any suggestions?"

Cole knew you could Google any and everything, but he still trusted the word of locals over the information on his phone any day.

Marge laughed and said, "I remember you. You bought the old Westfield place. Weren't you going to bulldoze it to the ground and build McMansions?"

"That's me, and yes, I did plan that, but I changed my mind. I'm staying. I'm Cole Houston," he said with a smile.

He might not like most people, but he did know how to be cordial when necessary. He did, after all, run a successful business. He knew how to act.

"Nice to meet you, Cole. You had a lot of people all fired up about vernal pools and contaminated water. I enjoyed those meetings. Good times," she said happily.

"That's your idea of a good time? I think they wanted to chase me out of town with torches and pitchforks."

"Nah, they were just protecting their own. But now that you're staying and fixing it up, you'll probably become Longview's golden boy."

"Good to know," he replied.

"As for a place to stay, you've no doubt realized that hotels are thin on the ground here. There are a couple, but they're miles away. If you want to be close by, your best bet is your new neighbor, Cora. You've met Cora, right?" she asked.

"Yes, I've met her. How can she help me?"

"Well, she has the only Airbnb around, and I don't think she rents it out very often this time of year. It would be perfect for you, almost like being right on site as you work on your place. But she's at school by now. You should check with her this afternoon."

Cole didn't quite know how to process all the information Marge had just given him.

"She lets people stay in her house?" he asked, clearly appalled. That wasn't safe.

"Oh no, it's the bungalow right beside her house. I don't know if you can really see it from the road because there's a fence between the two houses. It has its own driveway and everything."

He had to admit he noticed very little except Cora when he saw her. He hadn't seen the bungalow, but he had noticed an extra driveway up the road from Cora's that seemed to go behind her house. Now he realized it was the driveway for the Airbnb.

"I'll stop by there this afternoon. Thank you very much," he said.

"You're welcome. Let me know if you need anything else."

With that, Marge moved on to check on her other tables, and he settled in to eat. The food was delicious, but nothing could distract him from the fact that he now needed to visit Cora and ask if he could rent the bungalow.

After breakfast, he took a walk down Main Street. He

stopped in a few businesses he thought might be useful in his renovation, introduced himself to a few people, and popped into the local florist to buy Cora a pot of early-blooming daffodils to take with him when he went by there this afternoon. Then he went back to his house to start clearing out decades of junk left behind.

The afternoon passed swiftly as he sorted through box after box of old stuff. In what was the formal dining room, he created a staging area with piles for donation, stuff to toss, and a few things he thought had some significance to resell. He arranged for a dumpster to be delivered as well as someone to come and take a look at the furnace.

Chances were high he needed a whole new system, and he needed to get started on that right away. Always, he kept track of the time, figuring she would be home in the late afternoon. He could see Cora's driveway from his house, and he gave her plenty of time to get settled before he drove down the hill to talk to her.

Cole found himself a bit embarrassed as he knocked on the door of her stone cottage, holding the little pot of daffodils in front of him. Stepping back from the door, he took notice of the smoke wafting from the chimney, the warm glow of lights in the winter afternoon. It was an inviting place for sure. He heard a bark from Atticus, and then Cora opened the door.

"Hi Cole," she said. "What brings you by?"

She was wearing pink sweatpants and a white t-shirt with those furry boots women wore. Her hair was piled on top of her head in a mess, a dishtowel slung over her shoulder, and a wooden spoon in her hand. If Atticus hadn't come barreling down the stairs to the door, he might have stared at her a little too long. She was lovely.

Just as the huge dog made a move to jump on Cole, Cora let out a sharp "Sit," and to his surprise, the hulking beast changed modes instantly, sitting obediently at her feet. "Good boy," she said as if it was nothing.

"I was asking around town about a place to stay, and well, you kept coming up. I didn't even realize there was another house here." Remembering the flowerpot in his hand, he added, "Oh and I brought you these. Just to say again how sorry I am that you fell this morning."

She laughed and took the flowers.

"That's very kind of you, and I don't know any girl who would turn down a daffodil in January. Thank you very much. As for the house, yes, it's tucked away down the hill, and luckily, it's available for a few weeks. To be honest, I don't usually have a lot of guests in January. Is it too cold and bare for you up at Westfield?"

She was friendlier and more relaxed than she'd been this morning. Clearly, she'd moved beyond their awkward meeting.

"That's about right. I thought I could tough it out, but that's not going to work. I seriously underestimated how cold it would get up there and how drafty."

"Come in. I need to stir my soup and grab my coat," she said.

Cole stepped in and was instantly enveloped in the warmth of her cozy home. There was a fire roaring in the stone fireplace that dominated the opposite end of the room. The news played on the TV in a corner cabinet but muted. He heard her say, "Atticus, bed." The dog wandered over to a plush dog bed by the fire. Cora was in the little kitchen around the corner, stirring a pot on the stove. The smell made his mouth water.

"I've made some chicken noodle soup if you want to stay for dinner after we look at the bungalow," she said easily.

He was shocked that she felt safe asking him into her house, let alone for dinner, but his answer was an unqualified yes.

"That would be great. Thank you."

In minutes, she was bundled in her coat as they headed out. She led him to a gate in the fence that ran down the side of her house, a fence he'd noticed from the road but not seen beyond. As they stepped through, he realized that a whole little world existed beyond it. Immediately, there was a bungalow. It was small but very well kept. They walked a pathway that led to the front door. She unlocked the door, stepped inside, and flipped on some lights.

"Well, here it is. It's small but has everything you might need; kitchen, bedroom, living area, washer and dryer, bathroom. I offer meals delivered for an extra fee. I can make you breakfast and dinner and deliver it most days."

"Wow, it's perfect. I'll be up and out early every morning, so I won't be in the way, but here's the thing. I need it for a while, at least until I get my house warmer and a few things fixed. Is it available for at least the next month?" he asked without even touring the entire space.

"Actually, I don't have my first reservation of the year for another six weeks. So, I can guarantee it until then. Will that work?"

"Definitely. Thank you so much."

Relieved that it was settled, Cole wandered into the living room and stopped short. The modest little bungalow was a hidden gem. Floor to ceiling windows lined the back of the room, showcasing a view of land that sloped steeply down to a patch of woods and a waterfall that was frozen solid at the moment.

"What a view," he said quietly.

"It's what keeps guests coming back year after year," she said proudly. "Let's go warm up and eat dinner. I have the contract for you to sign in my office at home."

Later, he found himself settled at her small dining table as she served up bowls of soup with homemade focaccia bread and a salad. The table was set with yellow placemats and blue napkins, and the daffodils had pride of place as the centerpiece. She moved around the tiny kitchen with ease. Atticus stayed settled on his bed, possibly the most obedient and chill pup he'd ever met.

"Will you add another log to the fire?" she asked.

"Sure."

Cole was happy to be given a task to do. He was fidgety and restless. His huge body was too big for this tiny room. This little cottage and this woman were foreign to him. The cozy, peaceful home was not something he knew, and the fact that she was creating it all by herself was something he didn't understand. Settling back in his seat, he took in the sight of the meal and the table.

"Do you always cook like this for yourself? And set the table?" he asked bluntly.

"Are you asking if I did this for you?" she asked, her voice tight and a bit terse. Before he could answer, she continued, "Well, if you remember, I didn't know you were coming, Cole. It's dinner time, and I made dinner. That's how it works. Even if it's only me."

"I didn't mean to imply you didn't deserve a nice dinner. I just, well, I live alone too, and I tend to eat cereal standing up at the sink more often than not. It's really nice. Thank you very much for letting me stay."

He was eager to put her at ease, put himself at ease, just

generally feel anything other than this chronic itchiness that being near her made him feel.

"No, I shouldn't have been defensive," she said, her voice now softer. "My husband and I cooked and ate dinner together every night. It was our thing, and after he was gone, I kept it up because the alternative is too painful."

"Gone?" Cole asked.

"He passed away five years ago."

"How?"

"His heart," she replied simply. "Now let's eat. Our soup is going to get cold."

A million questions raced through his head, but now was not the time to ask them.

"This looks delicious," he said as he began to eat.

CHAPTER 3

CORA

THERE WAS ALWAYS silence following any discussion of her husband. The world simply didn't know what to do with a widow, especially a young one with no children. She had effectively tossed a rock on the table, but it wasn't in her nature to hide her heart. Cole asked a question, and she simply answered it.

Jeff was the love of her life, a love so strong that four years of dating and five years of marriage had given her enough to last a lifetime. She was good at being alone. It was a choice. Most people expected her to move back home to Iowa or to remarry one of the local bachelors.

No one expected her to keep on renovating the cottage, taking care of the land, or running the Airbnb. But she had to live. Jeff's life had ended, but she was still here. There was still so much she wanted to do, so many of their dreams she wanted to make come true. Cora let the silence linger a few moments, concentrating on her meal. She took a sip of water, ate a bite of salad, and offered Cole the butter.

"Was your day productive?" she asked in an attempt to shift the awkward tension in the room.

She looked up from her plate and was shocked to feel

the intensity of his brown eyes focused on her. She'd only seen him in full tough man mode. Even when he'd stood awkwardly at her door earlier holding a pot of daffodils, there'd been a taciturn resignation in his stance. Right now he was looking at her with some emotion she wasn't sure how to label. Was it tenderness? Was it compassion? She didn't know him at all so there was no way to discern his mood at the moment. When he spoke, she was even more shocked.

"I'm really sorry that happened to you." His voice was low and soft, and she felt the words all the way to her soul.

She, who had heard a thousand *I'm sorry for your loss* darts that never hit the mark, felt this one fly straight to her heart. Without even realizing it, she placed her hand on her chest as if to brace for the impact. The statement was simple and to the point, said by countless others over the years since Jeff's death. Yet, Cole's delivery was so genuine, it hit her with more force than all the others combined.

"Thank you very much," she said quietly.

"Do you mind telling me more?"

Once again, she found herself surprised. After the stilted silence that followed the widow bombshell, people usually turned back to small talk as quickly as possible. Few ever dug deeper or invited her to talk about it at all. Humans, she'd found, always sought comfort, and grief was anything but comfortable.

"I met Jeff the second week of my freshman year of college. He just walked up to me on my way to class, introduced himself, and went right along with me. He was there after class to walk with me again, and that never changed. We ate lunch together, went to the gym at the same time, took walks, and studied at the library every night. Week three he asked me out on an official date, and before I said yes, he said *I need to warn you. If you say yes, that's it. It will be me and you forever. I plan to marry you.* I said yes, and the rest is history."

"Wow, direct kind of guy," Cole commented.

"He was this tall, handsome guy, so sure of himself, but also gentle and kind. He was exactly what I needed. I was smitten from day one."

"Were both of you from here?"

"Neither, actually. I'm from Iowa. I never really fit in my family, always just seemed extra. I went away to college to the place that gave me the most scholarship money. Jeff was from Manhattan, an only child, very wealthy parents with lots of expectations that he continue to chart the course they'd planned for him. He refused and went off to my no name college, and that's how we met. Both of us escaping."

"Why here then?" he asked.

She noticed his soup bowl was empty and offered him seconds, answering as she went to get more.

"He found it online if you can believe it. It was a disaster, but both houses came on the land, and he had an inheritance from his grandmother. We both wanted to create something that was just ours. So here I am."

It made her smile to see Cole start eating the second bowl of soup with just as much gusto as the first.

"What did Jeff do for a living?" he asked, all his questions short and to the point.

"He was a teacher too. High school. So, we were able to pay for the house with the money from his grandmother, but two teachers don't make a lot of money. We did most of the work ourselves on the weekends and during the summers."

"How long have you had the Airbnb up and running?"

he asked as he finished the second bowl of soup and his third piece of focaccia. His salad bowl was still untouched. Not a veggie and greens kind of guy, she thought.

"We got it up and running as fast as possible in the first year. We needed the extra income."

She laughed thinking of how steep the learning curve had been at both DIY restoration and running the Airbnb. They'd made so many mistakes, but it had been so much fun, just like everything with Jeff.

"That was absolutely delicious," he said. "I can't remember the last time I had a home cooked meal that good."

Cora hid her surprise. Cole was a huge, healthy man with a matching appetite. He was also handsome and must be successful. That land up the road did not come cheap, and to keep it for himself, instead of developing it, meant he had plenty of money. So why was he single? Or was he? Maybe he had a girlfriend who just didn't cook.

"I have some caramel brownies if you would like a little dessert."

"I never turn down dessert," he said with the first wide smile she'd seen from him.

Oh yes, there was definitely something there to attract a woman, she thought.

"Coffee or milk?" she asked as she cleared their plates and walked to the kitchen.

"Milk for sure," he said, still smiling.

She had to blink and force herself to look away. She cut an extra-large brownie for Cole and poured him a glass of milk, cutting a smaller treat for herself. He was busy adding another log to the fire when she returned to the table.

"That's huge," he said and laughed, as she placed the dessert in front of him. "But I'm here for it."

"Well, if you haven't had a home cooked meal in forever, I figured you probably didn't have too many homemade desserts either. You have to make up for it when you can."

She laughed when he bit into the caramel brownie and closed his eyes as if savoring the moment.

"This is amazing," he said. "I shouldn't talk with my mouth full, but damn."

After dessert, he offered to help clean the kitchen, but Cora was feeling a bit crowded. She was used to living alone, eating alone, just generally minding her own business. This huge man in her small space was too much, and she was experiencing a touch of sensory overload. Plus, she felt guilty, which surprised her.

Jeff had been gone for five years, and she was just as committed to staying his wife in death as in life. And that had always been easy until this moment. That scared her. Something about Cole got to her even through his clipped questions. No, he wasn't staying to clean up. He needed to leave immediately.

"Actually, you need to get settled in next door. Let me get the check-in paperwork. I just need to run up to my office," she said as she dashed upstairs, eager to take a breath of air that didn't smell of Cole.

She grabbed the paperwork quickly and took a moment for some deep breaths to calm herself down before making her way back downstairs. Cole was waiting for her at the kitchen table.

"Here you go. The rate is $200 per night, but since you're staying for four weeks in the off season, let's make it $150. You have a washer and dryer in the bungalow, so you can just take care of the sheets and towels since you'll be here for a longer than usual stay." Cora said.

"Absolutely. You won't even know I'm here. As for knocking the price down, absolutely not. You're doing me a favor letting me stay now, and I really appreciate it. I can give you the full amount right now in cash," he replied.

"That's not necessary. Let's do it weekly. Just put it in an envelope and stick it in the door at the start of each week."

"Okay, but I'm giving you this week's right now," he said as he took out his wallet and counted out a stack of hundred dollar bills, handing them to her.

"Thank you. Do you want me to bring you breakfast and dinner? I should be able to do that most days, and I'll let you know when I can't. I won't charge extra since you're paying full price," she offered.

"I don't want to make more work for you."

"Nonsense. It's my standard offer, and since it's only one person, I'll probably just bring you a portion of whatever I'm making for myself. Any food allergies or aversions?" she asked.

"No allergies, and I'm happy to eat whatever you prepare. I'll pay the standard fee for meals, which according to this contract is $50 per day. Stop selling yourself short," he muttered sternly as he counted off more crisp bills.

"Hold on. That amount is for up to four people. Make it $20," she said, putting her hand out to stop him counting.

"Deal," he said smiling.

"You can park your truck in the driveway that leads straight to the bungalow. It's the only other one on this side of the road. Here's the key. Let me know if you need anything," she said as she opened the door.

Then he was gone. Cora didn't watch him go, didn't wave. She just closed the door and walked away. Cleaning the kitchen was always a peaceful task, almost a meditation of sorts. She usually turned on music she could dance to, and tonight was no different.

With no dishwasher, Cora soon found herself elbow deep in hot, sudsy water with Miley Cyrus singing about all the things she could do for herself. Singing and swaying at her farmhouse sink with a roaring fire, her sweet Atticus asleep on his bed, and the peace of her little cottage on a cold winter's night, Cora settled back into herself.

It had been so long since she'd shared a meal alone with a man, and the only other man had been Jeff. So, of course, she was rattled. She was a loner, an introvert, and a grieving wife. Cole had cleared her snow, helped her when she'd fallen, and now eaten dinner at her cozy kitchen table. It was all out of her routine and no wonder at all that she was a bit off kilter.

She was going to make herself a hot toddy, take an even hotter shower, read in bed, and forget today ever happened. Nothing would make her unfaithful to Jeff and the love they'd shared. Nothing would ever make her settle for less than the magic of their relationship, certainly not a grumpy man like Cole Houston.

Jeff had been gentle and kind, sweet in a way that was as natural and honest as breathing. Sure, there was passion, but there was also deep friendship and unity, as if they were one and the same person. Both of them lonely and out of place in their own families, they'd found in each other everything they needed. Anything else would be second best.

However, as she did the nightly chores, checking on the animals, letting Atticus out for a potty break, shutting down the kitchen, even during her shower, she kept asking herself one question. Why did Cole make her feel differently?

She'd only known him a handful of hours and spent most

of them irritated. Yet, she couldn't stop thinking about him. This morning he was rude, yet helpful, and this evening he was kind and curious, asking her thoughtful questions and really listening to her answers. He was unexpected, a novelty, she thought. It was just something out of the ordinary. That had to be it, she promised herself. No other reason mattered.

CHAPTER 4

COLE

He was a man who focused on work and making money. His childhood had been a study in disappointment and pain. Born to a mother who didn't want him and neglected by her until she simply walked away, Cole had then spent years with a series of foster families or in group homes.

As a result, he made a vow to himself that he would never depend on anyone else ever again. Emotion was a waste of time. His heart wasn't so much hard as it was dead. He reckoned once your own mother said you were a waste of space and time, there was no coming back from that.

Yet, here he stood outside Cora's front door, trying to make himself walk away. It was cold. It was dark. He still had to get his things from his wreck of a house to bring over to the bungalow, but he couldn't move. From this vantage point by her front door, he could see through a front window into her cottage. What he saw glued his feet to the ground where he stood.

She was dancing and from the looks of her mouth moving, also singing as she cleaned up after dinner. The music was turned up loud enough he could hear it faintly outside, and she was giving it her all while she cleared the table. As she moved to the kitchen area, she disappeared from view, but he could still hear the music and her.

A classic rock fan, he wasn't a fan of the pop song, but it had a nice beat, and she sure could move. For a moment, he thought of himself as the voyeur he clearly was, standing outside staring at her while she danced in her own home unaware. Still he couldn't make himself move. It wasn't just the sight of a beautiful woman. It was her.

Everything about her, from her face to her voice, her body, her smell, her smile, pulled him to her like a magnet. He'd never experienced it before in his life. Sure, he liked women, had spent some pleasant hours with a few. He was no monk, but he lived for work and solitude. He didn't share meals with women, didn't shovel their snow, and for damn sure didn't fret over their injuries. He enjoyed the company of a willing female and moved on, no promises, no regrets.

But tonight somehow reminded him of the one good time in his childhood. When he was ten years old, he lived with the only decent foster parents he ever had. Rick and Betty Evans were stable and dependable, if not affectionate. Rick was a mailman, and Betty was a nurse. Their only son had joined the army after high school, and they felt they still had something left to give a needy child. It was the first time he'd ever felt like he might belong, like there was a place in their home just for him.

Betty was not a great cook, but she tried. Mostly, she heated up frozen dinners and cans of soup. They ate together, the three of them, at the table in the old, outdated kitchen. While they weren't particularly talkative, the atmosphere there was always peaceful. For the time he lived with them, those meals were Cole's favorite part of any day. That's what he remembered now, what his time with Cora had brought to his mind.

Right now, what he wanted scared him, undid him in ways he didn't understand. What he wanted was the right to dance with her, the privilege of being the one who cleaned the kitchen by her side, the one who would turn off the light as they made their way upstairs for the night. But that was folly.

Nothing good ever lasted. It was all just an illusion. Rick Evans died when Cole was twelve, and Betty got sick soon after, no longer able to care for him. Before he turned thirteen, he was back in a group home just trying to survive. Remembering the loss of that one good season of life had his feet moving away from the sight of Cora and her cozy home.

He walked to his truck. Within half an hour, he'd collected what he needed from his house and pulled into the driveway of the bungalow, where a light was shining by the front door. He unlocked the door and began getting settled, moving around the little house with very few lights on, just eager to get to bed and forget this day.

He stopped at the large picture windows that lined the back wall of the living room, taking in the dark night with only the moon and the snow to give any brightness at all. He saw a pinprick of light moving down the hill to the little valley and out toward the barn he'd glimpsed a bit earlier when Cora had shown him the house. What was down there? He opened the French doors that led to the patio, turning on his phone flashlight to enhance his view. Walking to the edge of the patio, he was able to make out the source of the light.

It was Cora. Why was she roaming around in the dark and cold at this time of night? Then he heard a sound. Was that a bray? He remembered that Cora had mentioned taking care of animals. She was out there checking on a donkey and probably goats and chickens too. He heard a bark that wasn't Atticus and the sound of laughter. Clearly, there was another dog, possibly a livestock guardian, down there too. Out there in the cold, dark night, she was laughing.

He wanted to rush down there and warn her of all the ways she could get hurt out there alone. He wanted to scoop her up and take her back to her warm house, check on everything for her, and make sure she was safe. However, he knew that wouldn't be welcome by Cora, nor should it be. She was clearly a capable woman who'd been living life quite competently on her own for a long time.

More, he wasn't that guy. He didn't do those things. He didn't want those things. Cole had never thought of women as anything but capable and independent, and he wasn't sure what was bringing up all these protective instincts toward a woman he'd only just met.

So he walked back into the house and closed the door, but he didn't go to bed until he saw the tiny blip of light move back up the hill toward her cottage. From his bedroom window, he could just make out the lights of the second story of her house. He didn't let himself sleep until the little cottage was shrouded in darkness, knowing then that she too was tucked in for the night.

Surprisingly, Cole slept so well that the sun was high in the sky when he awoke the next morning. A glance at his phone told him it was after nine. He sat straight up in bed in shock. He never slept in. He was up with the sun, already hours into work by this time.

After a hot shower and a cursory making of the bed, he went into the kitchen, hoping to find what he needed to make coffee. He felt almost hungover from all that sleep, but he also felt good, rested and eager for the day. Not only was there a coffee maker and coffee, but there was also a reusable shopping bag on the counter with a note taped to it. He carefully unstuck the note.

Good morning, Cole. I hope you found everything you needed. It was too cold to leave your breakfast out in the snow, so I took the liberty of just leaving it here. I'll be out this evening and unable to bring your dinner over, so I put some lasagna in your fridge. Just pop it in the oven at 350 for about 25-30 min when you want it. There's garlic bread in there too. Just let it heat up with the lasagna for about 10-15 min. Have a good day-Cora.

Cole opened the bag and discovered several still-warm white chocolate raspberry muffins and a cup of fruit. He bit into a muffin as he opened the refrigerator to find an aluminum pan of lasagna with a foil-wrapped loaf of garlic bread on top. He felt like a king.

He'd enjoyed a lot of good meals since becoming an adult, usually at restaurants. The poverty of his childhood left him with a deep desire for good food once he was able to get it. He loved a good steak dinner, seafood, a deluxe burger, and he was willing to pay handsomely for the meals. Homecooked food, however, was a luxury he'd rarely experienced.

That muffin tasted like all the things he didn't have. It tasted like someone cared, and he'd eaten three before he even realized it. He tucked the note in his wallet for no reason other than he couldn't bear to throw it away. When he headed to his truck, it was with a pep in his step that both made him happy and terrified him in equal measure.

The day passed quickly. By ten that morning, a team was replacing his entire boiler system while he continued with his general clean-out. He had a roofing company scheduled to stop by for an estimate after lunch, and a contractor was coming later in the afternoon to check out the exterior restoration job.

Cole could do a lot himself and wanted to, but at over seven thousand square feet of absolute deterioration, he knew it would take him forever working alone. He needed a team, and he wanted them to get working quickly. For lunch, he munched his way through a fourth muffin, drank more coffee, and kept going.

Around four the furnace crew left with a plan to finish the job the following day. Both his afternoon meetings yielded results which meant he would have a team working on the structural issues by early next week. January was an unusual month to begin a renovation with low temps and possible blizzards making the jobs hard to start and harder to finish.

He was determined, and he knew that there was more than enough work inside to keep them busy even if it snowed or the temperature plummeted, preventing them from working outside. The new boiler system would have the house warm enough for the work. That also meant he could move back to his own house sooner.

Money might not buy happiness, but it did get you what you wanted faster. What he wanted was to get out of the bungalow and back to his house. He would pay Cora for the full four weeks he'd asked for, but he needed out sooner. He'd eaten one of the best meals of his life, slept like a baby, make that overslept, and then gorged himself on homemade muffins while whistling a happy tune. He couldn't afford that kind of softness or that kind of care. It would make him forget who he was and where he came from.

All he could count on was what he built for himself.

People, in his experience, rarely stuck around for the long haul. That's why he needed to get back to his own house where he could live off take-out and peanut butter and jelly sandwiches, where he could get up at dawn and work himself to exhaustion, where he could remember he was a man born to be alone.

By the time he had the upstairs nearly halfway cleared, he realized it was dark outside. Glancing at his watch, he saw it was past seven. He was happy with his progress. It felt good to see a few empty rooms ready for work. There were six bedrooms upstairs and three bathrooms, to include a huge primary suite.

All the carpet needed to be pulled up. A different color decorated every room, and he wasn't even sure what color some of it had started. Whatever it was, it wasn't that color anymore. A combination of fading, stains, and general filth made it disgusting. He'd pulled back enough to know that hardwood floors were hidden underneath. They were in a sad state, but that wasn't a problem. He knew just how to return them to their former glory. The bathrooms were either blue or pink tile which had chipped and cracked. They represented yet another demolition job to add to his list. There were three claw foot tubs, though, which he would get fully restored.

Looking down, he realized he was covered in dust and grime from a day of hauling out trash. He needed a hot shower and some of that lasagna Cora left him. He shut the house for the night and drove down to the bungalow, immediately noticing that her house was still dark. Clearly, she was out tonight. He rubbed his hand over his heart, wondering why that bothered him.

CHAPTER 5

CORA

CORA HAD A faculty meeting followed by yet another meeting at the local library where she volunteered weekly. She led story time in the summer, helped out with the little bookstore in the back, and just generally promoted the small town institution for the gem it was. After the meeting, she'd promised to meet Eliza for dinner.

Eliza was her first and best friend in Longview. They taught together for almost five years before Eliza left teaching to stay at home with her first baby. She'd known Jeff, and Eliza and her husband had often met them for Friday night pizza or line danced at a bar a couple of towns over. She and Eliza hit it off immediately, both full of passion for teaching. They did yoga together, took long walks, and talked about most everything. Or at least, they had until Jeff died just as Eliza was celebrating the birth of her first child.

Cora retreated into herself then, and Eliza felt guilty for having a healthy husband and a beautiful new baby. The timing had been rough. Eliza didn't return to school after giving birth to baby Gracie at Easter, and Jeff died just as school let out for the summer. That left Cora with loads of time alone. Summer had always been when she and Jeff tackled their largest home projects.

Those long summer days together had been bliss. After rolling out of bed, they would plan their day over breakfast. Then they would work all day, stopping only for homegrown tomato sandwiches and sweet tea made in a jug that sat in the warm sun. And then, it was back to work until they stopped for dinner, something simple they cooked together before they crashed for the night. There was passion and companionship along with a sense of building something good together.

Then he was gone, and she was left with a summer staring at her like a yawning hole she didn't know how to fill. Just as Cora's life had come to a grinding, grieving halt, Eliza's had soared as she embraced full time motherhood and family, something Cora knew she would never have now that Jeff was gone. It had taken them time to figure out how to navigate their friendship in those new circumstances.

In the end, it was Eliza who conquered the growing distance between them. She just showed up at Cora's house one Saturday about six months after Jeff died. Cora had been outside gardening. That was how she grieved.

Eliza got out of the car, marched right up to her, and said, "I've called. I've sent you texts. I've invited you for dinner. And you always say no. Well, enough. We're friends. I love you. I know you're grieving. I know it's hard to hang out with people who are just going on with regular life when your own is so different and so hard, but enough. I miss you."

Cora crumbled. The two of them collided in a weeping hug right there in the front yard with Atticus looking on.

"Brent's got Gracie, so I'm going to stay and garden with you, or do you want to go to Taco Fiesta and gorge on chips and salsa while drowning ourselves in margaritas? Your pick," Eliza said as they finally stopped crying.

"It's going to be chips and salsa for me," Cora said in gratitude and relief. "I've been grieving and gardening for weeks, and I'm exhausted. Come inside while I change and grab my purse. We can eat on the patio at the restaurant, so Atty can come too."

While their couple dates were over, Cora made it a priority to connect with Eliza daily through texts and promised to have a girls' date once a week. Sometimes sick kids or bad weather got in the way, but more often than not, every week since that long ago Saturday in Cora's driveway, the two women got together.

Today her library meeting ran long, so she was ten minutes late walking into the restaurant. She saw Eliza instantly at their favorite corner booth, chips, salsa, and giant margaritas already on the table. She would have to stop at one since she was driving, but it would still be a treat.

"There you are," Eliza greeted with a big smile.

"I'm sorry, El. Mrs. Grissom got started talking about the need for more large print books in the fiction section, and there was no stopping her," Cora explained.

This was said as Cora unwound all the layers winter required in their part of the world. Finally, with her scarf, gloves, hat, and coat piled high and wide on the bench beside her, she dug into her first salsa-covered chip and washed it down with a hearty gulp of her margarita. Taco Fiesta was a local favorite. It offered both the cheerful décor expected in a Mexican restaurant, but also a certain dimly lit, private feel that made it easy to enjoy good food *and* good conversation.

"Oh, that's good, just what I needed." Cora said as she

scarfed down more chips. "It's been a week, and it's only Tuesday. Not a good sign."

"I went ahead and ordered our usuals. With the way you're motoring through those chips, I'm guessing you're okay with that," Eliza said with a smirk.

"For sure. How are my two favorite little girls in the whole world?" Cora asked, referring to Eliza's two daughters, Gracie, age five and Claire, age two.

"A hot mess with a mama that is only too happy for a night out of the house," Eliza said with a laugh. "I adore those two and their daddy, but my goodness, I need this tonight. You sound like you do too. So, go ahead. Spill. What's going on with you? Your text about a new male guest at the bungalow has me all kinds of intrigued."

Cora quickly brought Eliza up to speed on the arrival of Cole Houston right from the beginning. She didn't leave anything out, from her embarrassing fall in her pajamas to their cozy dinner just last night to dropping off muffins and lasagna this morning. She might have also included the color of his eyes and the way his muscles moved in his flannel shirt.

"So, you like him? That's what I'm hearing, right?" Eliza asked.

"What?" Cora replied, clearly embarrassed. "No, of course not. He's just a guest staying at my bungalow and who tried to do a neighborly deed which caught me off guard. What part of that means I like him?"

"I don't know. Maybe the part where you told me about his chocolate brown eyes. And then, there was the description of how giant he was, accompanied by the suggestion that I should see his muscles. Oh, and if that's not enough, I'm not sure you're aware, but your eyes go soft and dreamy when you just mention his name. Yep. I think you like him," Eliza spelled out for her, clearly delighted.

Cora always appreciated Eliza's no nonsense approach to life, the fact that she called it just like she saw it. *No bullshit ever* was El's personal motto. But right now, as Cora stared at her friend across the table, she really disliked that quality.

Luckily, their food arrived, and they put the conversation aside for a moment as they settled in to eat. Cora always ordered the chicken enchiladas, and Eliza always ordered the Burrito Supreme. And without fail, they each immediately split their portions and gave half to the other. When all that was done, Eliza gave Cora a pointed look.

"I don't know what you want me to say. I can recognize he's a reasonably attractive man. Can't I? That doesn't mean anything. I can see that's true of Chris Hemsworth too. And I'd like it noted that I also said he's gruff and a bit scary," Cora explained.

"You took him your white chocolate raspberry muffins and your lasagna," Eliza said before scooping a bite of enchilada into her mouth.

Cora stopped eating, literally holding her fork in mid-air.

"Oh no. I did," she said quietly.

And with that, she placed her fork back on the plate.

"Why did I do that? Those were Jeff's favorites. I've never made those for anyone else ever. In fact, I rarely even make them for myself, and it usually makes me sad. Oh no. This isn't good," she said with fat tears rolling down her cheeks.

She was trembling. Eliza got out of her seat and made her way to Cora's side, sitting down next to her friend and wrapping her arms around her.

"It's okay, sweetie. It's really okay. It doesn't have to mean anything."

Cora looked up at her just as the waiter appeared.

"Do you ladies have everything you need?" he said, only just noticing that one of them was crying.

He looked panic-stricken and took a noticeable step back.

"Thank you for asking, but I don't think you have what we need right now in the kitchen," Eliza replied with a sad smile, and he scurried away.

"That wasn't very nice," Cora said, her face streaked with tears.

"A little situational awareness would be good. That's all I'm saying. Did we look like our problem could be solved with a little extra queso? I don't think so," Eliza said. "Plus, I said it with not a hint of snark, just concern for you."

"El," Cora said, bringing their attention back to the topic at hand. "You automatically thought I liked him just from what I shared. And I made him food I've never made for anyone except Jeff. How can it not mean anything? Now is not the time to go easy on me. That's not who you are."

"Cora, I know that Jeff was the love of your life. I also know something that you refuse to believe. There can be another. And if there is another, it won't cancel out what you felt for Jeff. True love multiplies. It doesn't diminish. But even if this is just you finding another man attractive, that's a good thing. That's healing. Sweetie, that's living."

"I made a vow," Cora said simply.

"Oh honey, I know you did. But that vow wasn't to Jeff. He was gone by then. It was a vow to yourself, and it was made in a time of raw pain and grief, the likes of which many people wouldn't survive. But Jeff, the Jeff I knew and loved, would never want you to be alone. And you know that," Eliza said gently.

"I do know that. You know that's not what this is. I

found my great love, and I know in my heart that nothing will ever surpass it. Nothing will ever even come close to equaling it, so why would I settle? I'm happy and content as I am. Period," Cora said firmly.

"What if you look at it this way? Maybe it doesn't have to be about your vow at all. Maybe it's not even about Cole in particular. What if this is just a sign that you're a healthy, young woman who is slowly moving back into the land of the living? Like you said, you've appreciated Chris Hemsworth. This is no different. It doesn't mean you're going to marry the man. A little flirting, a new friendship. Those aren't bad things, Cora."

Cora nodded and smiled. After a moment, Eliza moved back to her side of the table, and they finished their food, even ordering their favorite sopapillas for dessert. The conversation shifted to Gracie's upcoming dance recital and Eliza's husband's promotion at work. They laughed and talked until nearly ten.

It was much needed time spent with Eliza, but all the way through dinner and all the way back to her house, their earlier conversation played in Cora's mind. No matter how she spun it, she wasn't comfortable with Cole Houston. He made her feel things she didn't want to feel. She needed him out of the bungalow as fast as possible. Sure, the unexpected money was nice, but it wasn't worth her peace of mind, and it certainly wasn't worth her vow.

CHAPTER 6

COLE

COLE SETTLED INTO bed early hoping to read and fall asleep, but he couldn't get Cora off his mind. Where was she? His thoughts were filled with worry and questions. It was past ten on a Tuesday night. Was she stuck somewhere with a flat tire? Her car was ridiculous, small and old, with all the fortitude of the car Fred Flintstone drove in the cartoons he'd seen a few times as a kid. She could be in a ditch, on the side of the road, or bleeding from a head wound.

Then it hit him. She could be on a date. He dismissed that immediately. He couldn't even think about that. He was so agitated by the time he heard her tires crunching on the gravel, he shot up out of bed, stalking to the door like a lion. Before he even knew what he was doing, his hand was on the doorknob.

"Get a grip," he muttered to himself. "What are you thinking?"

He got a drink of water and headed back to the bedroom, only to stop short when he caught a glimpse of the little pinprick of light from her phone moving down the hill past the bungalow. She was clearly going to care of the animals he'd still not seen.

He waited there in the dark, clad only in his t-shirt and boxers, still there twenty minutes later as she made her way back up the hill, his eyes following the little dot of light. Only when her lights went off upstairs did he finally lay his head back on the pillow, but it was hours before he slept. What was it about this woman that got to him? More importantly, how did he stop it?

The next morning Cole was up at dawn. He estimated he'd slept two hours total, but he was itching to get over to the house and get to work. The sooner he got it livable, the sooner he could get away from Cora. Other than Joe, his mentor and the man who'd helped him transform his life at age eighteen, Cole didn't let himself get attached to people. To some degree, he even kept Joe at a distance.

He might be light years from the boy he'd been, but that feeling of living life unwanted left a scar. He figured his heart, broken so many times when he was young, had simply healed crooked and sharp. Cole remembered walking home from school the year he was in first grade. He was staying with his second foster family in a neighborhood filled with the happy, messy chaos of life.

Children and dogs were everywhere. Bikes were left scattered in driveways. Toys were strewn across lawns. He saw mothers tending to babies, children playing after school, and fathers teaching kids to ride bikes or throw baseballs.

The house he stayed in was full of chaos and noise too, but it had an edge to it. His foster parents were not gentle. Voices were always raised. They had too many kids and too little money, and as he looked back, he wasn't even sure how they'd ever qualified to foster kids at all.

For the most part, he was left on his own, making cereal for breakfast and dinner, shoving his shoelaces into his sneakers because no one took the time to teach him how to tie his shoes. Everything there rocked along just fine unless one of the kids asked the wrong question or made trouble, and then it went sour fast. A slap, a shove, the sting of a harsh word were all regular occurrences in that house.

It had been another lesson learned young that what was possible for others wasn't for him. He might live in the same neighborhood, but he would always be on the outside looking in when it came to the warm glow of a real home. Cora was like those houses he'd walked by as a child. He was drawn to her warmth and beauty, to the safety and peace that surrounded her.

It wasn't lost on him that he spent his life building houses for others. When he sold them and walked away, he was once again a little boy staring into the windows of homes that would never be his. To believe even for a moment that he could be part of something more was foolish. That's why he needed to get away from her as soon as possible.

He was showered and dressed, standing at the sink finishing a cup of coffee when he heard a knock at the door. Even as he vowed to avoid her, he felt his heart beat faster as he moved to open it.

"Oh good, you're up," she said. "I felt funny yesterday coming in, but I didn't want to leave your food out in the cold. I hope I didn't overstep. I just put the food down and left. I promise."

This was all said in a rush of breath, as if she rehearsed it in her mind as she walked over. Cole thought she was the most adorable human he'd ever encountered. He couldn't help smiling, and wasn't that a first?

"It was fine. I slept late, and I never do that. All of the food was delicious," he replied.

Just like that, the nervous woman who greeted him with her hurried words vanished, and Cora's face bloomed at the praise.

"Oh good. I'm so glad." They stood there staring at one another as if in a daze, until finally she said, "Well, I'll be around this afternoon, so I'll bring dinner by then. What time is best for you?"

"Just text me when you have it ready. I'm just up the road. It's easy enough for me to stop working and come get it," he answered.

She nodded and handed him the stack of containers in her hand.

"Well, for breakfast I've brought you some sausage and biscuits, scrambled eggs, and hashbrowns. I thought it might be enough for leftovers at lunch if you got too busy to go grab something in town," she explained.

"It's only seven. How in the world have you already had time to get ready for school and make this much food? When I said yes to breakfast, I was imagining a bagel and some cream cheese. This is too much. I don't expect this kind of meal."

"I'm an early bird. I get up to take Atticus out and tend to my animals. I love cooking, so it's really not a problem, and I promise I'll tell you if there is a day I can't do it. Well, you have a good day," she said, turning to leave.

"Thank you, Cora. I really appreciate it."

She turned the knob and opened the door, a gust of cold air filling the room.

"Cora," he called softly.

He wasn't ready for her to leave, and it occurred to him that he hadn't checked on her enough after the fall yesterday morning.

"Yes," she said, looking back at him.

She was blushing now, and he realized he was staring, maybe a bit too intently. He couldn't help it.

"How's your back?"

The blush crawled down her face and right into the neck of her sweater. Oh, to be that blush.

"Just a bruise. It's fine. Thank you for asking."

Her pretty green eyes were wide and a bit shell-shocked. And not for the first time, he had the impression that he scared her. He didn't want to scare her, not ever.

"Alright then. You have a good day too."

She smiled and walked out the door. But her scent lingered in the air, and her food was on the table. Cole felt surrounded by the one woman who might be the undoing of him.

His day passed much as the one before, clearing out junk to get the house ready for the real work to begin. The detritus of the long abandoned property reminded him yet again why he preferred new things. Cole bought the house from the Westfield estate when Walter Westfield, the sole heir, passed away at the age of ninety-seven. While Walter had spent a very happy childhood there, he hadn't lived there since his early twenties. After his parents died and he inherited the property, it sat vacant for the rest of his life.

When Walter died, he'd lived in Wyoming for more than sixty years, visiting the house only occasionally. On those trips, he would mow the grass or clear some brush, but he never tackled any of the major issues that decades of neglect had caused. He was a wealthy man, and the hefty property tax bill that came due every year didn't cause him any stress. He simply paid it and went about his business while the house quietly deteriorated.

Other relatives who lived nearby had implored him to fix it up or sell it, and Walter always refused. It was as if the man had preserved the happiest time of his life in that house, never realizing the structure was falling down around those memories. All of this information Cole gleaned from the people who'd been involved in the sale of the property. He had to admit it intrigued him to think of someone so enamored with his childhood home that he made it a shrine. It was certainly the opposite of Cole's own experience.

Cole was working steadily to clear the second floor, but that left the attic, the basement, and the first floor all still packed to the gills with junk. George and his team were back on site to work on the new boiler system, and it was George who suggested he call Angelo DeSanto to come take a look at the furniture and other items that still had some life in them.

Apparently, Angelo ran a local store that collected, refurbished, and repurposed old items like furniture, windows, and doors to sell in their store on the waterfront, a huge warehouse called *Alive Again*. He'd called him first thing that morning, and now he was waiting for him to arrive. Soon, he saw Angelo's truck pulling up the long drive to the house. He stopped his work, did his best to wipe off a layer of grime, and went to greet him.

"You must be Angelo," he said. "I'm Cole. Cole Houston. Thanks for coming out so quickly."

"Very nice to meet you. As for getting here quickly, I've been dying to get inside this house for years. Are you kidding me? The Westfield Place is legendary around here," Angelo replied.

"Well, I need to warn you. It's a complete mess, but you're welcome to look around. I've staged a bunch of items in the dining room that I think are still good enough to use. The second floor is nearly empty, but everywhere else is fair game. If you see something you think you can sell, have at it."

"I'd love to think I could afford everything I might want, but I'm not sure. This is a huge house. Let me take a look and see what you've got." Angelo answered.

"Let's talk money right off the bat then. I don't want any. I just want you to haul off whatever you think you can work with and hopefully, you'll turn a profit from it. Will that work?" Cole explained.

"Are you sure? Typically, we pay a fair price for each item. We take donations, but usually that's for a small amount, nothing like this. You might not need the money, but every little bit helps. Right?" Angelo responded.

"I appreciate that, but right now, I'm just happy to get rid of as much stuff as I can. Honestly, I can't even begin to work on this place until it's cleared out."

"Alright, well, that's huge. Thank you. Thank you very much," Angelo said sincerely.

Within minutes, Angelo was in the dining room, looking over everything Cole had already gathered. A big guy with tattoos crawling out of the neck of his flannel shirt and a gold earring winking from his earlobe, Angelo looked more like a bouncer from a high-end nightclub than a connoisseur of reusable junk. And yet, here he was, eyes alight while he sorted through dressers, mirrors, and lamps that had seen better days. Cole just stood and waited for Angelo's initial appraisal.

Finally, Angelo looked up and said, "We would be happy to take all of this and probably a ton of whatever you haven't sorted yet. If you agree, I'll call my guys at the shop to bring the trucks over. Hopefully, we can get this stuff out of your way by late this afternoon."

"Perfect," Cole said.

Angelo was soon ensconced in the basement, which he'd deemed the right starting point. Happy to have the job of clearing out junk off his plate, Cole retreated to the second floor to start tearing up carpet. Hours later, Angelo had moved on to the first floor, and his guys were up and down the basement stairs, hauling his finds to the two large trucks now parked in the driveway.

Around noon, Cole was ready for some lunch and a stop at the building supply store. He found Angelo in the grandest room in the house, a huge, cavernous space with tiled floors that felt like a ballroom. There was a grand piano in the corner and a few small chair groupings oddly placed around the room, but for the most part, the space was empty.

An elaborate Italianate mural had been painted on one side, and large floor to ceiling windows lined the opposite wall. The other two walls had smaller windows with marbled wallpaper falling off in long strips around them. The whole room smelled like mildew and decay. Cole hated it. Angelo looked like he'd found the Holy Grail.

"This space is unbelievable. It's got to be a ballroom. Right? Who has a ballroom?" he said, his thick New York accent coming out strongly in his excitement.

"Unbelievable is one way to describe it," Cole said, as he walked down the four steps from the French-doored entrance into the grand room.

"Come on. Can't you just imagine the music and the parties in this room? It must have been something else. This piano is an absolute treasure. I have a guy who can restore this easy-peasy. You could make a fortune off some of this stuff."

"I told you I just want it cleared. I'd be happy for you

to make a fortune off of it, but I just want it all gone." Cole said, uncomfortable amongst all the old relics.

He didn't understand the concept of home as most others seemed to enjoy it. This ballroom with its history of festive times was as unfamiliar to him as the meal he'd eaten at Cora's the other night. More than that, the junk that filled the house simply reminded him of all the hand-me-downs of his childhood. He'd lived with other people's cast-offs for too long. Every foster home was filled with toys, clothes, and stuff that belonged to someone else. Nothing was ever his own.

He didn't think most people realized how every house had its own distinct smell. The apartment he'd lived in with his mother had been small and messy. It smelled of garbage that needed to be taken out and toilets that needed to be cleaned. The Evans' house, the only one that left him with good memories, always smelled of Pine Sol and laundry detergent. Betty might not have been a good cook, but she was stickler for a clean house.

This house smelled like decay. Angelo might see treasure, but Cole saw only the leftover bits of someone else's life. He wanted no part of it. Not for the first time, he wondered what he was doing. He wasn't a man who restored homes. He built new, shiny, state of the art ones. So, why was he here in this old, abandoned disaster cleaning out equally old, abandoned junk?

"I'm going to grab lunch and head over to Pace Building Supply to order shingles. Do you guys have a plan for lunch, or would you like me to bring back pizza?" Cole asked, eager to get away from the house for a while.

"We're going to break soon and go grab some food at the café. I feel like we can still finish today, but if not, I'll come over with a couple of guys tomorrow and finish up first thing. Is that okay?" Angelo asked.

"Sure, I'll be here for what feels like the rest of my life," Cole said, as he turned to leave, the magnitude of the undertaking getting the better of him.

"Hey, man, you aren't staying here. Are you? It's damn cold in this house, and I see you've got George and his guys working on the furnace," Angelo called to him as he was leaving.

"More like putting in a whole new system," Cole responded. "And no, I'm not staying here."

"Where are you staying then?" Angelo asked.

"I'm staying down the street at Cora Lane's Airbnb. Do you know it?" he replied.

"Aren't you the lucky one?" Angelo responded and let out a low whistle.

Cole felt a host of unfamiliar emotions in response to Angelo's comment, and they were all feelings he had no right to feel. There was some possessiveness, a little jealousy, and even a hint of anger. None of them were warranted or welcome, just another sign that he needed to stay away from Cora.

"Excuse me," he said.

"Come on. She's a looker, that one. Absolutely gorgeous and sweet as well. Every man around here knows Cora Lane, but she doesn't care. Only cares about Jeff. Never was there a luckier guy than Jeff Lane. That woman is as devoted to him in death as she was in life. But hey, a guy can look. I thought she closed up the bungalow in January."

"She was gracious enough to open it for me for a few weeks since it's close to my house," Cole replied stiffly.

That was all Cole was going to say about Cora Lane to

Angelo. Angelo spent a moment staring at Cole with narrowed eyes, clearly reading something into Cole's stiff reply and demeanor with regards to Cora.

"Well, I better go. Thanks again, Angelo," Cole said as he made a speedy getaway to his truck.

CHAPTER 7

CORA

CORA'S DAY WASN'T going well. A parent came in early that morning and chewed her out for giving his son a conduct mark after he hit another child at recess yesterday. Her computer kept freezing, and she realized she'd forgotten her lunch in her rush to get Cole his breakfast. She found herself in the cafeteria eating a wilted salad and some chicken nuggets that in no way resembled chicken.

To put the exclamation point on an already messy day, at recess, Atticus, who was the school's therapy dog, got sick. Apparently, a student fed him an entire birthday cupcake. Thankfully, it wasn't chocolate, but still, dog vomit was the best way to summarize her afternoon. So, she headed to the vet's office instead of her classroom soon after. Luckily, Dr. Brenner wasn't too busy, and he could fit in their unscheduled visit quite quickly.

"Hey Cora," Dr. Brenner said as he came into the exam room. "Connie tells me Atticus here enjoyed a cupcake at school today."

Cora had to admit the vet was handsome in a clean-cut, wholesome way, much like Jeff had been. But he didn't make her heart beat faster or cause her to stumble over her words, not like Cole. It would make much more sense for her to feel a pull toward Dr. Brenner. She couldn't for the life of her understand how a woman who was madly in love with a man like Jeff Lane could somehow be attracted to Cole Houston. Yet, as she stared at the handsome man in front of her who was speaking so tenderly to Atty, she felt nothing.

"When is the last time he vomited?" he asked as he ran his hands gently over the lethargic dog.

"It's been about thirty minutes. Now he just seems listless and sleepy," Cora replied.

"That's normal. Connie said you knew it was one of the vanilla cupcakes from Anita's Bakery so I can confirm there were no toxic ingredients. I eat them more frequently than I should," Dr. Brenner said with a grin. "He probably has the worst of it out of his system, but he will be lethargic and likely still feel a bit sick at least for tonight. I'd hold off on any food, let him have water, and if he seems hungry much later tonight, stick to a small amount of his regular food."

"Thanks, Dr. Brenner. I really just needed peace of mind."

"Call me Sam, Cora. We've known each other too long to keep up this Dr. Brenner business."

"Alright, Sam," she said with a smile as she gathered her things and got ready to leave.

"Cora?" he asked hesitantly.

"Yes," she responded, knowing all too well what was coming next.

"If you ever decide you're interested, that invitation to dinner still stands."

It was something he always said when she brought Atticus in for a check-up. He was gentle and respectful, but he always asked, and she always declined.

"I'll let you know," she said.

She was ready to leave. The whole day had been too much. Unfortunately, Atticus had gotten comfy on the floor and was now refusing to move when she clipped his leash back on.

"Come on, Atty. Let's get you home."

He just stared at her. So, she gave a gentle tug on the leash. Again, nothing.

Dr. Brenner, who was now standing in the open doorway, said, "I'll carry him to the car for you."

"I'd appreciate that. Let me settle the bill with Connie, and then we can go. I'm literally parked right in front of your door," Cora said gratefully.

"No charge today, Cora," he said as he scooped up a sleepy Atticus and walked past Connie to the front door.

It was only steps to her car, and Atticus was soon settled comfortably in the back seat, giving the vet an affectionate lick in thanks. Once the door was closed, Cora turned to talk to Dr. Brenner. She never thought of him as Sam.

"I insist I pay," she said, giving him her best tough teacher voice.

"Don't turn that teacher talk on me. I can resist it. It was nothing, Cora. He didn't need x-rays or meds or anything. You were here for all of fifteen minutes."

"Are you sure?"

He responded by putting his hand on her arm and saying, "Yes, I'm sure. Now take Atticus home, and have a good evening."

"Thank you so much," Cora said as she turned to make her way to the driver's door when Cole suddenly appeared in front of her.

"Are you okay?" Cole asked her. "What happened?"

"And you are?" Dr. Brenner responded quickly before Cora could answer.

"I'm Cora's new neighbor, Cole Houston," he said.

"I'm Cora's vet, Dr. Sam Brenner," the vet said, stepping closer to Cora, which she noticed made Cole's nostrils flare.

Cora wasn't sure what was going on, but there was a heavy dose of testosterone in the air, coupled with a tension so thick she was surprised she couldn't see it. She needed to cut right through it, not let this scene continue to play out on Main Street.

"Atticus gave me a scare this afternoon at school, and Dr. Brenner was kind enough to see us quickly to check him out," Cora said easily.

"It's Sam," Dr. Brenner turned to her and replied.

"Yes, of course," she said to Dr. Brenner before speaking to Cole. "Anyway, we were just leaving. I need to get Atty home and in bed."

She was getting in the car as she heard Cole say, "I'll follow you in case you need help getting him in the house."

Cora simply nodded, which Cole clearly took as a sign she was accepting his offer of help, judging by the size of his smile as he walked away. In truth, Cora just wanted to go home. About fifteen minutes later, she sighed with relief as she pulled into her driveway. The familiar crunch of gravel and the sight of her cozy cottage with its stone and white wood façade calmed her heart as it always did. Sometimes she felt like she spent most of every day just trying to get back home.

Glancing back, she saw that Atty was conked out, his breathing relaxed. She was so grateful he was okay. It was a constant blessing to have him at school with her during the day, not having to leave him behind, but there was always a risk that something like the cupcake incident could happen. Kids and dogs were precious, but they could be precocious together.

Just as she opened her door, she heard Cole's tires crunch behind her. He was out of the car almost before it came to a full stop, slamming it into park, and rushing toward her.

"Why don't you let me carry him? I'm certain you can do it, have done it, and will do it again. But right now, I'm here, and I can help," he said, even as he opened Atty's car door.

"I've got him, but thank you. If he wakes up, it might scare him to find a stranger holding him," she replied.

"Cora, he's out cold," Cole said, gesturing to Atty, who was snoring on the backseat. "He's not going to notice who's holding him."

"I've got him," she repeated.

She could feel the annoyances of the day building into a mountain of frustration. And while she realized Cole was only trying to help, this encounter reminded her of their first one when she fell in the snow. She didn't need to be rescued, and he didn't need to be so pushy.

"He's a hundred pounds of dead weight right now," he said. "Just let me help. You go unlock the door, and I'll take him straight to his bed. It will be done in two minutes flat."

"Fine," she replied, huffing out an exasperated breath. "But only because I'm tired, and it's been a long day. Let's be clear though. You cannot just drive up here and start taking over. That's not acceptable."

She was well aware that he towered over her, outweighing her by at least one hundred pounds. But she didn't back down. As she finished her little rant and stared up at Cole's face, she wasn't sure what she was seeing. He seemed equal parts concerned and possibly about to laugh. Was that humor? Did he think she was funny? Obviously, this only added a heaping dose of fuel to her already burning fire.

"Is there something funny about this situation to you,

Cole? Is my terrible day and my poor sick dog making you laugh? Or maybe you just don't know what to make of a woman who isn't all impressed with your bossy, arrogant ways," she said, now on a roll and happy to let off some steam after the day she'd had.

He stared down at her with surprised eyes.

"What? No. I'm not laughing at you. I'm not happy you had a bad day or that Atticus is sick," he said in obvious confusion.

"Then why did it seem you were holding back a laugh?" she prodded.

"Well, if I'm honest, I never know what to expect with you. Sometimes you're polite and offering me food, and other times, I think you want to throat punch me. It's kind of entertaining. Most people just don't get that close."

He seemed so embarrassed and confused by his own explanation, some of the fury left her. Heaven knew, he made her act out of character as well.

"We do seem to rub each other the wrong way which is unusual for me. I generally get along with most people," she replied.

He frowned and dropped his eyes, as if hurt by her comment.

"I don't like that," was all he said in reply and then moved immediately to open the door to retrieve Atty. "Why don't you go unlock the door? I'll get Atticus."

She didn't understand why his unhappiness over her comment bothered her, but it did. Somehow she sensed that he was vulnerable underneath that hard exterior. She'd seen it last night over dinner and again just now when he admitted he didn't like what she'd said about them. He seemed as confused by their interactions as she was.

She heard him murmur soft words to Atty as he lifted him from the car. Glancing back, she realized that Atty was so wiped out he hadn't even woken at the sound of their voices. He was usually her stalwart defender, but that cupcake had really waylaid him.

She quickly unlocked the door to the cottage and held it open as Cole came behind her, cradling the large German Shepherd in his arms. Atty's eyes were barely open, just slits, but he seemed content to let Cole carry him over to his bed. Once he was settled, Cole stood up as Cora remained on the floor talking softly to Atticus and making sure he was comfortable. He sighed and went right back to sleep.

"Do you mind if I make a fire while you tend to him?" Cole asked.

It was clear from the tension in his body and the tightness of his voice that he expected her to say no, and that was fair given how she'd responded to his offer of help outside.

"That would be nice. Thank you."

Cora spent a few more minutes with Atticus and then set about doing her usual after-school chores. She took off her coat, turned on some lights to combat the early darkness, and went to the kitchen where she was happy to be reminded that she'd left her favorite beef stew simmering in the crockpot all day. The room smelled delicious, and her stomach rumbled, attesting to the pitiful lunch she'd choked down at school earlier in the day.

Once Cole had the fire going, he said, "I'll be heading over to the bungalow. If you need anything tonight, if you have any trouble with Atticus, I'd be happy to help out."

Without waiting for a reply, he headed to the door.

"Cole, why don't you stay and eat dinner here? It seems silly for you to go over there only to wait for me to bring your dinner to you. It's ready. All I need to do is warm up the bread and set the table, and we can eat." She could see refusal in his eyes so she added, "Please. It would make it easier on me."

"I can always just take a bowl with me. That way I'm out of your hair. The last thing you need to end your terrible day is to have to spend your evening with me. Like you said, we don't get along too well," he replied, and once again she could hear the hurt in his voice.

"Actually, I was thinking it would be my way to thank you. You really helped me this afternoon, and you were so gentle and kind to Atticus. Plus, I'd like to think we could start fresh, maybe try to get along a bit better. That's what I make my second graders do, so it only seems fair I hold myself to that standard as well." This last part was said with the hint of smile, teasing in her voice.

"Okay," he said softly. "I'd like that."

Within minutes, Cole was pouring them each a glass of wine at Cora's insistence.

"It's been that kind of day," she said as she slathered slices of homemade sourdough bread with butter and put them in the oven to toast.

"I'll just go wash up. There's a bathroom through there. Right?" he asked pointing to the room behind the kitchen.

"Yes, but be careful. When you step up to go back there, I think you're tall enough you might bump your head on the ceiling. These old houses have some odd proportions," she said and smiled as she watched him duck his head as he walked that way. By the time he returned, she had the stew served and was sitting down with a sigh of relief.

"That sigh sounds like someone is glad to be home for the day," he said as he joined her.

"Oh, I am. I'm a homebody, so I'm always glad to be home, but today I'm extra glad."

Once they were settled and eating, Cole said, "So, tell me about this terrible day."

"It all started about seven this morning when an angry father came in before school to chew me out for giving his son a conduct mark yesterday. Then my computer froze," she began, stopping abruptly when she noticed the concerned look on Cole's face.

"An angry man just gets to come into your classroom before school? Were you alone? How did he get in?" Cole asked, his voice clipped and eyebrows raised.

"Well, for starters, it was not just some random angry man. It was my student's father. Parents often stop by in the mornings with a quick question or just to chat, especially when the kids are as young as my students. I'm trained to handle irate parents, Cole, and I'm quite good at it," she explained.

"I'm sure you're brilliant at everything you do, but it seems like that set-up leaves you without any protection if a situation goes south. What if he started yelling or tried to touch you?" he continued.

"He was just mad. He's in the middle of a nasty divorce, and his son is suffering. The boy got into a fight at recess yesterday and threw a punch. He's been increasingly angry lately and not himself. I had both students speak to the principal which is standard for physical altercations, and I gave him a conduct mark. He told his dad a different story. I told his dad the truth. Case closed."

"Even if you know the parents well, it still feels risky," he said. "You never know when a situation can escalate beyond your control."

It was obvious he was not going to let it go. On one hand,

it was nice to have someone so concerned about her safety. She'd been alone a long time and forgotten how good it felt to have someone else look out for her. On the other hand, she was a very competent human who didn't need someone questioning her ability to take care of herself. Cole didn't have the right to any commentary on her life.

"Eat your dinner, and let's move on. That alone wouldn't have made my day terrible. I have more to share," she said, pleased to see her teacher voice worked on grumpy men just as well as badly behaved eight year olds.

"I do believe I just met the teacher," he commented with a smirk.

"And that's all you'll get if you can't have a conversation with me without going into macho protection mode," she continued primly.

"Fine. What happened next?" he said, grinning at her cheeky reply.

"Well, like I was saying, my computer froze so I couldn't access my email, my attendance record, even some of the programs I needed for the Smart board. So, I had to re-plan on the fly, which is something any teacher can do, but I just wasn't at the top of my game today."

In fact, she realized that she didn't actually feel very well. All day she'd had the sense that something wasn't right, a general malaise. She'd hoped that being home would make her feel better, but that wasn't the case. Her body had begun to ache, and her head felt foggy.

"And then?" he asked, clearly wanting the whole run-down of her terrible day.

"And then I realized I'd forgotten my lunch. I tried to stomach some cafeteria food, but it made me queasy, and when I got out to recess, someone came to tell me that a child fed Atty an entire cupcake with mile high blue frosting. I found him vomiting in the teacher's lounge. And so, I left early to take him to Dr Brenner, and here we are." She laughed. "I sound like the boy from *Alexander and The Terrible, Horrible, No Good, Very Bad Day.*

"What is that?" Cole asked, looking confused.

"You've never read it?" Cora asked, astounded.

Cole just shook his head.

"It's a classic children's book by Judith Viorst. Obviously, Alexander has a crappy day, and the book does a list of all the terrible things he says happened to him. I laughed because I sounded just like him when I was telling you about my day."

"I think I must have missed that one," he said, his gaze fixed on his bowl of stew instead of her.

"Oh well. I read it as a kid, so I thought maybe you did too," she said.

He just shook his head and kept eating. Cora had the distinct impression he was uncomfortable, and she couldn't figure out if it was the children's book she mentioned or books in general. Regardless, he was distant now when only moments ago he'd been completely invested in her story of the day.

"Anyway, that's it. It's not really terrible, considering all the horrible things that can happen to human beings, but it wasn't great." she said, trying to pull him back into the conversation.

"You said someone came to tell you about Atticus. Does he not stay with you at school?"

"No, he's the school therapy dog so he stays with the guidance counselor during the day. He has a bed, food, toys, the whole nine yards. I check on him at set points in the day. Usually, he comes out to recess a few times a week, which the kids love. But mostly, he helps sad or hurt or troubled kiddos. If a child needs to see the counselor, Mrs. Price checks to see if they like dogs, and if they do, Atty is part of the session. Also, he goes with her to visit classrooms. Everyone loves him!" she said and heard the pride in her own voice.

"So, Mrs. Price is trained to work with him?" Cole asked.

"Yes, she was already trained when I met her, even before Jeff and I adopted Atticus as a puppy. We were friends with her, and when she came over one day and met Atty, she was instantly smitten. She encouraged us to have him trained and certified, and it was honestly one of the best things we ever did. He's a natural, and it means I don't have to leave him alone all day. The truth is it helps me to have him at school. I can see him whenever I want to. Plus, Shepherds are a working breed, so they need a job."

"That sounds pretty ideal for you and for him." Cole said.

"It is. Atticus is my best friend, and he's the only other soul who knows how it feels to lose Jeff just like me," she said as her gaze shifted to look at her precious furry friend snoozing in front of the fire.

"May I ask you a personal question?" Cole asked after a few silent moments.

"Well, ask it, and I'll tell you," she replied.

He smirked. "Have you dated Dr. Brenner?"

"What? No. I haven't dated anyone since Jeff died, and I won't. But Dr. Brenner does ask every time I take Atticus to his office. I always say no," she responded.

"Wait a minute. You don't date at all?" he asked.

"No. I made a vow to Jeff right before he died. He will always be my one and only. Nothing else could ever match what we had together," she said.

Cole just stared at her.

Finally, he said, "You haven't eaten, Cora. I've kept you

talking instead of letting you eat, and you have to be hungry after your bad lunch."

It was true. But, as soon as he mentioned eating, she realized that she didn't want to take another bite. Just the sight of the bowl of stew, which had earlier made her mouth water, now made her queasy.

"Actually, I'm not feeling all that well. Maybe that's why I was such a mess today."

Something in her face or voice must have alarmed him because he said, "Let me clean this up for you. You can go on up and lie down, and I can let myself out."

"No, I can't let you do that. It won't take me long to clean up, and I need to take Atty out before we settle upstairs."

She made a move to get up, but she was instantly dizzy and sat right back down.

Cole put his hand over hers, and said, "Cora, let me help."

She just nodded.

"I'm going to lead you up the stairs. Then I'll clean up and take care of Atty," he said softly.

He held out his hand for her, and she took it. Even in her present state, she felt the warmth of his touch and the awareness it brought. She couldn't tell if he felt it too. He helped her up and led her gently up her narrow, twisting staircase.

At the top of the stairs, she said, "I'm good from here. Thank you, Cole."

She made her way straight to her bedroom, the aches intensifying, and a terrible chill settling in her bones. She took off her shoes, pulled back the covers, turned on the electric blanket, and was asleep in minutes.

CHAPTER 8

COLE

COLE MADE QUICK work of cleaning up the kitchen. Cora was neat and tidy, so it wasn't a hard job. It was much trickier coaxing the usually alert Atticus to wake up and go out. He could see Atticus looking for Cora, but the dog didn't seem to feel any threat from Cole. He sniffed and licked him and then tried to stand up.

"Why don't we do it this way, Atty, my man?" Cole said as he lifted the big dog into his arms. "I'll carry you out there, set you down, and you do your business. Then you can come in and be with your mama. You need to look out for her tonight. Okay?"

Atticus did just as he was told. Cole was surprised to find it snowing fairly hard when they stepped outside. How had he missed this in the forecast? He knew snow was coming, but he was certain they'd only predicted an inch or two, which didn't amount to much for people around here. But this seemed like it had more potential than predicted.

When he set Atty down, the snow already completely covered his paws. Once they were back inside, he dried him off with a towel he found on a rack in the bathroom. It had dog bones on it, and the name *Atticus* was stitched in black across the top. Once he made sure the pup had a little water, he picked him back up and carried him upstairs. This time Atticus whined a bit when Cole lifted him.

"We both know you aren't climbing these stairs feeling like you do tonight. You and your sweet mama are quite the pair this evening. Let's get you settled with her. I'd bet a hundred bucks you sleep in the bed with her," he murmured to the sleepy dog.

Cole had only been as far as the top of the stairs, so he didn't know how the second floor was laid out. He found himself in a large living room with a massive stone fireplace. There was a very small office that opened off the living room, and through another doorway, he could see what had to lead to a bedroom. He didn't want to intrude, but he needed to check on Cora and get Atticus settled with her.

Sure enough, he passed into a long room that seemed to be a dressing room of sorts. One long side was devoted to an open concept closet area with shelves and hanging space running the length of the wall. At one end of the room was the bathroom, and at the other end, a set of small wooden steps led down into Cora's bedroom.

He stood at the top step and saw she was snuggled down in her bed, a few wisps of hair the only part of her he could see. She didn't budge even though every step he took seemed to make the floor creak. Atticus saw Cora and began to squirm in Cole's arms, whining again.

Cole heard Cora mumble, "Atty, come here, baby. Come go to sleep."

He could tell from her words and the dreamy tone of her voice, she wasn't fully awake. She was simply responding to Atty as she would any other night. Cole moved quickly down the wooden steps and set the now wiggly dog on the bed. In a series of automatic moves that seemed like a dance they did every night, Cora raised her covers, and Atticus circled three times before he settled in close to her. She put the covers back down over them, and instantly, they were both asleep.

He didn't let himself linger there. He'd only known Cora for a matter of days. If she was her usually healthy self, she wouldn't want him in her bedroom or here at all, for that matter. He simply made sure she was breathing easy and turned away. But for a moment he thought he'd be more than happy to spend the night watching over the two of them, the beautiful woman and the dog who ate a cupcake.

Cole moved back up the odd little stairs and moved to turn a light on in the bathroom. He didn't want Cora to get up in the night and be afraid. He knew she slept here alone every night, but being sick often made people feel vulnerable. He left a light on in the staircase as well. He then banked the fire in the dining area, left a lamp on in the kitchen, and locked up with a spare key he found in her key bowl.

He found himself back in the bungalow at a little before seven o'clock. They'd eaten an early dinner, and this left Cole with a lot of time on his hands. He was normally exhausted at the end of a workday. Construction work was like that, and even though he was in charge now and didn't do most of the work himself, he still liked to get his hands dirty. With this old house, he was doing a lot more than that. However, today he'd spent several hours just ordering building supplies at the shop in town, and he wasn't as tired as usual.

His plan had been to return to his house and keep working, but seeing Cora in town had changed that. He'd been driving down Main Street, contemplating a stop at *On the House* for one of their cinnamon rolls and a hot cup of coffee to clear the cobwebs from his mind before he got back to work. He'd even considered leaving Cora a note that he would not be back for dinner intent on working himself to exhaustion long into the night.

Then, he'd seen her rushing out of the vet's office, scrambling to open the car door as a man followed behind her holding Atticus. Never in his life had Cole felt so many disparate feelings all at once. His first thought was worry. Even from where he sat at the street's only redlight, he could feel Cora's anxiety. What was wrong? Was she okay?

His heart kicked up a hard beat at the thought of her in distress. He saw the man holding her dog and had to admit to a moment of jealousy even though he knew he had no right to that emotion. It was then that he read the sign on the building and realized that Cora's distress clearly had something to do with Atticus.

Once the light turned, he'd slid into the first parking spot he found on the narrow street and began to make a beeline for her. Up close, he could see the man was handsome and also clearly, the vet. But he could also see the interest in his eyes. Of course, any man would be interested in such a beautiful woman. After his chat with Angelo, he wasn't surprised. Clearly, the men of Longview recognized what a gem she was.

Cole's genuine relief when Cora seemed to accept his offer of help was huge. He didn't understand what was happening, but from somewhere so deep inside him he didn't recognize it, Cole knew that if anyone was going to look out for Cora, he wanted it to be him.

Now as he stood in the bungalow kitchen in the early evening, he was at a loss for what to do. The snow was coming down hard, so it seemed foolish to trek up to the house to work. Angelo's men had been the last on site, and Angelo had sent him a text that they were gone for the day and had secured the house. Cole wasn't sure what there was to secure in the decrepit old place, but he was grateful.

He guessed he would just take a hot shower and then settle in with a book. Cora's question about the children's book tonight at dinner, something to do with a kid named Alexander and his bad day, had cut him, but he'd done his best not to let her see. He hadn't learned to read proficiently until he was a teenager. Rick and Betty Evans had tried to help him in the few years he spent with them, but they couldn't afford the kind of tutoring he needed. His teachers simply did the best they could without the resources needed to really make a difference.

After Rick died and Betty couldn't take care of him, he returned to the system. It hadn't been a good experience. He was a scrawny kid, forever underfed and slow to grow, an easy target for bullies. The rest of his childhood was an exercise in trying to be invisible so he didn't get beaten up or worse. Reading wasn't a priority when he was just trying to survive.

He spent the last few years of his adolescence in a group home. It lacked most every creature comfort, but he did get enough to eat on a consistent basis. It wasn't good food, but it was filling. He finally hit a growth spurt. That extra size gave him a little bit of power, and sadly, he used it to become a bully himself. It was a relief to be the one who caused fear instead of the one who was afraid.

Cole became an expert at sneaking off the grounds of the group home no matter how much of an eye they kept on him. He skipped school and stole beer from the gas station nearby. He picked fights and threw punches at the least offense. He let every ounce of anger and pain pour out of him in a raging torrent. He'd tried to be a good boy for most of his life, just hoping for someone to love him, and no one ever did. So, he became a bad boy instead.

By the time he was released from group care at eighteen, not a single adult he encountered was interested in whether or not he could read and write. They just wanted him gone. Most people in the Texas town where he lived probably expected him to become a drug dealer or any other thing that would land him in jail. And that was a distinct possibility.

Without regular meals and a safe place to sleep, Cole quickly became defenseless all over again. He was nothing but a taller version of the scared little boy he'd once been. Then he'd run into Joe in a convenience store late one afternoon, and that meeting saved his life.

He was attempting to steal a bottle of Gatorade and a honeybun when Joe had walked up to him in the back of the store and simply said, "Hand it over. I'll get that for you the right way."

Cole's first instinct had been to run, but something in the man's kind eyes and determined stance stopped him. He stood there defiantly, keenly aware of the pitiful state of himself. He was dirty, scrawny, and skittish. He hadn't had anything to eat in a few days and only water from someone's hose to drink. His hand had trembled as he reached into his filthy jacket pocket and handed the items to the man.

"I'd like to buy these for you and then take you across the street to *The Taco Shop* for a real meal. I won't touch you, and I won't turn you in. You have my word. I think I can help you. We'll be in public the whole time. I'll drive over to the restaurant, and you can just walk," he said, reaching out his hand.

Cole merely stared at it. Was this man offering to shake? He knew he smelled bad. And even if he didn't, he'd grown used to being invisible. No one ever really saw him, much less treated him like a human being.

"My name is Joe," the man said gently.

He was a tall, muscular man who looked to be in his forties or fifties. Cole wasn't any good at figuring out people's ages. Joe's clothes were rugged and a little dusty. He had a worn brown leather jacket over a snap-up western shirt and dark jeans. A cowboy hat sat on his head, so Cole could see only the hair that spilled out from the edges. It looked silvery. Even over his own stench, Cole could detect the cologne the man wore which smelled woodsy and clean. He lifted his trembling hand, and Joe grabbed it gently in a strong shake.

"I'm Cole," he said, and his voice sounded rusty even to his own ears.

"Nice to meet you, Cole."

At that moment, Cole's stomach let out more of a roar than a growl, and the man laughed.

"Let's pay for this and then get you some real food."

Together they walked to the register where the cashier looked at Cole with skeptical eyes. She had to know they hadn't come in together, and certainly they didn't look like they belonged together in any way. Cole knew she probably suspected his stealing. It wasn't the first time he'd done it, but she'd looked the other way. That wasn't exactly help, but it wasn't unkind either.

In his experience, even the people who might feel some compassion for him didn't actually want to get involved, as if his misfortune was somehow contagious. Humans liked to be comfortable, and Cole knew he didn't inspire comfort. Letting his theft go unreported likely counted as the cashier's good deed for the day, and what he stole never amounted to much anyway.

Once Joe finished the transaction, he handed the bag to Cole, and they left the store.

"I'll meet you over there," Joe said as he climbed into a hulking black truck.

Cole walked across the street and waited in the parking lot far from the door. He knew all too well how he would be treated if he loitered any closer. In just a few minutes, Joe joined him, and they walked to the door.

"I don't think I'm clean enough to go in there," Cole said, starving for the food he knew was inside, but certain no one in there wanted to smell him while they ate.

"There are some tables out back. Why don't I go order for us, and you can wait there? Anything you like or don't like?" Joe asked, clearly not wanting to scare him off.

"They won't want me hanging around anywhere, even out back," Cole answered.

"I'll speak to them when I go inside. It will be fine. Now, what do you want?" Joe asked.

"I've never eaten here. I don't know, but I pretty much eat anything I can get my hands on," he said, his stomach growling again even louder.

"I bet," said Joe, chuckling. "I'll just order a bunch of different things. You go get a table."

Hesitantly, Cole made his way to the small set of picnic tables at the back of the parking lot in a grassy area. He knew from passing by that a lot of construction workers stopped here for lunch and often ate outside if they were dusty or dirty. Maybe he would be okay back here. There was a door open to the kitchen, and Cole could smell the most amazing scents coming from inside. In just a moment, Joe joined him. He held a tray with chips and salsa and two large cups of soda.

"Here you go. This should hold you over until the real food gets here," he said as he sat down.

Cole knew he should be embarrassed that he fell on the chips like a starving dog, but he couldn't find it in him to care. He was a lot like a starving dog. After gorging on chips and salsa, he looked up to find Joe just watching him, having not touched a single chip.

"I'm sorry. I was just so hungry. I guess you don't want to touch them after me," he said, more than a little embarrassed as he wiped his mouth with his sleeve and put his hands in his lap.

Joe grabbed a chip and crunched it.

"Nope. You're just hungrier than me. I've been there. Eat all you want."

"Why are you being nice to me?" Cole asked skeptically.

He'd heard stories. He knew that there were predators looking for vulnerable kids like him.

"Well, for one thing, I want to help you. And more importantly, I was you many years ago, and someone helped me. It changed everything. I made a promise I'd do the same if ever given the opportunity," Joe said.

They were interrupted by a waitress coming toward them with a tray of food. A waiter came behind her with another tray. Both of the servers stared at Cole with wide eyes, but the sight and smell of the food was too good to pay them any attention.

"I ordered a little of everything. We have beef as well as chicken soft tacos, a couple of burritos, some refried beans, rice, guac, and quesadillas. There's got to be something in here you'll like," Joe explained.

"I think I'll like all of it," Cole said as he dug in to the meal, polishing off two tacos before Joe had even finished filling his plate.

Cole shook his head in the present, still able to taste and smell that delicious food all these years later. Joe had saved his life that day and many days after. Thinking about books always made him think of Joe, for it was Joe who finally taught him to read just like he taught him how to build a house.

Later, when Cole was showered and dressed in gray sweats and a navy-blue t-shirt, he decided to build a fire in the living room. The lights were off so only the glow from the kitchen lit the room. The snow was falling outside, and it was, he thought, a magical sight. Once the fire was lit, he walked to the long wall of windows.

It was definitely a night that made a person glad to have a warm house to shelter in, but as he stared out into the night, he heard a sharp bark and then a cry almost like a wolf. The sounds continued, and Cole grabbed his heavy coat, stepped into his boots, not bothering to tie them, and stepped out onto the patio to get a better look.

The sound was coming from the hill down into the valley, the same path Cora walked each morning and night to feed and care for the animals. The bark continued but seemed to get closer to him. The whines and howls stayed put, and he could make out a bit of motion. As he stepped further onto the patio, Atticus came running out of the snow and lunged onto the patio barking sharp, short sounds of alarm.

Even Cole, who had little experience with dogs, recognized that Atticus had come for help. Cole's heart raced at the knowledge that Atticus being outside meant that Cora was outside too. Atticus didn't stop moving or barking. He clearly wanted Cole to follow him. He kept circling him, herding him to the edge of the patio and out into the snow.

"Okay, boy, I'm coming. Take me to her."

Cole followed the loyal dog down the hill, slipping a bit on the slick snow. Soon, he could see another dog, a large white one he'd never seen before, standing guard over Cora's small form, collapsed in the snow. Cole rushed to her, the white dog stepping away, clearly trusting the human that Atticus brought to help them.

"Cora, Cora, can you hear me? I'm here," he asked frantically, checking her over.

As he brushed the snow off her face, she moaned, seeming to wake up.

"Cole, is that you?" she whispered in a thin voice.

"Yes, it's me. Are you hurt? Can I lift you? I need to get you back to the house."

"Yes please. I'm so cold."

As he scooped her up, he could feel her small body shivering through her coat and clothes. He climbed back up the hill, making sure that each step was sure. Atticus followed, but the other dog disappeared further down the hill.

Soon, they were back at the house, and Cole didn't stop until he had Cora back upstairs in her bedroom. He eased off her coat and tucked her back in the bed. Then, he grabbed a towel from the bathroom and returned to gently dry her hair and face. She was shaking hard. He reached over and turned her electric blanket to the highest setting. Then he pulled it up to her chin and rubbed her arms over the covers, trying to get some heat into her.

"That feels good. I'm so cold," she mumbled, burying her face deeper under the covers.

"Cora, can you listen to me for a minute?" he asked, and he could make out a slight nod from under the blankets.

"Did you take anything earlier? Any medicine?"

"No, I just went to sleep."

"I'm going to go look in the bathroom and find something for you to take that will help get your fever down," he said.

Cora didn't respond, but her shivering had lessened. Still, he spied an extra quilt and tucked it around her. She let out a deep sigh of relief at the added layer. In the bathroom, he was easily able to find what she needed in the medicine cabinet.

Sitting on the edge of her bed, he said, "Cora, let's sit you up just enough to take these tablets."

Thankfully, she was able to do that without too much trouble, and he let her wash the pills down with the water glass from her bedside table. Then he helped her settle again under the covers. She seemed a little more alert for the moment, and her brow furled.

"Where's Atty?" she asked.

"He's right here at the foot of the bed. Once I'm sure you're okay, I'm going to dry him off."

This seemed to reassure her. She let out a soft *my good boy* before slipping back to sleep. He took a moment to towel off Atticus, making sure he was as dry as possible. It was likely he was going to get right back on the bed with Cora, and Cole didn't want him to make her cold again.

Sure enough, once he was dry, Atticus leapt on the bed and snuggled right into Cora, but the sweet dog didn't try to get under the covers. In fact, he seemed more careful than usual as if he sensed that she didn't need to be jostled or disturbed.

Cora reacted by pushing closer to the dog and whispering, "Hey, sweetie."

"Do you want to tell me what I need to do for the animals?" Cole asked.

"Oh yes, please."

She then proceeded to give him a fairly lucid run-down of what needed to happen for the chickens, the goats, and the donkey, all of whom were sheltered safely and just needed to be checked on to make sure they were warm enough.

"Will you be okay while I take care of them?" he asked. "I'll stop by the bungalow and grab what I need on the way back up. Then I'll stay here and look after you."

"I can't ask you to do that. I'll be fine," she said in what Cole assumed was meant to be Cora's fiercest voice, but it came out as soft as fluff from a pillow.

"You didn't ask. I'm offering. I just found you passed out in the snow. You're sick. I'm guessing the flu. I'll camp out on the couch, so I can let Atticus out in the morning. He needs me too," he said in a tone that brooked no argument.

In his brief time with Cora, he knew she would normally argue, but sick as she was, she simply said, "Thank you."

With her settled, he headed out to check on the animals. Cole hadn't yet ventured down to the barn and the chicken coop, but he wasn't surprised to see them neat and tidy. All was well with the little crew who were clearly well loved and tended.

For a man like Cole who'd been neglected and mistreated, then abandoned by his own mother, Cora was a revelation. This woman seemed to mother everything that crossed her path; students, dogs, donkeys, goats, chickens, guests at her bungalow, and even him since he'd arrived. She was a person who took care of others, who had a knack for tending. He'd had precious little of that in his life.

His mother had been young and disinterested in tending to anyone but herself. At her best, she simply forgot he was there. At her worst, she left marks on his body and mind. April Houston had been only nineteen when he was born. What he remembered was a pretty but volatile girl who wanted life to be so much better than it was. Sometimes they stayed with her friends. Occasionally, she could afford a ratty apartment of their own for a while. She flitted from job to job and man to man, but nothing stuck. She was often drunk and sometimes high.

She used Cole as a prop when she thought it would help her catch a man's attention, and in those rare moments, she would smile and cuddle him like he imagined real mothers would. But more often than not, he was an obstacle that she needed to get around, a burden she'd didn't want, and she told him that with both her words and her actions. He had not only the mental scars but also the physical ones to prove it. There were the marks of cigarette burns on his back, as well as a litany of hateful words etched forever in his memory.

Years later, after April simply left him in the parking lot of the Shop & Save, Betty Evans had come into his life as the only mother figure who ever truly cared for him. She'd taken an interest, but she'd done it all in an automatic, fairly detached way. She was a nurse, and while she tended with care, Cole always felt a bit like one of her patients. And then, even that comfort was taken from him when she could no longer keep him.

There were other foster mothers, other caregivers at the group homes, but not one of them ever made him feel like anything other than an obligation. Cora, on the other hand, seemed to care for others as an instinct, as if it would never occur to her to act in any other way. It wasn't something Cole understood, but it certainly appealed to him.

As he left the barn, he ran right into the huge white dog he'd seen with Cora earlier, the one who had stood guard over her. He saw now, without the haze of panic, that it was a Great Pyrenees, a livestock guardian. As such, he wouldn't live inside the house like Atticus whose job was to guard Cora. This dog would live down here with the animals he protected, constantly roaming the borders to scare off predators. He would certainly be welcome in the barn especially on a frigid night, but most of the time, he worked. He'd done his job admirably tonight.

Cole reached out his hand to the big dog, letting him have a sniff before trying to pet him. The huge dog took a light sniff and then licked Cole's entire gloved hand. Before he knew it, Cole was fully engaged in a belly rub of the huge beast who apparently loved a good cuddle. Cole laughed to himself.

Of course, he did. No animal that lived with Cora would be a stranger to love, cuddles, and belly rubs. She was probably even affectionate with the chickens. Right then, he promised himself that as soon as she was healthy again and the weather let up, he was going to watch her tend to these animals. She probably treated them just like another classroom of students.

He found himself muttering to the dog, "Thank you for watching over her. She's safe now."

Before he could think of how foolish he sounded, he got up and climbed back up the hill to his temporary home. He quickly grabbed his phone, his book, a few toiletries, and a change of clothes for tomorrow. He stuffed it all in a ragged duffle bag and locked up the house, eager to get back to Cora.

CHAPTER 9

CORA

CORA SLEPT DEEPLY, warmed both by the electric blanket and Atticus snuggled next to her. The medicine kicked in bringing her fever down and lessening the aches. At some point in the wee hours of the morning, she woke achy and cold again, shivering so hard she thought her bones rattled. Her mouth tasted disgusting, and her eyes were dry and scratchy. Before she could even process what to do, she heard Cole come down the stairs to her room and felt his weight dip the mattress.

"Here. Your meds wore off," he said, gently lifting her head and pressing two pills into her hand before holding a water bottle to her lips.

"Thank you," she said softly, laying her head back on the pillow.

Cole straightened her covers as best he could with Atticus lying heavily next to her. At some point, she'd apparently thrown off some of the layers in a blast of fever. Now, she was trembling with chills again. Cole made sure she was covered and comfortable, never turning on the light, just quietly tending to her.

"You're most welcome, Cora. Go back to sleep now."

The next time she awoke, the room was brighter but not sunny. Through the window, she could see the snow still falling thickly outside. She took a brief assessment of her aches and pains before moving. Everything hurt but not as terribly.

She was cold but not shivering. Her mouth was dry, but the nauseous feeling in her stomach indicated food or drink might be a mistake. She rolled over gingerly to snuggle with Atty and discovered he wasn't there. Cole had no doubt taken him out and was probably wondering what to feed him and all the other animals.

Looking at the clock by the bed, she saw that it was after nine in the morning, well past her usual wake up time and certainly later than her furry and feathered crew was accustomed to eating breakfast. At least the heavily falling snowing made her confident that there was no school today. She sat up carefully. Just as she was about to throw one leg over the side of the bed to get up, Cole came bounding down the small steps.

"Let me help you."

He rushed to her and eased her back into the bed. She wanted to be a bit miffed at how he took over, but she had to admit it felt a lot better to be lying down again. She was dizzy from simply sitting up.

"Whatever it is you need, I'll do it, but unless you need to use the bathroom, I really think you should stay put," he said.

"I need to feed Atty and the animals. I didn't tell you what to do, and it's a little more involved than just checking on them like last night. And yes, I do need the bathroom and my toothbrush," she said.

She looked at him as he leaned over her on the bed. His hair, which on any other man she would label as too long, was still damp from a shower, one he'd likely taken in her bathroom. She'd only seen it pulled back, and this glimpse of him with his hair down, smelling of soap and shampoo while he tended to her in her bedroom, felt incredibly intimate.

He was wearing a short sleeved gray t-shirt, clearly not warm enough for this day, which meant he'd likely rushed down here to stop her getting up while he was still in the middle of dressing. She could see a tattoo peeking out the bottom of the short sleeve on his right arm. It looked like the wings of a bird, but she couldn't see enough to be sure. She was not a tattoo kind of a gal, but once again, Cole seemed to invoke feelings in her quite the opposite of her normal preferences and opinions.

"Tell me now then. I'm a pretty sharp guy. I think I can get it done, maybe not as well as you, but everybody will be fed and alive. As for Atty, I just had to wing it. He was starving. I did two scoops of his dry kibble. Hope that's okay," Cole explained.

The way he was looking at her, so intently, his eyes tender made her heart beat a bit faster. When he reached up and smoothed the hair out of her face, she felt a little light-headed all over again. She told herself it was just the illness, nothing to do with the man.

"I'm sure he's fine. Where is he now?" she asked looking around.

She was surprised Atticus wasn't snuggled back up with her. He usually stuck pretty close.

"I did a little snow shoveling this morning while he did his business, and he had time to run around. I think it tired him out. After breakfast, he went straight to his bed by the fireplace and conked out."

"He's probably still recovering from yesterday," Cora

said before going over the details of her morning routine with the animals.

She was pleased with how intently Cole seemed to listen to her. He smiled when she finished going over it all for the second time.

"I think I've got it, mama bear," he said.

"Okay," Cora replied. "I'm guessing there's no school. Right?"

"I didn't know who to call, so I turned on the television downstairs and saw it on the news. We've had almost a foot of snow, and it's still falling, so they are urging folks to stay home."

"That works out well for me. I hate making sub plans. It's almost more trouble than being sick," she said, thinking of other mornings when she'd woken up sick and alone, texting her principal and typing up emergency lesson plans to send out while it was still dark outside.

A snowy day was a pleasant reprieve from that. She could just give in and be sick until she wasn't, especially with Cole here to help her. It was rare for Cora to have anyone to lean on. Sure, there were many friends and sweet people in town, but they all had their own families and lives. For some reason, Cole felt different. Maybe it was simply their odd circumstances, but letting him help her felt natural.

"Let's get you up to the bathroom before I head out to the take care of your little flock," he said.

It should have been awkward, she thought. She'd known him for a matter of days and still only barely. And yet, as he lifted her from the bed and carried her to the bathroom, all she felt was safe and grateful. With the door closed, she quickly got down to business, using the bathroom and brushing her teeth, aware that she felt weak and woozy. He was waiting just outside the door when she came out and carried her right back to bed.

When she was settled again, he said, "Well, the snow is good because it means you don't have to think about school, but it does mean seeing a doctor will be tricky."

"No need. Three kids in my class have had the flu in the last few weeks, and I forgot to get my shot last fall, so it seems clear that's what I have. I think I just need to tough it out, keep taking meds for the fever and aches, and let it work its way out of my system. It's not my first rodeo. Teachers are exposed to almost the same number of germs as health care workers. It's always something." She was getting sleepy, her eyes growing heavy. "You probably shouldn't get so close to me. I don't want you to get sick too."

"Nonsense. Besides, I think the germ ship has sailed. It's too late to worry about that now."

She felt him tucking the covers under her chin, tightening them up around her.

"Before you fall asleep, is there anything that sounds good? I hate to keep giving you medicine on an empty stomach. Crackers, dry toast, soup, anything?" he asked.

Her stomach turned at the thought of food, but she knew he was right.

"Maybe dry toast when I wake up and need the meds again," she suggested.

She felt the bed shift as he stood up and left the room, and then she knew only the pleasant numbness of sleep. Hours later, she felt the bed dip again, and recognized the comforting smell of Atticus as he circled the requisite three times before settling right up next to her. She pulled her arm out from under the covers and reached over to stroke his fur. It was chilly to the touch, so she knew he'd been out with Cole again.

Soon she was asleep again, waking sometime later to find herself drenched in sweat and so hot it felt like she was on fire. Clearly, she was in the midst of another fever cycle. Atticus was gone again. She was thirsty and nauseous and needed to go to the bathroom.

Carefully, she sat up, closing her eyes as a wave of dizziness hit her. When that passed, she got to her feet and stood still for a moment before beginning to move to the stairs, leaning on the bed and then the railing as she went. She made it halfway to the bathroom before she had to sit on the small settee that sat next to the window in the dressing room that connected her bedroom to the bathroom. That's where she was when Cole found her.

"Cora, what are you doing?" he asked, and his voice was loud and hard, almost frustrated.

Why was he mad at her? Sure, he was helpful and kind, but sometimes he was harsh in the way he spoke. It caught her off guard. She was a gentle woman, strong and independent, but gentle. She spoke softly and walked lightly in the world. He came in all loud, gruff words and forceful stomps. She didn't really know what to make of it. And right now, feeling fragile and weak and so sick, it just made her burst into tears.

He was on his knees in front of her immediately.

"Why are you crying?" he asked.

"You. You're so mean to me. I'm sick, Cole. I'm just trying to go to the bathroom. And you just come in here yelling at me," she said with all the anger she could manage.

"I'm sorry. I saw you slumped here, and it scared me. You seem to do that a lot. And I just want to take care of you."

"Being scared doesn't make it okay to yell at me. That's just an excuse for poor behavior."

"You're absolutely right. I'm sorry," he replied, his voice much softer now. "Let me help you up."

He led her to the bathroom where she quickly closed the door and leaned heavily against it. He seemed genuinely sorry he'd made her cry, but she couldn't help but remember the gentle way Jeff would've cared for her. She couldn't help thinking of the differences in the two men.

Jeff exuded kindness and care, was trustworthy and faithful. He'd showered her with all the attention and affection she'd craved as a young girl, always overlooked in her big, busy family. To him, she was *the* one, not just another one of many.

Cora was the fifth of sixth children and the only introvert in the bunch. Every one of her siblings was successful in some way, and she always felt utterly plain by comparison. While they were playing sports or dancing or riding horses or making straight A's, Cora was playing school with her dolls.

It wasn't that Cora wasn't a good student or a good kid. It was more that she was unremarkable. That feeling was reinforced by parents who clearly favored her more outgoing brothers and sisters. It felt like their love was doled out in direct proportion to the accomplishments of the child. Cora's portion of that love was, in her opinion, quite small.

Every night at dinner, there would be a mad rush of voices vying for attention, everyone clamoring to share the best story at the table. Cora didn't even bother to participate. She simply ate her food and smiled or laughed at all the appropriate places. When she was about nine years old, her father suddenly noticed that she wasn't taking part in the dinner conversations. Her quietness, in his eyes, was shyness, and he didn't like timid people. And so, she became his focus for a time.

"Come on, Cora. There has to be one thing you can share with us, something good or possibly funny. It's very important to be a person who can hold their own in conversation," he said, after a few nights of trying to coax her into talking.

And while his voice was completely calm and cordial, Cora saw the glint of steel in his eyes, the determination to make her speak. Her father was good at what he called *tough love*. It involved him taking a firm stance on something he expected from one or more of his children and simply making life difficult for them until he got his way. Cora agreed that it was indeed tough. However, she wasn't sure there was much love in the mix.

If one of them needed to be faster, he made them run until they threw up. If another needed a higher grade on an exam, he drilled them for hours until they could recite the answers in their sleep. And when one of them succeeded, he took as much credit as possible. Conversely, if one of them failed or got into trouble, his disappointment, as well as his punishments, were heavy. Cora decided early on that if being remarkable wasn't possible, then being invisible was the way to go.

That Saturday night at dinner she knew she was perilously close to becoming the recipient of some tough love. With nothing particularly special to share, she proceeded to tell them about helping Mrs. Cranston in her garden and checking Mr. Shumacher's mail. She told them about walking one family's dog while they were on vacation and about helping a classmate with her book report.

When she was done, there was silence at the table. Her father didn't say a word, simply nodded and took another bite of his chicken. She didn't think she'd impressed him, but she had satisfied the requirement. After that, he left her alone as if he'd determined early that she was always going to be a disappointment.

That was why Jeff was such a surprise and delight to her. Right from the start, she was more than enough for him. Her dreams of a quiet, fulfilling family life, of teaching school, and restoring an old home had appealed to him as if they were his dreams too. And when she spoke at their dinner table, he was always engaged and eager to hear her stories, no matter how mundane.

Cole was entirely different. Or was he? He certainly looked different, and his delivery was not as polished. But the truth was he looked after her with a steady care that was stunning. He was never far when she needed help. He seemed genuinely concerned for her. Maybe he was more like Jeff than she thought. Maybe that was the reason she was drawn to him.

Relieved to have made some sense of this odd situation, Cora finished in the bathroom, happy to feel remotely human and stepped out. Cole was there instantly, holding out a hand for her. Regardless of all her logical thoughts, her heart beat faster and something fluttered low in her belly. She pushed it away and simply smiled.

"I almost came knocking on that door. If I hadn't heard you moving around, I would've been worried something was wrong. Your ability to terrify me is unreal," he said.

Even though this was what she was coming to know as typically Cole, she also noticed that he was trying to soften his delivery.

"Sorry. I felt really disgusting, so it took a while to freshen up."

"I understand. I just keep reliving that moment I found you passed out in the snow, and it gets me going all over again."

He helped her get settled back in the bed. She noticed that the sheets were fresh, now bright white instead of the light floral that had been there only twenty minutes ago. He must have noticed her spying the change.

"I hope it's okay. I saw the sheets on the shelf in the dressing room, and I could tell by the tangled state of the bed that you'd had the fever sweats. No one wants to get back in the bed after that. So, I changed them. Sorry if that was a mistake."

"No, it's wonderful. Thank you," she said as she snuggled into the lavender scented sheets, their cool, freshness absolute heaven to her. "I'm sure I'll have the chills again soon, but right now, these cold sheets are just right."

"Good. I'm glad. Now how about some dry toast and more medicine? Also, your phone has been buzzing like crazy. I imagine a lot of folks are checking on you."

"It's probably a bunch of school texts and then Eliza, my best friend. And maybe Dr. Brenner, checking on Atty. I should answer them before they send out the cavalry," she said, chuckling.

"Yes, definitely Dr Brenner would just be checking on Atty," he said, smirking at her. She laughed. And then he said, "Eliza?"

"My best friend. We taught together until she had kids. Jeff and I were best friends with her and her hubby. That's who I was with earlier this week when I couldn't get your dinner. We have a standing dinner date once a week just to catch up. Eliza has never once let me down. I would be lost without her."

"Well, let me go grab your phone off the charger so you can let everyone know you're fine," he said, as he left and returned with her phone.

"You take care of those messages while I get you some food and medicine. I'll be back in a minute. Just text me if you think of something else you need," he said as he left the room.

Cora did indeed have about ten texts and at least that many emails, all regarding the storm, the cancElization of school, and yes, from both Eliza and Dr. Brenner. She took care of the school messages first, pleased to learn they'd cancelled school tomorrow as well. It was Thursday, so she would have the whole weekend to recover. Next, she called Eliza.

"There you are. I was about to head out on skis to check on you," said her friend with a relieved laugh.

"El, you won't believe it. I have the flu. Cole has been taking care of me. What with Atty and the cupcake yesterday, and now me being sick and the snow, I've been a little overwhelmed. Sorry I didn't answer sooner."

"Cole is taking care of you?" Eliza asked.

"That's all you got from all that?" Cora asked, giggling.

"It's the most interesting part. Tell me everything."

Cora glanced at the doorway to make sure she didn't see or hear Cole coming. Then she indeed told Eliza *almost* everything, starting with their meet-up outside Dr. Brenner's office all the way to when he found her in the snow.

"Oh my," gushed Eliza. "This is better than Netflix. I would ask if you need anything, but it seems like your strong, sexy man has it all covered."

"Just stop. This is not a rom-com. He's just being a kind human, looking after a neighbor. He's definitely not *my* strong, sexy man."

"Okay, sure. He's just neighborly. Got it," Eliza said.

Cora ignored the sarcasm.

"How are you guys doing?" she asked.

"We are in a perpetual cycle of out in the snow, back in the house to warm up and dry off, and then do it all over again. It's a zoo, but it's a lot of fun, too. And I think nap time is going to hit hard today for all four of us."

They chatted for a few more minutes, ending the call just as Cole came in with a tray of food.

"Love you," Cora said to Eliza as she always did.

"Love you, too, sweetheart. Enjoy that man," Eliza replied.

"I'm hanging up now," Cora said, blushing.

She ended the call and put her phone on the bedside table. Cole set the tray on her lap and looked at her intensely, placing his warm palm against her forehead.

"Why is your face so red? Is your fever spiking?"

"I'm fine," she said, as he removed his hand. She glanced at the tray, smelling the scent of toasted bread. "This looks good."

"It's not much, but it will get something in your stomach. I made you a cup of weak tea too."

He seemed almost embarrassed offering her the tea. Cora recognized a fellow loner, someone used to looking after himself, but unlike her, not used to looking after others.

"Well, I don't think I could handle anything exciting anyway. Thank you."

"You're most welcome. Now eat," he said more like himself, and this time his bossiness just made her smile.

The dry toast tasted good and seemed acceptable to her poor stomach. The tea tasted like heaven to her parched throat. While she ate, Cole updated her on the animals.

"They're all fine. I fed them and made sure everyone had fresh water and was warm enough. I'm going to admit I don't know a thing about livestock, but no one seems to be in any kind of discomfort. Those goats are a hoot, though, and that donkey means business," he said with a laugh.

Cora laughed too and said, "His name is Mr. Rochester, and yes, he can be a handful."

"Mr. Rochester. I see a pattern. So, Atticus is clearly from *To Kill a Mockingbird*, and Mr. Rochester is *Jane Eyre*. You love books. That's something we have in common."

Cora had to admit she was pleased and surprised that he recognized the literary references. He hadn't seemed too keen on her children's book comment at dinner, so she'd wrongly assumed he wasn't a reader. Cole must have seen that in her eyes.

"I didn't have books as a child," he said. "But once I learned to read and had access to them, I've never stopped."

"It's one of my favorite things to do. I love to get lost in the pages of a book. It's like taking a trip without leaving your house."

"Definitely. Sometimes it's the only way I can even understand the world," he said solemnly, and though Cora wanted to push for more information, she instinctively understood that when Cole shared, he needed to do it at his own pace.

"So, tell me about the other dog, the Great Pyrenees. He was with you, right by your side, last night in the snow, but I hadn't seen him before then," he asked, changing the subject just as she thought he would.

"That's Mr. Darcy," she said with a grin.

He smirked at her and said, "Right, Mr. Darcy. I suppose it's fitting."

"How did you know his breed, you who says he doesn't know animals?"

"I read about it in a book once. He fit the author's description."

"Well, Mr. Darcy is a livestock guardian. He guards the property and primarily looks after the animals. But he is a love, and even though he doesn't live with me and Atticus in the house, he's still a huge part of my heart. I'm not surprised he and Atticus took such good care of me and found you."

"He does love a good belly rub. I learned that this morning when he rolled over after I fed him. It's easy to tell that he's used to affection," Cole said.

"Well, just because he has a job to do doesn't mean he doesn't need lots of cuddles. I love all my babies," she replied.

They chatted a few more minutes before her eyes began to drift closed.

"I think someone needs a nap," Cole said.

Atticus came in at that moment, jumping on the bed. He did his usual pre-sleep circles around her.

"Sleep well, you two," she heard Cole say softly as he left the room.

CHAPTER 10

COLE

RIGHT BEFORE SLEEP claimed her, he heard Cora say, "Cole, make sure you eat. There's plenty of food."

He wanted to stay. He wanted the right to cuddle up to her and Atty, to keep them safe and warm. It felt wrong to walk away. Even sick and half-asleep, she was tending to him, and it felt good. What surprised him, though, was how good it felt to tend to her as well.

He had precious little experience in caring for anyone other than himself. There were no pets, few close friends, and only his work crew to look after. He was a generous and fair boss, but he didn't involve himself in the lives of his employees.

His relationship with Joe was strong, but he was always aware that he was the recipient of care. Even now, twenty years after they first met, Cole hadn't found a way to help Joe in any way that matched all his mentor had done for him. Joe was a force of nature, independent and strong. He was always the giver, and that imbalance in their dynamic often left Cole feeling like less.

Somehow tending to Cora came as naturally as breathing. He simply thought of what Betty or Joe might have done in the same circumstance, and he did it. There hadn't been a lot of affection in his life, but from both of them, he'd learned that caring often meant just doing what needed to be done.

Words weren't his strong suit. He knew he often came across as stern or even harsh. It wasn't his intention. From his earliest memories, he hadn't ever been able to impress or even interest anyone with his words. He didn't know if he'd been any chattier than most young children, but he did remember his mom often yelling at him to shut up.

Most of his foster parents preferred he simply fade into the background, never needy and always quiet. Any time he did try to stand up for himself or speak out, he was usually rewarded with a litany of cruel words or even crueler fists. And so, he became the taciturn man he was, more comfortable doing something than saying something. It hurt him to think that Cora thought he was mean to her. He never wanted that. And wasn't that just a clear reason to stay away from her once she was better? She was too good for the likes of him.

She was right about one thing. He did need to eat. He was starving, so he headed downstairs to the kitchen. Passing through the upstairs living area, he stopped to stoke the fire. For just a moment, he let himself linger on the photos on the mantle and scattered around the room, photos of Cora and Jeff and the life they lived together. There were wedding photos, snapshots of holidays and celebrations, all kinds of images captured of the two of them clearly deeply in love with one another.

Cora's smile in each and every photo was bigger than any he'd seen since he'd met her. He picked up one frame to examine it closer. It seemed like a more professional shot. Cora and Jeff were dressed in summer clothes, tan and almost glowing. They were outside in the backyard under a large oak tree, flowers blooming all around them. They sat on an old quilt with Atticus right between them, and all three of them, even the damn dog, had the most brilliant smiles on their faces.

The Cora he saw in that photo was still clearly the same sweet woman he knew now, but she was alive in a different way than the Cora of today. She was still gorgeous, energetic, and sexy, but somewhere in the years of loss and grief, not only had her smile dimmed, but her entire being seemed more cautious, even guarded. He supposed losing her love had done that, made life less safe, less expansive, just less.

And Jeff? Well, Cole couldn't really stand to look at the other man, the one who had Cora's heart even now. He made himself stare at Jeff, if only to bring into harsh relief every reason he himself would never be a man that Cora loved. Jeff was lean but muscled, tan, and happy in the way of men who have everything they ever wanted.

He sure didn't look like a man with a weak heart, didn't look a bit like a man who would die years too soon. He looked at Cora in every photo like she was the answer to every question, like she was the sun itself. Their happiness with one another was almost a living thing, palpable even through a photo.

In every picture, Jeff gave off the casual, relaxed vibe of a man who was comfortable in his own skin. And why wouldn't he? Cora said he'd come from wealth, had inherited money from his grandmother. He had left behind the life he didn't want and bought his dream home with his dream girl and settled into the life he truly wanted.

Cole was a rough-acting, tough-looking man. Sure, he knew he was reasonably good-looking, but in an accidental way. His clothes were always of the sturdy variety, more about comfort and durability than fashion. His jeans were often ripped. His shirts were old. His boots were scuffed. His hair was long, often under a hat or tied back, not because he was fashionable or rebellious but rather because he hated haircuts.

As a kid, his hair had often been buzzed right off, either because he had head lice or because his mom or later, foster parents didn't want to deal with it. When his hair grew back out, he always felt like more of a real person, less like someone who'd been thrown away. Whenever someone turned on the clippers, Cole would feel a part of himself die. And when he looked in the mirror after the deed was done, he would be again the little orphan that no one wanted. As a result, he'd grown into a man who feared hair clippers and hated barber shops, a modern-day Samson.

He had tattoos, big ones and small ones, mostly covered by his shirt, but they stuck out of the edge of his sleeves. Some of them were meant to cover scars as if those old hurts could be erased by the magic of art. He chose images that signified strength; the face of a lion on his back up near his right shoulder, a small lightning bolt to cover a cigarette burn on his left side. A broken chain on one arm represented his hard-won freedom from the prison of his childhood. Only one tattoo was done in color. It was a red rose to represent Betty Evans, the only bright part of his childhood.

His muscles were big, the kind that came from tough, manual labor. They ensured he wouldn't be pushed around ever again. He was polite enough and law-abiding, but most gave him a wide berth. Everything about him now was an answer to the little boy who wondered if he'd ever be able to fight back and win.

In other words, he wasn't Jeff. He didn't know how to be light, how to joke, or make small talk. It wasn't that he didn't understand his strengths. It was more that he wasn't sure he had the kind of gentleness that a woman like Cora needed.

Downstairs he raided the fridge and had to admit that eating at Cora's house was no hardship. The woman was single and small, but she clearly loved everything that had to do with food. There were good leftovers, homemade bread, and all kinds of sandwich ingredients. He heated up a bowl of stew and made himself a grilled cheese to go with it. Then he stoked the downstairs fire and sat down to enjoy his lunch.

The snow was still falling, and all reports he'd seen called for a shift to ice by the evening. That meant potential power outages. He knew they had enough food, but he needed to bring in more wood and make sure the animals were warm and safe.

He wasn't accustomed to time off. Snow didn't fall often in Texas and certainly not like this. He built houses when the weather allowed, which was most of the time. In the rare times when it didn't, he planned and courted new business.

Cole worked. That's what he did, and while he was glad for the chores that could occupy this afternoon, he was still uncomfortable with so much down time. It left him far too much time to think. By early evening, he'd gathered wood, checked on everything that needed checking, even trekked up to his place with Atticus in tow to make sure all was well there. Now back at Cora's, both fires were going, and darkness was falling. She'd slept a long time, only waking to go to the bathroom or take more meds.

By the time his stomach was rumbling again for food, the predicted ice was clicking against the windows. He went to check on Cora, hoping to get their dinner heated before they lost power. He'd rummaged around in her barn earlier and found a small generator that would keep the heater on for the chickens, but he hadn't found anything that would power the house.

He found her tossing and turning in a sweaty mess of blankets when he got to her. She was moaning, clearly in pain. He went to get a cool, damp cloth for her face, something he remembered Betty doing for him once when he was sick, and returned quickly. Sitting beside her, he threw off the covers to get her some air and wiped her face with the cool cloth. She didn't open her eyes, but she did settle at the comforting touch.

His heart broke a little when she murmured, "Jeff, it hurts."

He just kept stroking her face with the cloth. He straightened the bed as much as he could with her in it, and when she seemed to settle further into sleep, he decided she needed rest more than dinner. Then he heated some leftovers and ate dinner, fed Atty, found some candles and matches, and made sure all was well. When all that was done, he settled on the couch to read. A couple of hours later, the power went out, and he heard a cry from Cora.

"It's okay," he said as he hurried to her room, carrying a large pillar candle on a dish. "The ice storm knocked the power out, but we're okay."

She was trembling when he reached her side.

"Are you cold or scared?" he asked as he sat beside her.

"Both," she said, and he could just make out the trail of tears on her cheeks in the candlelight.

He bundled her back under the covers and talked soothing nonsense for a moment.

"I thought it was just snow. I don't like ice, all the ominous clicking and the sound of branches breaking. And it always knocks out the power. I don't like it at all," she said.

"Well, it's going to stay with us through the night, but it should stop in the morning. The temps will climb on Sunday, and by Monday we should be able to leave the house again. You aren't alone. I'm here, and I'm not going anywhere," he told her.

She reached one hand out of the covers and rested it in his. He knew it was just for comfort, just out of fear, but he relished her touch just the same.

"Do you think I could sit on the couch for a while? I'm sick of this bed," she said.

"Absolutely, and it's perfect timing. You need to eat a little something and have some more medicine. Considering we don't have power, what sounds good?" Cole asked, not sure there would be anything that appealed to her.

"Could you just bring me up some crackers, the peanut butter jar, a banana, and a knife?" she asked immediately.

"Yes, ma'am. It seems like someone knows what she wants and has a bit of an appetite," he said feeling a rush of relief at her wanting anything at all, let alone something he could actually provide.

Soon, he had her settled on the couch, covered up and cozy. Just a few minutes after that, he brought her a tray filled with all her requests.

"I don't know how much I'll be able to eat, but this sounds good to me."

With the tray settled on her lap, she quickly dug in, slathering a thick layer of peanut butter on a cracker and topping it with a slice of banana. If the sounds she made as she chewed were any indication, she was happy with her dinner choices.

"Good?" Cole asked and couldn't help but chuckle at her.

She was adorable, even sick and weak.

"It's delicious. Want one?"

He wasn't hungry, but he couldn't resist her offer.

"Please, but just one."

When he took a bite, he had to admit she was right. Maybe it was the cozy room lit only by candlelight and the glow of the fire. Maybe it was just circumstance, but he suspected it was the woman sitting beside him. Regardless, the childish fare was indeed delicious.

"Why this combo?" he asked.

"It was what my mom always made us when we were sick. She's a nurse, and she always said that crackers with a tiny bit of peanut butter and a slice of banana were good to the stomach, bland enough to stay down but tasty enough to want. She isn't very affectionate or even that sweet, but this is one thing from my childhood that always makes me feel safe and loved."

She finished quickly after only four crackers and set the tray on the coffee table. They were silent for a while, both just enjoying the crackling of the fire.

"Are you comfortable? Do you need to lie down?" he asked.

"I'm fine, absolutely content right this minute. Thank you for taking such good care of me. It's been a long time since someone's done that."

"You're welcome. I'm certain you would do the same," he said, and she nodded. "I imagine your husband was good at taking care of you too."

"He was, or rather, we were really good at taking care of each other," she said with a sweet smile at whatever memory she saw in her mind.

"You can tell me about him if you want, if it doesn't make you sad."

"It doesn't make me sad. Talking about him always makes me remember how grateful I am to have had him even for a short time. What do you want to know?"

"Anything you want to share."

For the better part of an hour, Cora told him stories of her life with Jeff. And she was right. Talking about him brought her joy. As she spoke, her face glowed, even apart from the firelight. Cole didn't know what he'd expected her to share, but most of her stories were funny anecdotes from the restoration of the house. He'd expected less laughter and more tears simply because of the grief she'd experienced, but that's not what happened. Instead he found himself laughing so hard his cheeks hurt.

"Just one more," she said. "I promise."

He would listen to as many stories as she told because he enjoyed seeing her happy and also because he longed to know more about the man she still loved so much.

"It happened the first summer we lived here. I was in the backyard playing with Atty in the late afternoon. Jeff was working in the barn. I heard the shriek of a big bird, maybe a hawk, which is quite common around here. It was off in the woods, and I didn't think much of it. But all of a sudden, I heard the whoosh of its wings, and the hawk dropped something right in our yard, just a few feet from where I stood. Atty barked like mad and started running. I screamed."

"What was it?" Cole asked.

"I didn't know. I figured it was an animal, likely dead, so my first thought was to keep Atty away from it. Of course, he started sniffing around it immediately. I grabbed his little kiddie pool, the one we use to cool him off in the heat, dumped out the water, and flipped it over whatever the hawk dropped."

"Didn't you look to see what it was?" Cole asked.

Cora shook her head and scrunched up her nose.

"I looked away the whole time," she said.

Cole laughed at that.

"It was early in our time here," Cora protested. "I was a suburban girl who loved animals, but this place was entirely different. Early on, we had run-ins with bears and snakes. Everywhere I turned there were critters in and out of the house. It was a little overwhelming to me. I loved it, but it was wilder than anywhere I'd ever been."

"What did you do after you covered it up?" Cole asked, his laughter still evident in his smile.

"Jeff heard my scream and came rushing up the hill, armed with a metal rake. I just pointed to the kiddie pool. He walked over there, like a ninja on a mission, and flipped it over with the rake. It was a huge, headless owl, the size of a dinner plate."

"If the owl was that big, imagine how big the bird that dropped it was. No wonder you could hear its wings flapping," Cole said, completely able to visualize the whole scene in his mind.

"I know. Jeff carted it off to the woods. Atty and I went back to playing. But for weeks after that, Jeff teased me. We both loved Harry Potter, so he would say I'd been rejected from wizarding school."

"If you were used to the suburbs, why did you choose this place?" he asked when they'd both stopped laughing.

"My grandmother," she said. "She lived on a small farm. My favorite memories of my childhood are all from the time I spent there with her. I guess I wanted to recreate that feeling."

When she fell silent after a time, he asked, "How did he die?"

"You remember how I said he told me he was going to marry me if I went on that first date with him?" she asked.

Cole nodded.

"Well, the other thing he told me was that he had a weak heart, a congenital condition that could shorten his life. He said I needed to take time to consider what that would mean for us and for me. I'll always remember this part. He said, *If you say yes, Cora Lane, you need to know that I'm already in love with you. It was instant. If you say yes, then this is it for me for however long my life is. Consider if that might be what you want.* Then he walked away."

Cole was stunned. She'd known he might die right from the beginning. He felt a mix of emotions like a witch's cauldron bubbling inside him. There was astonishment that someone would be willing to say yes to that deal, but there was also anger that Jeff would even put the offer on the table. There was admiration for a love so great but also a deep sadness that this precious woman had been through so much.

"How long did it take you to decide?"

"There wasn't anything to decide. From the moment he walked me to class that first day, I was a goner for him. He offered me something I'd never had, unconditional love. No one is guaranteed that. I would have been a fool to say no to something so wonderful just because I couldn't have it forever. To be someone's only love, the focus of their devotion; that's all I ever wanted."

"But you were always going to lose him. How could you live knowing that?" he asked.

This was what baffled Cole. Sure, he understood wanting something that your crappy childhood hadn't ever offered you. But to say yes, knowing you would end up right back where you started—all alone—what kind of deal was that?

"We didn't live that way. He was well most of the time, occasionally more tired than he would've been if healthy, went to the doctor more than most. But it was monitored, and he was careful. He coached basketball because he couldn't play. He took naps. Truly, it wasn't even something I thought of every single day," she said.

"That's admirable, but it had to be at the edges of your mind."

"True. Usually at night when he was sleeping. It was part of the reason we made a point to be a big part of the community, why we had so many animals, why we had Atty trained as a therapy dog. It was always to set me up for when I might be by myself," she said with a sad smile.

"You loved him a lot."

"I did," she said. "We were exactly what the other needed. I don't mean we always agreed or that we never had bad days. Certainly, we did. But I think both of us felt that we were more fully ourselves together than we'd ever been before. I felt both safe and free with him, and he with me. And, of course, it was a bonus to live with someone who wasn't forever telling me to keep up or speak up."

"Who said that to you?"

"My parents, my siblings, sometimes even my teachers. I was small for my age and had little legs, so I was always falling behind when went anywhere. Plus, I often stopped to watch birds or look at flowers. I spent too much time making daisy chains in the yard instead of improving myself in some way. I made good grades and never got in trouble, but that wasn't enough. In my head, I can still hear my mother's voice. *For goodness sake, keep up, Cora.* It happened so much my brothers and sisters started calling me *Keep Up Cora* as a nickname. I hated it."

There was such sadness in her voice, an acceptance that except for Jeff, she really wasn't enough for anyone. It broke his heart.

"That's ridiculous. Look at you. Look at everything you do for your students, for your animals, in the community. Any parent would be proud."

He'd never been one to gush over anything or offer praise very much, didn't really know how it worked, but these words fell out of his mouth before he could check them.

"Not mine," she said. "But thank you for the kind words. I can't even really complain. We had everything we wanted or needed. My parents were successful in their careers. I wanted for nothing."

"Except love and attention," Cole added.

"Yes, but from what you've barely said about your childhood, I have no room to complain. Will you tell me about it?"

If anyone else asked him that, the answer would have been an automatic no. Even with Joe, he'd only ever told bits and pieces of the story, and that had taken years. To his surprise, he found himself wanting to share with Cora, not just because she'd opened up to him, but also because it felt like his stories and wounds were safe with her. And so he started at the beginning and just kept going. Before he knew it, he was telling her some of the scariest parts of his childhood.

"After Betty, I lived in a group home again for a while. It was a different kind of set-up, not an orphanage but a house where a bunch of us lived with house parents. There were about twelve of us boys, all between the ages of ten to maybe thirteen or fourteen. A married couple lived there full time, and another adult would come and help at busy parts of the day like before school and at dinnertime."

"That sounds nice, more like a real home," Cora commented.

"That was the idea, but it's not how it worked out. Even though the adults in charge were nice enough, they were clueless about what was going on behind the scenes. Stuff fell through the cracks, got overlooked. We were supposed to be like a family, but twelve adolescent boys in one house was too much. A few of the older boys were bullies."

"Their idea of fun was scaring us, making the younger, smaller boys afraid all the time. It was four boys to a room with two sets of bunkbeds. Let's just say that what they whispered in the dark, what they threatened, was scary enough to make a little kid stop sleeping at all."

When he'd told her all of it, they were both quiet again.

"We are quite the pair this evening," Cora said, breaking the silence. "But I'm happy to call you my friend, Cole. You took a bad start in life and made yourself something wonderful from the ground up."

He lit up inside from her praise.

"I think we both did that," he said.

Neither said anything else. Cora was tired, and Cole settled her back in bed. He sensed a wall between them had come down. Some distance had been crossed. Something in him must have settled at that thought because he slept deeply and untroubled that night, with the knowledge that Cora had called him her friend.

The next few days passed much the same with Cora getting better each day. By Monday evening, she felt well enough to return to school the next day, the first day back for everyone after the ice storm lasted longer than expected.

She had a touch of cabin fever, and he knew that this unexpected time alone with her was coming to an end.

She was still moving slower than she had before getting sick, and her appetite was only mildly better. Her usual bright face had the pallor of illness to it, but she was determined and wouldn't be swayed when he urged her to stay home one more day.

"No, absolutely not. I can sit more than I usually do, and I'll ask for help if I need it. But it's easier to go to school feeling terrible than to plan it all and stay home. I've been fever-free for twenty-four hours so I'm good to go," she argued.

She was up and moving around, able to go downstairs to eat, and get her school bag ready. He insisted on packing her lunch, making her more of the peanut butter crackers that seemed to be the one thing that she would eat. He helped her change her sheets, and he did the outside chores, but she insisted he go back to the bungalow and sleep in a real bed without having to be on sick duty.

"I'm happy to stay one more night, just to be sure you're okay," he offered for at least the third time.

"Go. I'm fine. You've done so much for me these last few days. I appreciate it more than you know, but it's time for me to get back to it."

As he turned to leave, not the least bit happy about it, she said, "If you have time, you're welcome to stop by and eat dinner here tomorrow night." He thought he saw a bit of a blush. "I mean, instead of me just dropping it off for you."

He grinned at her flustered state and said, "I'd love to."

"Around six work for you?"

"Absolutely. And Cora," he said before he walked away, "please call me if you need anything."

She nodded but made no move to close the door, and they

just stood there staring at one another. Worried she would get cold, he finally broke the stare and said, "Go inside before you freeze. Sleep well."

He walked away before he could think of another reason to stay.

CHAPTER 11

CORA

CORA TOLD HERSELF that she asked him to dinner because it was easier to serve it all once rather than packing his up and taking it to him. She told herself she was just being neighborly. She told herself it was her way of thanking him, but underneath all those perfectly good reasons, she knew it was because she wanted him here.

Even as she turned off the lights and readied herself for bed, she missed his presence. All the while she brushed her teeth and settled in for the night, she kept repeating one phrase to herself. *Just a friend, Cora. Just a friend.*

Cora slept deeply and woke early feeling much more like her usual self. A hot shower and actual clothes instead of pajamas made a big difference. Even though she looked pale even to herself, she looked better than she had for the last few days. She forced herself to eat some oatmeal, knowing she needed the energy. She took care of Atticus, even made breakfast to take to Cole, and headed out to feed the animals.

She could hear the chickens squawking as she approached and the braying of her loud donkey, but she also heard something else. She heard the deep timber of Cole's voice, talking softly to the animals. When she entered the barn, she found he was already there handing out food to everyone, shifting them to their daytime spots, and giving them all scratches and pets. Her heart melted a bit at the sight.

"You beat me to it."

"I've got this. Go back inside," he said, his tender voice of moments ago as he tended to the animals gone, exchanged for a stern tone and terse words.

"Well, I guess we're officially back to normal now. You're barking at me again," she said, ignoring him and turning to help with the chores.

He stopped what he was doing and looked at her.

"You think I *bark* at you?"

"Not for the last few days. While I was sick, you were mostly sweet, but now it's back to the bossing and the barking."

She was now flinging feed at the chickens with vigor, stomping around, and just generally tiring herself out which made her even madder since she'd been feeling so good just a few minutes ago.

"For goodness sake, Cora, you were so sick. And today is the first day you're going back to work. You can't do it all, and I'm here to help. Coming all the way down here by yourself was foolish. You're not back to full strength yet."

"There is nothing foolish about doing my normal chores. These are my animals, and I have tended them rain or shine, sick or well, for many years. You are not the boss of me, Cole Houston."

For a moment she glared at him, but then she broke into a rueful smile and began to laugh.

"I'm sorry. That sounded exactly like something one of my students would say, and they're eight years old," she said when he looked confused at her laughter.

"Look," he said, his voice gentle now. "I'm sorry for

speaking harshly. I'm worried about you overdoing it. That's all. Let me start over. Cora, I've got this for today. Why don't you go back up to the house? I'll gladly let you start back on the chores tomorrow morning. Is that better?"

"Yes, thank you. I'll put your breakfast on the counter in the bungalow. Have a good day," she said and turned to leave.

"You didn't need to make me breakfast today. I can look after myself too," he said before she could get away.

"It's part of our deal. You're paying me for it, and I always keep my end of a deal. Plus, it felt good to do my usual chores. I'm sick of being sick."

"Thank you. Be careful. It might still be slick in spots, and take it easy. Don't go charging through the day. Cut yourself some slack."

"Yes, sir," she said giving him a salute as she walked off.

"I know you're mocking me," he shouted after her, but she just kept walking.

Hours later, Cora would never lie and say the day had been easy, but as she pulled into her driveway after school, she was happy to say it was done. It hadn't been terrible either. Cole texted her throughout the day just to check on her, and now, he was already making his way over to her car, clearly waiting for her. She had to admit that his texts and the sight of him walking toward her gave her heart a thrill. She reminded herself that his friendship was all she wanted, all she could allow herself to have.

"Hey there. Why aren't you up at your house working?" she asked.

"I'll go back up there in a minute. I wanted to check on you as soon as you got home."

Without warning, he laid the flat of his hand against her forehead, and she leaned into the warmth of it, as if it was his right to touch her and hers to enjoy it. She filed that away, not eager to analyze it at the moment.

"Well?" she asked.

"No fever," he said but his hand lingered, sliding down to her cheek. "How do you feel?"

"Tired but okay. I'm definitely on the mend."

"Let me get your bags and get you and Atty settled."

He ushered Atty out of the car and placing his hand at the small of her back, led Cora to the house.

"I can manage getting in my own door. You need to go work at your place. You missed a lot of time there because of me this weekend."

"I missed the time as much because of the snow as you, and I can spare a few minutes to look after you."

He stayed, watching her as she hung up her coat and changed out of her snow boots. While Cora got Atty some water and a treat, he got the fire going.

"Now, I want you to rest a bit while I'm gone. I'm going to pick up pizza for dinner and have it here around six. No cooking for you."

"I'd like to argue because you're so bossy, but that sounds like heaven. I'll leave the door unlocked. Just come on in when you get here," she said.

"I was prepped for a fight about the cooking."

She raised her hands in surrender which made him laugh.

"But you will absolutely not leave the door unlocked," he said, his voice turning just a bit stern. "Just give me a spare key to use, and lock the damn door."

"Fine," she said with a huff. "But I have no neighbors other than you, and this country road gets no traffic. Plus, I have Atticus. I think you're being over the top."

"I don't care what you think about it. You could fall asleep.

A bad guy could give Atticus enough chicken, and that damn dog would likely just let him have you. Any damn thing could happen. Lock the damn door. I mean it."

"That's a lot of *damns*. You sure are surly this afternoon. Go rip out walls at your big, old house and settle down. I need a nap," she said, ushering him to the door.

"Now who's being bossy?" he asked, but he was smiling.

Once he was gone, Cora went upstairs and changed into a set of soft, pink sweats she loved. She made a nest on the couch and was asleep in minutes. When she awoke, it was dark upstairs, but she smelled pizza. She made a move to get up, but Cole clearly had eagle ears.

He shouted up the stairs, "Stay put. I'm bringing it to you."

Within a few minutes, he appeared at the top of the stairs with the pizza, two plates, and some napkins.

"Oh yummy. That smells so good. I may eat the whole thing," she said as she moved things around on the coffee table to make room for the food.

"I'd enjoy seeing that for sure," he said, handing her a plate with a large slice of cheese pizza on it.

She dug right in. Moaning as she took that first bite, she looked up at Cole and found him staring, the muscles of his throat tense.

"I'm sorry," she mumbled around the food in her mouth. "It's so good."

Any shot of making up for her lack of manners was lost as she talked with her mouth full of food. She just put her head down and kept chewing. After days of toast and peanut butter crackers with bananas, she was so glad to be enjoying this slice of pizza.

"I'm glad I chose something that tastes good to you," he

said, relaxing a bit. "I thought cheese pizza was the plainest, safest choice since you'd been sick. And I still need to pop back to the kitchen and grab us drinks. What would you like? There's wine, root beer, or soda, but to interject my two cents, I don't think you should have wine quite yet."

"Did you say root beer?" she asked, clearly surprised since she knew she didn't have any in the fridge.

"Yep. It's my drink of choice with pizza. I picked up drinks at the store on my way back with the food."

"Out of the bottle?" she asked.

"What?" he asked, clearly confused.

"Is the root beer out of the bottle?"

"Is there any other kind?" he asked with a grin.

"No wonder we decided to be friends. You're a genius. There is nothing better than a bottle of root beer with a pizza. Nothing," she said with glee.

"I better get down there and get it then. You seem a little impatient," he said laughing.

In just a few moments, they were both settled on the couch with their pizza and root beer, which to Cora seemed like the most delicious meal of her life.

She was finishing off her third slice when he asked, "Have you eaten anything else today?"

"Some oatmeal this morning that tasted like cardboard, but after that, nothing. This is the only thing that's appealed to me all day."

"No wonder you're starving, but slow down. You don't want your stomach to revolt."

"I'm all done," she said as she put her plate on the table.

"Let me clean this up and start the fire before I leave," he said, rising from the couch and collecting the plates and pizza box.

She wanted to stop him, put her hand on his arm, and urge him to sit a while with her, but she didn't allow herself that luxury. And besides, if she asked him to stay, she would want more. Cole had awakened feelings in her that she thought died with Jeff.

Right now, as she looked up at him, his hands full of the remains of their dinner, she had to admit to herself that what she felt was desire. She wanted those hands on her. She wanted to bury her nose in the crook of his neck and take a deep breath of his scent. She wanted to know what his lips would feel like pressed to hers. But she wasn't going to do any of those things. The last few days of his company had been so lovely, but it was best to rip that band-aid off quickly. She began to get up to see him out.

"Stay put," he said, pushing her gently back onto the couch and settling the blanket around her. "I'll clean up and put the leftovers in the fridge for you to take to school tomorrow. Let Atticus come down with me, and I'll take him out before you settle in for the night. I have a key, so I can lock up. Got it?"

"Got it," she replied, feeling a rush of heat at the bossy way he spoke to her mixed with the tender look. "Thank you, Cole."

He was at the stairs when she called out to him.

"Cole," she said, and he turned to look at her. "Tomorrow is my day to get back to all the usual chores. Leave the animals to me. But feel free to come for dinner at six again if that works for you. Got it?"

His grin was as big and happy as she'd yet seen it.

"Yes ma'am. I got it."

She settled in and closed her eyes, enjoying the sounds of him moving around downstairs, talking to Atty as he cleaned up the kitchen. She heard the door open as he took Atticus out and then returned a few moments later. Finally, she saw the lights blink out downstairs and heard the lock turn in the door. She was so cozy and drowsy she didn't move to her bed, just slept on the couch with Atty eventually coming upstairs to lie by the fire next to her.

The next days established a pattern that continued for weeks afterward. She delivered Cole's breakfast, chatted with him for a moment, and headed out to check on the animals. More often than not, he followed along to help out. Then, a bit later, he saw her off to school. When she came home later that afternoon, he was working at his house, but at six on the dot, he was at her door for dinner.

He began to let himself in, always stoking the fire, playing with Atty, or setting the table. It was a comfortable routine that put an extra pep in her step. She chose not to overthink it. For now, she was content to enjoy herself. Experience had taught her that most good things came to an end eventually anyway.

CHAPTER 12

COLE

COLE HAD BEEN on his own for a long time, and he liked to tell himself he enjoyed that freedom. But there was something about the routine he and Cora developed that was deeply satisfying. The peace he felt after spending time with her, even in silence, was overwhelming. He'd come to crave it.

More, it brought to mind the few nice memories he had of his youth. He remembered doing homework at the Evans' kitchen table while Betty heated up frozen dinners and holding the flashlight for Rick when he worked on the perpetually leaky pipe under the kitchen sink.

He thought of Joe and the tiny apartment over his garage where he let Cole stay for so long when they first met. In exchange for a free place to live, Cole agreed to clean out and fix up the space which had been used for storage for many years. He saw now that it had been a proving ground, a place where Joe taught him the basics of construction, where they learned to work together and trust each other.

Those memories were a relief to him. He usually tried not to think about his early years at all. When those thoughts did come, they usually involved the darkest experiences of that time and played on his mind like the slimy dregs of a nightmare. He'd forgotten that there was anything good to remember until his time with Cora sparked something inside him, peace calling to peace.

They didn't discuss their fragile friendship and certainly never acknowledged that it skirted the edges of a far deeper connection. Instead, it felt like both of them were holding their breath, afraid of how little it would take to burst the bubble they'd created.

For Cole's part, he was just happy to spend time with her. Knowing her vow never to fall in love again, he was afraid the slightest hint of romance would have her closing the door on him forever. So, he was careful to tread lightly, never overstaying his welcome, always trying to be of help.

The work at his house was progressing pretty well for bleak midwinter. The big needs were met with heat, electricity, and water all sorted. He and Cora had talked about the fact that he would move back there permanently at the end of the week.

He'd ordered a bed and bedding for the room that would be his and made sure the attached bathroom was in working order. The floorboards were bare, and there was still a bathroom renovation to be done. However, he could move into that room immediately and fix it up when the rest of the house was done.

Cora offered to keep making his meals when he moved to his house, but she refused to take any money. So, he'd offered to help her with some projects at her house she had planned when spring came. This exchange delighted Cora, but Cole felt guilty about it.

The truth was he'd heard her phone call with a man named John, who apparently often helped her with odd jobs. Cole had just let himself in her front door one evening for dinner when he heard her laugh like a wind chime as she spoke with someone on the phone. At first, he thought she was chatting with Eliza.

Then he heard her say, "John, you're the best. I always look forward to our projects."

If that wasn't bad enough, when Cole turned the corner into the little kitchen where he could see her, she was beaming that gorgeous smile of hers right through the phone. *Hell no, he thought.* He was going to shut this John person down ASAP. If any man was going to get Cora's giggles and breathtaking smile, it was going to be him.

He stopped himself right there. Cora was not his. She could smile and giggle with anyone she chose. He didn't have to like it, but he didn't have the right to comment on it. Cora waved to him in greeting and kept talking to John for a few more minutes. He smiled at her and went about his usual pre-dinner routine, stoking the fire and setting the table. Later, over dinner, he'd broached the subject of moving out, and when she offered the food but refused payment, he went in for the kill.

"I don't know what project you were talking about on the phone when I got here, but how about this? How about you let me help you with that work in exchange for my meals? Then you don't have to pay for help on the project. It's a win-win," he said with an odd combination of pride in his plan and nerves at her possible refusal.

She looked up at him and lit up like the sun after a rain.

"Really? You would do that? I would love it, but you have to let me tell you what I'm doing first. It's kind of a big project, could take a lot of time, and you have so much to do at your house."

"Cora, I don't care if you want to knock this whole house down and rebuild a new one, my offer stands."

He worried he might be overselling it, but she just smiled in that way that made his insides melt into honey.

"Thank you, Cole. That would really be wonderful, but let me tell you what I'm planning really fast before you agree," she said.

She got up and left the room for a moment, returning with a piece of paper in her hand.

"It's this," she said, placing the paper on the table.

What Cole saw was a very detailed drawing of a greenhouse. As a builder, he had to admire its precision and detail.

"Did you draw this?"

She nodded.

"I'm impressed," he said. "And the offer still stands. I'll build this for you."

"Really?"

"Cora, I'm a builder. This is what I do."

"Thank you so much. Speaking of your move, how should we do breakfast? Do you want to come and get it, or should I drop it off on the way to school?" she asked.

"I'll come and get it when I help you with the morning chores."

"You can't be traipsing down here every morning to help me. I'm more than capable of doing it. I did it myself for years. That's too much once you're back at your house," she said, talking in her firm teacher voice, stern but kind.

"I enjoy it. I haven't been around many farm animals in my life, and I like helping you. We're friends, right?" he asked.

"Yes, we're friends," she said. "Just promise you'll tell me if ever you can't make it or just don't want to do it. Promise."

"I promise."

"You're welcome to keep coming over for dinner. I enjoy your company," she said.

He watched a wicked blush sweep right down her face starting from her hairline and sliding down into the neck of her sweater.

"I would love that," he said, both delighted with her and uncomfortably turned on at the same time. "And I have one favor to ask of you."

"Sure," she said, as she began clearing the table.

"I'm in over my head at my house. I've always built shiny, new houses, all modern and sleek. In fact, I've never been a fan of old stuff. My childhood was nothing but hand me downs. So, this restoration business is not exactly in my wheelhouse. Angelo nearly had a heart attack the other day when I suggested we knock out some walls and try to make it open concept. I think I need your help."

"So, what I hear you saying is you hate old stuff, and I love old stuff," she said with a laugh. "So you need me to pick out old stuff for you that you aren't going to like anyway?"

"Something like that," he said, laughing with her.

"You don't seem to hate my house, or are you just being nice?"

They were now working side by side in her kitchen, cleaning up, and he was aware of her scent and her body in that small space even more than he had been at dinner. It was both the most torturous and the most pleasurable part of each day.

"I actually love what you've done here. It feels like it honors the age of the house without being too old-fashioned. That's why I thought you might come over and help me," he replied, trying to keep his focus on the conversation and not her nearness.

"You have no idea how long I've wanted to get inside that house. Jeff and I were obsessed with that property from our first day here. We would walk through the grounds just itching to get inside. I've been waiting for you to ask me to see it, but I didn't want to overstep."

"I'm sorry. You're welcome anytime."

The truth was that Cole had been doing his best to keep some boundaries in their relationship. In fact, he'd had the idea to ask for her help weeks ago, but he wouldn't let himself do it. Then, just this afternoon, Angelo, who was now helping him source some age-appropriate materials for the renovation, had suggested Cora outright.

"She and Jeff did such a good job at their place, and they learned it all as they went. She's a fount of information. I worked with both of them and then just her so closely on many of her projects. It would be a waste not to get her input."

Cole knew he was right. He wanted Cora's stamp all over the place, even if she was just his friend and never anything more. Plus, it was a good excuse to spend more time with her. Looking at her face now, bright with pleasure at his request, he knew he'd done the right thing.

"I could visit after school tomorrow. Would that work?"

That's how he came to be pacing the front foyer of his dilapidated old house the very next afternoon, impatiently waiting for the sound of her tires on the gravel drive. He knew her schedule better than his own these days, so he knew she would arrive any minute. Just as he thought he might wear a hole in the hardwood floor, he heard her drive up.

The smile that split his face was too much. He knew it, so he took it down a notch as he approached the door. Hearing her footsteps, he rushed to meet her. He was instantly greeted by Atticus who bounded up to greet him. He stooped down to give the sweet dog some affection.

"I hope it's okay that I brought him. I was so excited I didn't even want to stop at home before coming straight here. It's all I've thought about all day, finally getting to see inside this old beauty."

Her cheeks were flushed with the cold. Her hair, which had started the day in a sleek updo, was now messy with some tendrils curling against her cheek. Her smile was like that of a child going to Disneyworld for the first time, or at least how he imagined it. His heart felt raw at the sight of her.

"You know Atticus and I are buddies now, ever since that night we found you in the snow. He's always welcome. We just need to watch him. There are a lot of construction tools and random crap spread out everywhere. I wouldn't want him or you to get hurt."

"I can keep him on his leash if you want."

"Nah, just let him go. He's so well-trained. He rarely leaves your side anyway," he said, realizing that he and the dog had more in common than he cared to admit. "I've been coming and going from the side kitchen entrance, but I think you'll like this formal entry better. Even in its decrepit state, it's still quite grand."

He led her through a set of wooden double doors that were half-rotten, half peeling gray paint into a small vestibule with enough cobwebs to be its own haunted house. A huge arched wooden door that looked like it belonged in a castle stood open waiting for them.

Cole put his hand to the small of her back and said in a low voice, "Step up."

He felt a shiver run through her at his touch. It gave him a thrill of hope to know she was affected by him. *Me, too, he thought. Every time.*

The formal foyer had a high ceiling with a magnificent chandelier that currently didn't work and served only to prop up dust and spider webs. The floor was wood, still in good shape, just dirty from years of abandonment and in need of sanding and staining. The space was round, branching off in multiple directions to other parts of the house.

Immediately behind them was a grand staircase that wound up and around to a landing with a stained-glass window. To the left of the staircase was the entryway to the formal living room. To the right, a hallway led to the grand ballroom. Immediately off the entry to the right just beside the hallway was a spacious formal dining room with intricate built-in cabinetry. Cora spun herself around trying to take it all in.

"It's amazing. I always knew it would be. So much detail. Look at the crown molding up there," she said, pointing to the rounded details near the ceiling. "And that ceiling is meant to look like a rotunda, only a bit smaller. Even chipped, that pale blue paint is just beautiful."

That's how the tour went, room after room, Cora exclaiming over the most minute details.

"That banister. Look at the carving," she said as she moved her hand over the age-smoothed wood.

"Okay that makes five fireplaces," she said a little later. "That's just bragging if you ask me."

He simply followed along, taking her in while she took in the house.

"This kitchen is a disappointment, though. It looks like

someone tried to modernize in the 1970's, and it's just all kinds of bad," she said, frowning.

He chuckled at the disdain in her voice for whomever had done such a thing.

"Were these servants' quarters?" she asked when they stopped at two tiny bedrooms located behind what had once been a butler's pantry and now served as his makeshift office.

"I think so. There are service bells in the upstairs bedrooms that connect to these bells on the wall."

"Ooh la-la, very fancy, Mr. Houston."

When she'd taken in every space, every deck, every balcony, every closet, even heading down to the basement that Cole still found a bit scary, he said, "Well?"

"It's a fairy tale house from another time. I'm so happy to have seen it as it is, to be able to imagine all the life lived here before you modernize it."

"That's why I need you, Cora. I want to make it modern and livable but keep the history, keep the charm like you have at your house. I don't have the foggiest notion how to do that."

"Well, first you keep all the old elements that you can, things like the hardwood floors, the moldings, the fireplaces. All those things need to be repaired and salvaged, just put back to their original state. Anything that was done as a renovation in the 1970's or 80's has to go. No pale pink tile, no avocado green appliances. Those aren't era appropriate."

"I can do that. What else?"

"The kitchen could be bigger if you knocked down some walls and took in the room you're using as an office as well as the separate breakfast room. Make it one large space. Then use one of the servant's bedrooms as a laundry room and the other as a pantry. You can have an office in any number of other rooms," she suggested.

"Agreed, and I like the idea of a more open kitchen."

For the next couple of hours they walked through the house again with Cole making notes of all Cora's suggestions.

Finally, he said, "You have to be starving, and I know Atty is hungry."

She looked down at her watch and said, "I had no idea so much time had passed. Luckily, I put a roast in the crockpot this morning, so our dinner is done."

"Just let me lock up, and I'll follow you," he said, already turning off lights as they walked.

"No rush. Stay and take care of things here. I'll get a head start so I can get the bread in the oven and make a quick salad," she said, and as always, she was already on her way to do just what she was saying.

She had Atty loaded and the car started before Cole could catch up with her. He made short work of shutting everything down for the night and arrived at her house about fifteen minutes later. She was buttering slices of homemade bread while Atticus was chomping through his dinner. The ingredients for salad were spread out on the counter.

"Let me wash up, and I'll do the salad," Cole said, easily.

"Sure thing," she said around a mouthful of bread. "Sorry, I'm famished."

"Why are you sorry? It's your bread and your house. Plus, it's good to see you have your appetite back."

Soon, they were happily eating fork-tender roast with potatoes and carrots, slices of buttered, toasted bread, and a salad with hunks of butternut squash and avocado alongside dried cranberries and arugula. Cora could cook. That was for sure.

"How do you want this to work?" Cora asked when the first pangs of hunger were satisfied.

He knew instantly what she meant.

"Well, I'd like you to help me choose the fixtures, colors, stains, everything for each room, go with me to showrooms to check out appliances, and basically act as the interior designer. Man, that sounds like a ton when I say it straight out like that," he said frowning.

"Are you kidding? That's my idea of heaven. I'll love every minute."

"We can work together in the afternoons after school and maybe go look at showrooms on the weekends. Would that work?" he asked.

"Absolutely. I have a few commitments in the evenings each week, which will pick up a little once spring is here, but I'll always let you know in advance," she answered.

"What kind of commitments, if you don't mind my asking? We've only known each other through sickness and blizzards, so I haven't seen you go out much at night except to meet up with Eliza. Not being nosy. I promise. Just interested."

"Well, I'm on the Friends of the Library committee. I help out at the local animal shelter whenever I can. I go to the gym, and I line dance. Sometimes I do the Saturday story time at the library, and I tutor."

"I have so many questions, but only one that keeps playing in my head."

"It's the line dancing, right?" she said with a knowing grin.

"Yep. I can't say I pegged you as a line dancer. I'm a Texan, and I've spent a lot of time in honky tonks, seen a lot of line dancing, done a bit myself. But I just can't picture it."

The truth was he *could* picture it, all too well. It was easy to imagine her moving to the music. What he didn't understand was how she came to enjoy it, where she did it here in New York, and most importantly, who she did it with.

"I think I'm offended," she said, lightly. "I don't seem like someone who can dance?"

"Oh, I'm sure you can dance. I guess it's more the notion of you at the kind of place that has line dancing. You don't seem like a beer and cowboy boot kind of girl."

"Well, there's a bar a couple of towns over called The Lone Star that has line dancing a couple nights a week, and years ago Eliza and her husband, Brent, introduced us to it. We just loved it right from the start. It became a regular thing for us," she answered easily, and he could see the pleasure it brought n her eyes.

"And you kept doing it after Jeff?" he asked gently.

"Not at first. It took a while, but yes, it felt good to dance again, to remember. And line dancing is perfect for me because I don't need a partner," she answered with a sad smile.

He ached for her, aware once again of her strength and determination. She could have wallowed in grief, become bitter, lost herself entirely. Instead, over and over again, she'd made the choice to live a full life.

"I guess I'm not the prim little schoolteacher you think I am, huh," she teased him.

"The last word that would ever describe you is prim. I never doubted you could dance, just the rowdy atmosphere. I'd love to go along with you some time," he said, sure he had crossed the imaginary line that lay between them.

"Thank you, but you don't have to say that. I fit the prim description most of the time. I mean, I'm totally the old maid schoolteacher, so I can't argue with it."

Was she fishing, or was she genuinely clueless about her allure? He didn't see her as someone to ask for compliments, so it seemed she truly didn't see herself like he did.

"What are you talking about? You're gorgeous inside and out. There is nothing about you that fits the old maid description. You're a smart, badass woman who's endured so much pain and only gotten lovelier. Cora, you're a miracle. That's what you are," he said, and he couldn't keep the passion out of his voice.

Once again, he was keenly aware of the line in the sand and the full step he'd taken across it. But he couldn't have her thinking for one moment that he agreed with her assessment of herself. To his surprise, tears came to her eyes, hovering in the corners, and she blinked furiously to keep them from falling.

"Thank you, Cole. That's the sweetest thing anyone has said to me since Jeff. I forget how nice it is to hear sweet things."

She reached out and patted his hand, and he wanted to grab it and hold on, to grab *her* and kiss the hell out of her. He wanted to make her so certain of her beauty that it was imprinted on her skin, known in her soul. He wanted her so certain that she never again cried tears of appreciation at his praise or anyone else's. He'd never known anyone who deserved adoration and devotion like Cora. Yet, she was convinced that was something she would never have again.

He stayed to help her clean up and then walked with her down to the barn to check on the animals. The night air was fresh, not too cold, and the sky was clear and bright with stars. It was hard to believe he'd found Cora passed out in a blizzard only a few weeks before. He said as much to her.

"For sure, but this time of year the weather coasts back

and forth between winter and spring, always undecided. One day you can walk around in just your sweater, and the next you need gloves, and your heaviest coat. Years ago, when Jeff and I first moved here, I had to learn to go with it, just take whatever the day brings and not long so much for spring. She will come when she comes," she said.

"Wise words and easy on a night as nice as this one," he commented.

It was natural now for him to reach out a hand to steady her if she stumbled on a rock or a pine cone. She had laughingly told him that pine cones in winter became like roller skates if you stepped on them just right. It was natural for them to work in tandem to feed the chickens and goats, to check on the donkey. They were mostly silent, just enjoying the milder evening, greeting the animals, and watching Atticus and the guardian dog, Mr. Darcy, play for a few moments.

Cole had never been much of a talker, always prized solitude and peace. However, he noticed a quality to the silence he shared with Cora that was more satisfying and restorative than his time alone. Even without words, some unspoken thread of communication seemed to pass between them, some awareness that was soul deep.

He imagined that Cora thought it was no more than friendship. She seemed content to put all their interactions strictly in the friend zone. She had to know it was more. His only thought was that she must be denying it because admitting it would be breaking her vow to Jeff.

He dropped her off at her door when they made it back up the hill, laughing at the antics of Atticus who had taken off trying to chase a poor squirrel and then come running back panting when he couldn't catch it.

"Fooled you again, did he?" Cora asked him as he came rushing to the door.

"Ah! This squirrel is a regular foe?" Cole asked, smiling.

"Oh yes, that particular squirrel absolutely taunts Atty. He's his sworn enemy," she replied, her tone serious but her smile playful.

"You'll get him one day, Atty," he said, giving the pup a good scratch behind the ears.

"Well, good night. I'll come to your house after school tomorrow, and we can get started. Will that work?" she asked.

"Absolutely. Feel free to bring Atty."

"I'll stop at home to change into work clothes. Then, we'll be right over."

CHAPTER 13

CORA

To say Cora was excited about working on Cole's house would be an understatement. Just getting to look around inside had been a dream. To actually help restore it was a gift she'd never expected. She'd gone to bed with her mind brimming with so many ideas that she had to get out of bed and grab a notebook to jot down her thoughts, just so she could get some sleep.

Her teaching day was good and flew by, but she had to admit that she kept that notebook, now labeled *Cole's House*, close at hand. Already, there were sketches and notes filling probably twenty or more pages.

Once she was home, she changed quickly into a lilac thermal shirt and her favorite denim work overalls with huge pockets, deep enough for her notebook and pen. She put her hair up in a messy bun and slipped on her dusty work boots.

Atticus had fallen asleep, and she didn't have the heart to wake him. His days were spent with playful children so he didn't need a lot of stimulation after school. She made sure he had plenty of water and a treat in his bowl in case he woke up. Grabbing an apple, a protein bar, and her water bottle, she left, shoving her sturdy work gloves in her pocket as she went.

Cole was waiting in the driveway when she arrived. There were a few work vans already parked there. From their logos, she could see that there was insulation work being done as well as a plumbing crew at work. When she stepped out of the car, Cole was already making his way to her, a huge grin on his face. She had been munching the apple as she drove, so she was still chewing as she got out of the car.

"Hi there," he said, and she watched as his gaze took in what felt like every inch of her inside and out.

It was funny. Cora didn't like it when men looked a woman up and down. She didn't think many women did. It often felt demeaning and intrusive, the abhorrent idea that they were imagining what was underneath the clothes. However, with Cole, his gaze always lit a fire in her, made her a bit breathless. More importantly, it never felt intrusive or creepy. It felt like interest and appreciation.

Besides that, it was hard to be offended when she was doing the same thing to him. Wearing a navy work shirt with a gray t-shirt underneath, the sleeves rolled up to reveal his muscular forearms, he was ten kinds of yummy. At least if you liked that sort of muscly, tattooed, tough man, she thought. It certainly seemed to work for her.

His hair, which was long, was pulled back and tied at the nape of his neck, one lock having fallen out now sweeping over his eye. His skin was tan for a New York winter, hinting at his recent move from sunnier Texas. And that walk, that slow-gaited swagger, just about did her in.

There was no denying that she was attracted to him, but she had no intention of letting that attraction become anything more. She would keep her promise to Jeff. Nothing would change that, but she had to admit that it was fun to feel desire again. It was like some circuit in her blew when

Jeff died, and she hadn't replaced the fuse. And now there was Cole, and she was coming back to life.

"Nice outfit," he said and flashed her a sexy grin that caused her to stumble and choke on a huge bite of apple.

She had a bad habit of eating too fast when she was in a hurry to move on to the next thing. Jeff always told her she was going to choke one day, eating her food in such big bites when they were in a hurry to finish a project. Well, he was right. Her eyes watered as she tried to keep from swallowing the giant hunk of apple, all the while trying to keep her stumble from becoming a fall.

"Are you okay?"

Cora quickly sorted herself out, stepping back from him, when she thought he would reach out a hand to steady her. Right now, one touch of that hand was going to be her undoing. She put her finger in the air and pointed to her mouth, the crunchy apple making a deafening sound in her ears.

Nice, Cora, she thought. Very attractive. There he stood, more than six feet of edible man with a whole lumberjack meets superhero vibe going on while she was a tripping, overall-wearing mess of a woman with apple bits spewing from her mouth. Finally, she swallowed the last of it.

"Sorry. I took too big a bite and well, anyway, I'm here."

If she could have manifested a hole in the ground to swallow her up, she would gladly have done it. Had she ever been more ridiculous? She closed her eyes in embarrassment and shook her head to get a hold of herself.

When she opened her eyes again, she found Cole staring at her with the sweetest expression, equal parts affection and heat. No, that couldn't be right. Sure, she knew he was fond of her so the affection felt genuine, but she must be wrong about the desire she thought she saw in his eyes.

Worried, she ran her hand over her mouth, expecting to catch a piece of apple stuck to her lip, anything to explain the look on his face, which she now thought must be amazement that one woman could be so ridiculous. She came away with nothing.

"What? Is there something on my face that I'm missing?"

He ran a gentle hand over the curve of her cheek, setting her ablaze. A fresh, woodsy scent washed over her. She took a deep breath of it and nearly swooned. Okay, this was too much. How could the man smell so delicious after a full day of demolition in that old house?

"You are perfect. Absolutely perfect."

Cora had to shake herself out of a stupor just to form words.

"Are you making fun of me?" she asked, though he said it with apparent sincerity.

"Not a bit. I like the outfit. I like the enthusiasm. I like the way you eat an apple. You just carry on with all that, and I'll walk you through what I thought we could work on today. Sound good to you?"

The timber of his voice remained low and gravelly as if he was affected by her, attracted to her. Maybe that look *had* been attraction after all. She couldn't find words so she simply nodded and followed along. If this working together thing was actually going to work, she needed to get a firm grip on herself. She wasn't a woman who swooned in the presence of a handsome man.

Jeff had been strong but sweet and definitely not gruff or tough. He'd had a flannel shirt-wearing, Christmas-tree chopping, hot chocolate-drinking, snowball-throwing kind of charm like a Hallmark movie hero. He'd been safe and sweet and oh so good to her. They'd been very alike in that way. Cole, on the other hand, would not make the cast of a single one of those movies, and she was willing to bet he'd never sipped hot chocolate after choosing a Christmas tree in his life.

Everything about him overwhelmed her senses and made her dizzy. It was like the testosterone just wafted around him and knocked a woman down with its potency. She wasn't used to it. That was all. Once they got to work she would see him like any other man. He was just a new experience for her, nothing more. And yet, even as she thought it, she knew it was more.

Inside, he led her to the second floor where the bedrooms, save the one he claimed for his own, were now empty. The carpet had been lifted, and now only the scarred, rough wood floors underneath remained. There was an open living area at the top of the stairs with the bedrooms radiating out from it and three bathrooms if you counted the one in Cole's room. Most rooms had wallpaper, and some had rotten baseboards. The windows were old, and most of them were cracked and sagging.

"I thought we could start up here because the choices are fairly easy at this point. I need to get the wallpaper stripped, and all the bathrooms will be overhauled completely, but you can help me choose the stain for the floors and the paint for the walls. And I'm doing new windows everywhere, so you can help me select those."

"I'll strip the wallpaper. I actually have the steamer for that in the barn at home. I did a lot of that at my house. And, I think you should have a window restoration guy I know come out and assess the situation. Denny, a friend of Angelo, was able to help us a lot. Some of our windows just needed to be worked on, glass repaired, sagging sashes lifted, and so on. In the places where we needed a whole new window, Denny was able to source vintage ones to match. It's worth it to keep it authentic," she said as she took out her notebook to make a note to call Denny.

"What do you have there, schoolteacher?" he asked, clearly teasing her.

"I started a notebook last night with all my ideas. I couldn't go to sleep until I wrote it all down. I keep notebooks for everything, and this one is just for your house. See?" she asked, pointing to the cover where she'd written *Cole's House* with a magenta Sharpie and glitter.

She realized now that maybe glitter was not a Cole-appropriate choice, but in her line of work, bedazzling school supplies was just a part of the job.

"Very nice, and I must say, very teacher-like. I especially like the color you chose," he said as he ran his hand over the words on the notebook.

"Hot pink is very cheery. I like it." She heard the defensiveness in her voice.

Once again she felt like a teenage girl talking to the quarterback of the football team.

"Besides, I did it at school, so I just used what I had on hand." She quickly closed the notebook and put it back in her pocket.

"I like it," he said quietly. "I like it a lot."

There was some quality in his voice that had her looking up at his face. She frowned as she caught his expression. Once again, there was sweet affection mixed with a bit of heat that confused her, left her feeling not quite steady on her feet. The fact was she craved that look, wanted to give it right back to him, but her vow stood between them as surely as a wall.

CHAPTER 14

COLE

COLE HAD NO good memories of high school, but he imag-ined this was what he'd missed, this innocent flirting that made his heart race. Cora moved to the next room, turning back to see if he was following.

"Are you coming? We have more rooms to see," she called.

"Right behind you."

They spent the rest of their time before dinner making plans and arguing. He was insistent that they hire someone to strip the wallpaper. Cora was insistent that she would do it herself.

"Why pay someone to do what we can do ourselves? That's wasteful. Trust me. There's plenty you'll need to hire out. Don't ask for more," she said, hands on her hips and teacher voice firmly in place.

"Fine. But I'll need to see this all set up. I didn't ask for your help so you could do manual labor every afternoon. And you will not, I repeat, not do anything dangerous. Got it?"

"Got it," she said with a bite to the words. "I'll dig my steamer out of the barn tonight and bring it over tomorrow along with my ladder. Then, you can check that I'm capable of doing this very simple task without supervision."

"I'll go with you to the barn after dinner, and I'll bring the steamer and ladder here tonight and set it up appropriately," he told her.

"Oh, good grief. You do realize I live alone and continue to restore my own house with my own two, very capable hands. Don't you? I teach children, Cole. I am not, I repeat, not a child myself," she said with a slight stomp of her foot, which he thought ironically, made her seem quite a bit like a child.

"Don't get huffy. I'm just trying to keep you safe."

"I don't get huffy. Let's just keep moving," she said, already in motion.

In the bathrooms, she insisted she was an expert at popping off the old tile.

"It's boring and messy, but again, why pay for that kind of work? I'm good at it. Jeff said I was a champion tile destroyer."

While he understood all the references to Jeff, he was tired of feeling like he was in competition with a dead man. It made him feel small and mean, and it was a sport he wouldn't win.

"Okay, but here's the deal. If any of it becomes too much for you or if it's ever dangerous, you'll stop. Agreed?" he asked.

This time she didn't huff or stomp, merely shot him a glare and nodded her head.

"While you're working up here, I'm going to work in the kitchen. I want to build the kitchen cabinets and island you suggested. Could you draw me a picture of how you think the kitchen should look? I can work from that."

Now, her eyes lit up with joy instead of anger.

"I would love to. I can work on that at home. I have it all right here," she said, tapping her head.

"I'll be ready early next week to order the appliances, lights, sink, and other fixtures we need. Will you go with me?" he asked.

Again, pure glee. She actually clapped her hands which he took as agreement. A few moments later, they locked up the house and moved down the hill to hers for dinner. He parked behind her and waited for her to exit the car.

"You remember that I'm moving to the house tonight, right?" he asked as they walked to the door.

"I remember. Just leave the key under the mat, and I'll get in there to clean in the next day or two."

He noted that she didn't seem particularly happy and wondered if it was the cleaning or him leaving. He wanted desperately to believe it was the latter.

"I'll clean it before I leave tomorrow, while you're at school," he offered.

"No, you won't. That's not how this works. Besides, I do things a certain way."

He had to stifle a chuckle. Banter with Cora was more fun than anything else with anyone else.

"I can clean a house, Cora. I'm quite capable, and then you can go through and add your finishing touches. You can check my work."

"Oh, I'll be checking. After all that fuss about watching me with the wallpaper and tiles, you deserve a little payback."

"Sounds fair."

"Let's go eat dinner. I need food if I'm going to keep fighting you on everything," she said and laughed.

Dinner passed peacefully. Afterward, they went to the barn to get the steamer and the ladder. To Cora's relief, she was able to locate the wallpaper steamer easily, and Cole seemed to approve. However, he looked at her old, rickety ladder and shook his head.

"I'll take the steamer, but there is no way in hell you're standing on that ladder holding a wand full of boiling water. Just no. I'll get you a new ladder with a stable platform tomorrow," he said in a tone that brooked no argument.

He saw her open her mouth to argue and put his hand up.

"No, don't. I won't budge on this. In fact, that ladder needs to go to the trash immediately. You are not using this piece of junk ever again. It's a miracle you haven't broken every bone in your body."

He shook the offending ladder to prove just how unstable it was. Cora's face was a picture of embarrassment as they watched a rung fall off, and then the whole ladder collapsed. Cole thought steam was probably visibly billowing from his ears. This time she was the one to hold up her hand.

"To be fair, it wouldn't have collapsed if you hadn't shaken it," she said.

"Don't say another word," he said, glaring as her.

She actually took a step towards him, mouth open ready to speak.

"Not a word, Cora. I really can't handle one more snarky comment. I'm buying a new ladder. Period."

To his relief, she closed her mouth and simply began to move back to the house. The entire walk back she stayed well in front, clearly all done with him for the evening. He caught up with her at her door.

"I'll see you tomorrow afternoon, Cole," she said.

"Sleep well, Cora. Lock up."

She opened her mouth then shut it quickly, her lips pursing and her eyes sparkling with the attempt to control her tongue.

"I know," he said, winking at her. "You can look after yourself."

A little while later, he had to admit that it felt odd to be up at his house instead of her bungalow. There he could make out the lights in her cottage and felt close to her. It was also true, of course, that his house in its present state of renovation was simply lacking the comforts of Cora's bungalow.

The house was finally warm, but there were still drafts from the old, unrepaired windows and old doors that sagged instead of sealed shut. He'd bought only the most utilitarian bedding for the new mattress, which sat on the bare wood floor, making it a chilly.

In spite of the hard work of the day, he wasn't sleepy. Instead, he spent time thinking about Cora, about that incredible mixture of sweet and sour that seemed to be his weakness. Imagining her on that pile of sticks she called a ladder made him want to punch a hole in something. He had to admit to some surprise that her beloved husband had found that ladder safe for her. It was so old and slipshod that Cole figured it was already in bad shape five years ago when Jeff was still alive.

He was torn in his feelings about the much-lauded Jeff, so happy that Cora had been loved well, but also so irritated that someone else had been the recipient of her love. How could he not resent the man whose love might be enough, even from the grave, to keep Cole from ever having Cora for himself? And wasn't that a kick in the teeth, to be jealous of and angry at a dead man, who by all accounts had been good and true?

He'd been hellbent on getting to his house to get away

from the lure of her, away from the nagging ache for something he couldn't have. Now, he just missed her. He thought the ache was better than the absence. He tossed and turned on the new mattress, only finding comfort when he was settled in a spot that afforded him a view out the window. From there, he could just make out the chimney of Cora's cottage, smoke still curling out into the night air.

The next morning he overslept as a result of not falling asleep until dawn and found he'd missed morning chores with Cora as well as seeing her off to school. Yet another reason he didn't love living in his house instead of the bungalow. He rushed through his shower and made coffee, remembering that his breakfast was meant to have been picked up at Cora's hours earlier. Checking his phone, he found a text from her: *Hope you have a good day! Your breakfast is in the kitchen. You have a key.*

Just reading her words lightened his heart. A few minutes later, he was at her front door. He fingered through the keys on his ring, found hers, and let himself in. He found a brown paper sack with his name on the front, written in pink with a heart.

He chuckled, well aware that while others might think it was a sign of love, Cora was likely just reminding him of their banter the night before. And yet, when he touched her, she shivered. And there were moments he caught her staring at him, her eyes lit with what looked like desire. Could she actually be flirting with him in that note?

He didn't think she would mind that he just stood there at the counter and ate his blueberry muffins like a little kid. After tossing the paper sack in the trash, he locked up and went next door to clean the bungalow as promised. Then he drove off in pursuit of a new ladder.

Hours later, Cole had the new ladder and the steamer all set up in the first bedroom upstairs. Looking at his watch for the thirteenth time in as many minutes, he stepped outside to watch for her from the driveway. She was more than twenty minutes later than he expected. Granted, they hadn't set a time, and she'd only been coming to the house for two days, but he knew she was a creature of habit, reliable to a fault.

Looking down the hill, he could just make out the top of her car. She was home, so why wasn't she here? He sent her a quick text to check in and then resumed pacing. No reply. After ten more minutes, he got in his truck and gunned the engine, glad his was the only vehicle in the driveway at the moment.

He'd seen her sick. He'd watched her worry over Atticus. He'd seen her work herself to the bone. In his short time with her, Cole recognized that a silent Cora scared him. In his mind, he saw her again lying unconscious in the snow, his heart in his throat at the thought of something happening to her.

In just a moment, he was in her driveway and out of the car. A quick scan of the property revealed nothing unusual. He went to the door, surprised to find it slightly ajar instead of latched. Cora wasn't good about locking the doors all the time, but she always closed them, afraid of small critters coming inside to take up residence. His anxiety spiked immediately.

"Cora?" he called as he pushed the door open. "Cora?"

She appeared immediately, flushed and distressed, coming from the kitchen. Without saying a word, she gestured for him to be quiet. Her eyes were panicked. Her face was streaked with tears. It was then that he realized he heard another voice.

Cora turned back to the kitchen, and he followed her. She

pointed to the phone on the counter beside where she was working, a cutting board with apples and bananas beside her. To his surprise Atty was right at her feet on the rug in front of the sink, instead of his usual spot by the fireplace.

When he was done taking stock of Cora and Atticus, clearly both alive and physically fine, he focused in on the clipped voice playing through the phone's speaker. Cora just resumed chopping apples, a lot of apples. It was clear the apples were taking the brunt of whatever angst she was feeling. One thing she didn't do is take the phone off speaker mode, allowing him to hear whatever had upset her so much.

"Cora, we're not going to be home for Easter. We'll be with Meg, John, and the kids. They are too busy to make it to our house this year, so we've moved the whole thing to their house. I'm sure she wouldn't mind if you wanted to tag along," a voice said. "You know your sister. She'll go all out with the food and decorations."

"I'm sure she will, and of course, you want to see the grandkids. I was just asking in case we could be together." Cora's voice was dull, as if on autopilot.

"I appreciate you calling, honey, but I need to run. I assume all is the same in your little life," said the woman Cole was shocked to realize was Cora's mother.

Little life, Cole thought in amazement at the phrase. Cora's life was the opposite of little. He felt anger blooming inside him. He noticed Cora's hand shake and slip on the knife. He stayed her hand with his, indicating that he would finish the chopping.

She looked at him for one moment, eyes full of despair and what looked like humiliation. Then, this usually fiery woman just moved over and handed him the knife. She leaned against the counter, head hung low.

"Yes, Mom. All is still the same. The kids are getting restless, itching for spring. The weather here has been intense this winter."

"You know your brother just became the chief of staff at the hospital. He and Leslie are looking at building a house on the lake. Very posh," her mother said, as if Cora had not spoken.

One solitary tear dropped from Cora's eye to her cheek, and Cole felt equal parts sadness and anger. He began chopping a little too aggressively. The apple slipped and flew across the room. He dropped the knife, which clattered onto the countertop, tipping over the cutting board, and showering Atticus with apple slices which he happily chomped.

"Cora Leigh, what in the world are you doing? Did something just fall?" her mother asked with more exasperation than concern. "You always have been my clumsiest child."

Cole rushed to pick everything up, hoping to get to the apples before Atty ended up back at the vet with another stomach ache.

Cora just replied, "I was chopping fruit, and the knife slipped. Everything's fine."

She sounded like a robot. Cole wanted to punch something.

"I'll let you go now. Talk soon. Bye."

And she hung up. No *I love you*. No words of encouragement. No checking to make sure Cora hadn't cut herself. Cole didn't know a lot about parents, but he knew enough to know that Cora's mom wasn't winning any awards. Cora turned her phone over and bent down to help him clean up.

"Sorry you heard that. I should have sent you a text earlier or turned it off speaker, but," she trailed off before finishing. "I'm never at my best when I talk to my family."

They stood up and threw away the rest of the apple bits from the floor. Cora began washing the knife and cutting board. Cole was aware that by letting him hear the phone conversation, she'd given him access to a part of her life that made her feel small and vulnerable. He put his hand over hers.

"You have nothing to be sorry for. Do you hear me? I know that was your mother, and I know you love her. That's who you are, just pure love. But every word she said was a load of horseshit. Do you know that? You are perfect just as you are. You change the lives of children, of animals, of everyone you meet. You are kind. You are good. You are everything," he said and for that moment, he let her feel the full fervor of his feelings for her.

"Thank you for that. She has high expectations, and I never seem to meet them. I always call with hopes that this time will be different, but nothing ever changes."

Another tear made a trek down her cheek. Cole leaned in and wiped it away gently with his finger.

"If you hear nothing else I say, please hear this. She's wrong. Period."

For a moment, they were caught in each other's gaze, neither able to look away, a thousand words spoken in silence. When the moment passed, Cora simply nodded.

"Do you hear me?"

Again, she nodded.

"Say the words, Cora."

"I hear you," she said on a sigh. "I do. And in my head, I know it. But in my heart, she's my mama, and I'm always that little girl just hoping to please her."

Another tear welled in her eyes.

"Your tears are my weakness. Do you know that?"

This time he let his hand linger on her cheek once the tears were wiped away. She put her hand over his.

"Is that what caused you to rain apple slices down on my poor pup?" she asked, smiling through her tears.

Cole felt that smile like sunshine after rain.

"Poor pup, my ass. Atticus ate those apples as fast as they fell. He thought it was his lucky day."

"I was making us a snack, but I think we need to skip it and get going. At this rate, we won't make any progress today, and I was so excited all day about stripping some wallpaper."

"Well, I'll have you know, I stopped and got us some snacks and drinks for my house today when I was out getting your new ladder. You can eat when we get there. Go change. I'll finish cleaning up this mess," he said, happy to see her smiling as she left the kitchen.

CHAPTER 15

CORA

An hour later, Cora was standing on what she knew was the most expensive and safest ladder she'd ever seen. She was making steady progress on the first wall, but it was going to take a lot of time. Her first strip of wallpaper had revealed more wallpaper, and under that, someone had simply painted over yet another layer of wallpaper. She'd expected as much.

It had been several years since she'd used the steamer, and she was quickly reminded just how much of a strain it could put on the neck and shoulders. Standing for so long on a ladder, often reaching over her head, while holding the steaming wand took a toll. She was stretching her shoulders and turning her neck from side to side when Cole stepped in the room.

"I think it might be time for a break," he said immediately.

"I'm just stretching. I don't need a break."

He ignored her, simply walked over and lifted her down from the ladder as if she was a small child.

"You've got to be kidding me. I'm a grown woman. You can't just haul me around."

"There's my girl. I was worried for a while where all

that sass went," he replied, not the least bit offended by her outburst.

"Well, you're never going to see it when I'm talking with my mom. I turn into a child again whenever I talk to her. Always have. I just go weepy and silent and sad. It's pitiful. That was one of the few things Jeff ever got mad at me about, and man, that hurt, like a double whammy," she surprised herself by telling him.

"I understand. I had a few foster parents who made me feel like that, but that sadness made me angry, so I lashed out."

Cora just nodded, sad to think of Cole all alone and vulnerable with grownups who weren't reliable or kind.

"I really can't complain. I had everything I could want or need. We lived in a nice house. I went to a good school. There was always plenty of food and clean clothes. I was safe. I never went without," she told him, feeling guilty for complaining when his plight had clearly been so much worse than hers.

"Cora, there's more than one way to go without. You might have been safer, but you weren't more cared for. I heard how she spoke to you."

As they talked, she made her way right back to the ladder. He stopped her again.

"No, not yet. I brought snacks."

For the first time, she noticed what he'd brought with him. Sitting on a makeshift table made of sawhorses was a whole platter of fruits, nuts, cheeses, salami, and crackers along with two bottles of cranberry juice, her favorite.

"Oh yum. I was just about to give you a piece of mind, but then I saw this spread and well, yum," she said as she loaded a cracker with cheese and salami.

He laughed that deep chuckle that did something to her insides. She'd given up shoving her thoughts about Cole into a dark corner of her mind. It didn't work. They just spilled right out again. Instead, she convinced herself she could enjoy them without acting on them. That was her new strategy.

"So, the way to get you to agree with me is to feed you? Is that what I'm hearing?"

He put a clean drop cloth on the floor and set the tray and drinks down on it, so they could sit while they ate.

"It's a snack picnic. Very nice," she said. "You're quite the puzzle, my friend."

This was said around a mouthful of nuts and dried cranberries.

"Me?" he asked, clearly surprised. "I'm just a guy. I say what I mean, and I mean what I say. I'm no puzzle."

"You are to me. You're never quite what I expect, always surprising me. I've never known anyone like you."

"Like me? What does that mean?" he asked, and she watched him take a deep drink of his juice, the movement of his throat giving her a swirly feeling in her stomach.

She shook off that thought, trying to think clearly enough to answer.

"Well, you look like that," she said, sweeping her hands around him, like she was Vanna White on *Wheel of Fortune.* "You have the bad boy thing going on with the tattoos, the hair, the scruff on your face, and the gravelly voice. But then, you do and say all these sweet things."

"Sounds like stereotyping to me," he said, a challenge in his voice and a glint in his eye.

He was winding her up, and she knew it.

"No, I'm not. It's just that your outer image doesn't exactly match your ooey, gooey insides. If you were candy, you would be a marshmallow Peep with the shell of a peanut M&M."

He threw his head back and laughed. Inside she high fived herself for being able to entertain him. It mattered to her more than she was willing to admit.

"Definitely a schoolteacher. Not many in my line of work make candy comparisons. You are something else," he said, still chuckling.

Cora felt her insides light up. Usually, she was sad for an entire evening after talking with her mom, but here she was just an hour or so later, laughing with Cole.

"What can I say? I like my candy. And for the record, I wasn't being judgmental. I happen to like both Peeps and M&Ms. I just mean you're complicated. You keep me on my toes."

Cora was surprised to look down and see they had demolished the food. Both of them were sitting on the drop cloth with their backs against the wall, clearly relaxed and enjoying themselves.

"I guess we should get back to work," she said.

"I thought maybe the late snack could fuel us to work a little longer tonight. Then, instead of cooking, we could just order a pizza to be delivered here. Will that work?" he suggested.

"Well, yes, but I feel bad. Part of the deal is that I provide the food. And here you are doing snacks and dinner on day three."

"Cora, you've made a deal to cook the food and strip wallpaper for weeks on end. I'm not sure what kind of negotiator you usually are, but your end of this deal sucks. Take the pizza."

"When you say it like that, I think I might stage a protest.

Clearly, I'm overworked and underpaid," she said with a laugh.

They cleaned up their picnic, and Cole was adamant that he help her get back up on the ladder safe and sound before he left the room. When he was gone, Cora took her phone out of her pocket and turned on some of her favorite line dancing songs. As she got back to work, she realized she was happier than she'd been in longer than she could remember.

They fell into a groove that seemed to suit them both. At least, Cora knew it suited her perfectly. True to his word, Cole showed up each morning to help her with her little brood of animals. Then she gave him his breakfast and left for school. She'd grown accustomed to him waving as she drove off to work each day.

After school, she stopped at home to change, always giving Atty the option to go with her to work at Cole's house or to stay put in his cozy bed. Now that the weather was slowly warming up, still chilly, but not as frigid as before, Cora often walked up to the house, enjoying the exercise and fresh air. She imagined Cole was watching for her from a nearby window because he always seemed to know exactly when she arrived.

If she was walking, he often met her on the road, always asking about her day, greeting her as if they hadn't seen each other in weeks rather than hours. It became Cole's habit to make them a snack in the afternoons. Cora always scarfed it down, her hunger after school a monster. Cole usually chuckled, clearly amused at her daily chatter and ravenous appetite. She'd come to treasure their friendship and the way he made her feel.

Her marriage to Jeff had been safe and solid, a healthy mix of friendship and romance. She always knew where she stood, felt that she knew Jeff's mind almost as well as her own. It was comfortable and warm. Cole, however, made her feel entirely different. She wondered if the difference was simply that he was a bit older than her and had lived a much different life.

When he looked at her, it was with an intensity that made her stomach feel fizzy. He looked into her, not at her. It was as if he could see straight down to her toes, and he liked what he saw inside and out. It made Cora feel both seen and appreciated and absolutely naked and terrified at the same time, but she found she craved it.

No doubt, her years of widowhood had left her lonely for companionship on this level. She was probably romanticizing all of it, but the quality of his attention was absolute. It was as if he saw only her, heard only her. More, he acted as if she was the wittiest, most interesting person he knew. It was a heady feeling.

She was a thinker, a person who knew herself and held herself accountable, and yet, this man made her ignore all her usual sense. However, life was short, and at the end of the day, she didn't believe this would last. A man like Cole moved on. He would renovate this house, live in it for a brief time, and then move on to building the shiny new houses that were his bread and butter. At least, that's what she told herself in order to rationalize the relationship she was letting grow between them.

Today she'd decided to walk, and Atty had opted to nap on his bed. It was still early March, but the weather had been trending toward an early spring. Cora had foregone her heavy coat and was wearing her old, paint-spattered overalls and a long sleeve pink t-shirt with her work boots and a light jacket. She'd wrapped a colorful cotton scarf around her neck for a little extra warmth. The air felt fresh, and she relished the hint of spring in the air. It was one of those mild afternoons that reminds you of the exquisite feeling of the warmth of the sun in winter.

She was too well-versed in New York weather to trust there wouldn't be more snow, but she knew it was best to soak up the good weather when it came. As was her habit, she began singing as she walked with a happy skip in her step. She felt like she was living a dream: teaching, a pleasant stroll, beautiful weather, a renovation, and of course, Cole's friendship.

She knew from painful experience that it was important to seize every good thing and collect it for when good things were scarce. She must have lost herself in the wonder of it all because she was belting out the chorus of a favorite Pink song when she heard Cole's voice.

Her eyes were closed, and she was deep in the moment when she heard, "Bravo, Bravo! Encore, please."

He was clapping, and a bright smile lit his entire face. She had an insane desire to run and jump into his arms. She wanted to kiss that smile and breathe in his scent. She felt the heat of a blush rush down her face and into her shirt.

"Sorry," she muttered. "I guess I got a little caught up in this beautiful day."

Clearly embarrassed, she stared down at the road.

"Did you know that you have entire conversations with yourself that play out on your face even when you don't open your mouth?" he asked.

He approached her now, stopping right in front of her to smooth back her hair, which had become tangled in her face at the end of her impromptu street performance.

"I'm always talking to myself about something," she

said. "I can't seem to say and do the things I think I ought to a lot of the time. It's a constant battle. My parents say I'll never grow up, that I'm childish, but I think I do okay most of the time."

She felt tears well up in her eyes, dropping her head again so she didn't have to face him.

"Whoa there. You're not childish at all, but you do have a remarkable love of life that often comes across as childlike wonder. There's a difference. You're a responsible, capable woman. There is nothing childish about you, but you are definitely adorable. And I think we agree that your parents, as much as you love them, aren't exactly in touch with who you really are."

He wiped the tears away and stroked her cheek which left her feeling both shaky and oddly soothed.

"Better?" he asked.

She shook her head. Somehow just having him near was better.

"I have one more question. You up for it?" His eyes were teasing with a gleam of mischief.

"Sure."

"I think you just sang a word I've never even heard you say. In fact, Cora, I don't think I've ever heard you swear at all, but you belted it right out."

"It's a Pink song, Cole. Almost every Pink song has that word. It would be wrong not to sing it as written, a blatant disregard for the genius of Pink. Don't you think?"

She was surprised to find her former fragile state completely gone and in its place a certain cheekiness that only Cole provoked.

"Definitely. I understand completely, my prim little schoolteacher," he said as he slung his arm around her while they continued toward his house. "I figured you were eager to get back to the wallpaper stripping since it was going so well, so I got us some smoothies from the café when I was running errands earlier. I'll grab them from the fridge and meet you upstairs."

"Sounds delish," she said. "Peanut butter?"

"Would I get any other kind for you?"

To Cora, Cole was like the best friend you make on the first day of school, the one that becomes a soul mate, the one that makes you giggle even when you're sad. She was having such a good time with him. It was like being restored to a former version of herself that she'd lost when Jeff died, but this Cora was older and wiser. She was more aware of how much there was to lose, how precious good times were.

Grief, she knew, had stages. Goodness, she'd been the recipient of enough self-help books on the subject that she could recite them from memory. However, in her experience, while the stages mostly held true, they didn't always follow a linear path. Her grief journey was a twisting, often circuitous one that wound round and round her heart like vines. She'd experienced each stage multiple times. And here's what she knew. Grief never went away.

It wasn't something that ended after a neat pass through each stage. It wasn't tidy or reliable. Rather, it was an endless ache, a wound that refused to close, an awareness of absence that hit her at the most random of times. It didn't relent and move on. It lingered. It became, Cora realized, a part of her, something she lived with, a loss whose shadow lived in her heart.

She hadn't realized until she met Cole just how much she'd let that shadow darken her every step. Most days she felt she was living her best life, or at least the best one she could live without Jeff. She was engaged in the community, successful in her career, making strides on the dream list of projects they'd planned. She was physically in shape and mentally tough. Her students, her friends, her animals; they all brought her deep joy. She slept well, and she woke up content most days.

Now she realized, as she jogged up the stairs to the second floor of Cole's old house, she had in many ways been marking time, proving to herself that she could survive alone. Her deepest longing was to honor Jeff and the life they'd dreamed up together. And while that was honorable, it also had a price. How could a person truly move on when they were dedicated to the dead?

CHAPTER 16

CORA

FROM THE MOMENT she'd looked up at Cole's face from her spot in the snow that early morning only seven short weeks ago, he'd been challenging and changing her. As she fired up the steamer and set up her spot on a new wall, she thought about that fact. He shook up her cozy, comfortable world. He pushed her buttons at every turn, but somehow she was exhilarated. She felt renewed, energized, and more alive in his presence.

Certainly, there was attraction, and she was struggling with that. For starters, why him and no other man in five years? She'd made a vow and always found it remarkably easy to keep until now. Not only had she been resolved, but she hadn't even been tempted.

Cole, however, only had to walk into a room, and she felt a zing of attraction course right through her, head to toe, stopping at some interesting spots in between. Her marriage had been full of affection and yes, passion, but this was something different, something that made her feel equal parts dazzled and afraid. This connection made her fear for her vow.

He never made any overtures. They were affectionate

and flirty. She recognized that he was attracted to her, but he never crossed the invisible line that both of them knew was there. She was committed to Jeff, and Cole was a lone wolf who would likely move on when this project was done. Whatever this was between them was simply a moment out of time.

Cora was sheltered for sure. Her mother was a nurse, and her constant warnings that it only took one time to get pregnant had fueled her fears. Couple that with her religious beliefs and the fact that she was a late bloomer, and it was easy to see how Jeff had been her first and only boyfriend and then her husband. She'd been a virgin on her wedding night, and she still knew next to nothing about how to be sexy.

She figured maybe Cole was just flirty and affectionate with all women. Maybe he'd been intimate with so many women that nothing about her or their friendship was all that special to him. Or maybe, he truly only felt friendship. Part of Cora wanted to jump on that notion. If Cole really just felt friendship for her, then she could have him in her life forever. But she knew it wasn't true. She might be naïve when it came to sex, but she did recognize desire when she saw it.

Cora knew she wasn't unattractive. She had the wholesome sweetness of the stereotypical girl next door. She actually looked like someone who could be anyone's second grade teacher. She dressed fairly modestly, given her job. The closest she came to tight clothes was her workout attire.

Her long hair was almost always in a messy bun or a ponytail. She usually had dog fur and possibly some child's snot on her as well as dirt under her nails. She was cute, but she was no sexy bombshell.

Cole probably went out with tall, willowy models, women who knew how to be sexy without trying, women with short skirts and long legs. She could imagine him in some dark bar, music pounding, buying a woman like that a drink, inviting her to his place, and doing all manner of things with her. To her horror, she imagined he might be doing that here, heading out to some bar in a nearby town. While she was dreaming of him every night, he could be out there enjoying the company of other women.

She thought of her dreams now, of Cole next to her in bed, touching her skin, and pulling her close. She thought of the imagined pleasure, the feel of their bodies moving together in passion. Could she feel this way alone? She knew he wanted her, but that didn't mean he was waiting on her. Cora's face became a picture of defeat and maybe a little anger. These were the thoughts circling her mind when he walked into the room.

"What horrible thing happened while you were up here alone that put that look on your face? You look like doom and gloom," he said, handing her a smoothie.

She took a deep drink to calm the hangry attitude of her stomach that wasn't helping to level out the thoughts in her head. Drinking also meant she was distracted from punching him for his actions in her imagination. Was it fair to blame him for something she'd simply conjured in her head? Maybe not, but that wasn't going to stop her. It was possible, and that was enough to have her anger bubbling up again.

"I was thinking. And I'm sorry if I'm not all gorgeous and smiley like a super model. You sure know how to make a girl feel good, jackass," she snapped at him.

Cole's mouth dropped open, and Cora understood why. She didn't use that language, and she didn't call people names. She spent her life teaching young children to be kind, respectful, and all that other good, sensible stuff that just seemed like a load of crap as she stood looking at the completely baffled, but oh so sexy man in front of her.

"Jackass?" he asked. "Did you just call me a jackass, prim little schoolteacher?"

And there was his next mistake.

"Stop calling me that. I'm not prim. And who calls someone by their job? I don't walk in and call you Mr. House Builder. Do I? That's just stupid."

She was breaking all her adult communication rules now. Everyone knew that one of the rules of elementary school was that *stupid* was not a word to be used lightly and never about a human being. Goodness, he was making her crazy.

He threw his hands up in surrender.

"Okay. I get it. You're upset. The thing is I don't know why. Can you help a stupid jackass out here? Please," he asked in a gentle, almost pleading voice, the kind she might use with a stubborn goat or a recalcitrant student.

She felt her anger grow at the thought that he was trying to manage her like she would one of her students.

"How can that have made you even angrier?"

She shook herself off, as if to empty the rage. Rage? When had she ever felt rage? She was a calm, even-tempered woman. People trusted their young children with her. This was madness.

"Get it together, Cora," she muttered to herself.

"I'm sorry," she said. "I was thinking about something unpleasant, and it just made my blood boil. I took it out on you, and I shouldn't have. You didn't deserve that even if you prefer super models and smoky clubs."

Cole looked at her as if she might have suffered a head injury in his absence.

"Super models? Smoky clubs? Cora, did you hit your

head while I was in the kitchen? Are you having a seizure? What are you talking about?"

"Ignore that," she said, embarrassed that she'd let that last part slip out. "I don't know what's gotten into me. I think I just need to get to the wallpaper. It was a tough day at school. Must have gotten to me more than I thought."

Quickly, she put down the smoothie and moved to the ladder, the steamer now well and truly hot. Grabbing it too quickly, she felt a few droplets of scalding water land on her skin, the pain immediate.

"Damn it," she said as she hopped around, holding her wrist.

Cole was beside her in a moment, taking her wrist in his hand to examine.

"Let me look at it."

He bent over her arm, his hair brushing her nose as he moved. She took a deep breath, inhaling his woodsy scent, overwhelmed by his closeness.

"Stupid models," she murmured.

She couldn't have him, but she sure did want him, and that was messing with her mind. She nearly fell to the floor when she felt his breath on her wrist. He was blowing on the burn.

"I have some cream for this downstairs. I'll be right back. Sit your little ass on that ladder rung right there, and don't move."

She just nodded her agreement and then sat there miserably waiting on him. He was back in a flash, kneeling in front of her to apply the cream.

"Cora, I go crazy when you hurt yourself," he said, looking at her with such tenderness in his eyes. She looked away.

"I don't know what this super model nonsense is, but

believe me, it's nonsense," he said, placing his hand under her chin to steer her gaze back to him.

Cora felt tingly again as she stared into his tender eyes. He was close enough to kiss, close enough that she could smell the sweetness of the smoothie on his breath. His words were a balm to her. He couldn't know the wild thoughts in her head, but he managed to soothe her just the same.

"I'm fine. I was acting a fool, as my mom would say, and I got what I deserved. I think I'll just get to work and let you get on with it too. Sorry I've been so strange," she smiled, trying not to let her nerves show, desperate not to cry while he was still in the room.

He smoothed her hair back from her face and looked at her. He clearly wanted to say something more, wanted to push to know what she'd meant with all her nonsense.

Instead he stood up and said, "Okay, I'll be outside working on the new cabinets. Just holler if you need me."

Then he was gone. Cora wasted no more time. She picked up the steamer with care this time, climbed the ladder, and got to work. Soon the soothing monotony of the work relaxed her, and she let her cares fall away. It was hard to express just how much she loved restoration work like this, the act of putting something old and special back to rights. It was a particular kind of satisfaction to see something so abandoned, so desolate brought back to itself.

If she was honest with herself, she favored it even over teaching. Cora had wanted to be a teacher for as long as she could remember. She'd spent many happy hours playing in her room, her the teacher, her stuffed animals and dolls lined up in rows as students. She'd actually asked Santa for a chalkboard one year, but her mother refused. Chalk was too dusty and messy.

Cora loved school, and she loved kids. If Jeff had lived, she knew they would have filled the cottage with the sound of children by now. It was a dream not just delayed, but dead, a longing she never let herself think about anymore. Cora was one to focus on what she *did* have, not what she lacked, and so, her classroom full of students was her closest chance at that dream now. It would have to be enough.

Regardless of how much she loved teaching, she knew in her heart that she would be happiest restoring old homes just like hers and just like this one. It was the perfect combination of creativity and active hard work. There was a time for planning and designing, but there was also the kind of sweaty, messy labor that she loved. Jeff used to laugh at how much she loved demolition, at how giddy she got when it was time to rip out some tile or take a sledgehammer to some cabinetry from the 70's.

She supposed her love of old houses came from her grandmother and the small farmhouse in which she'd lived. It had a wraparound porch with a swing on one end, and the floors creaked when she walked. The kitchen wasn't sleek or sophisticated. Rather, it told the story of a hundred seasons of feeding a family, canning the harvest, and celebrating holidays. The garden was huge and bountiful, and chickens roamed free as if they owned the place.

Cora only got to go there a couple times a year. Her parents and siblings preferred their spot in the suburbs with all its conveniences, but Cora lived for those visits. Her father's mother was a no-nonsense woman who Cora felt could do anything.

Nonna was strong, sensible, and capable. And while she wasn't overly affectionate, she made Cora feel like she, too, could be all those things. Looking back, Cora realized her grandmother had also been a widow, and maybe sub-consciously she patterned her own path as a widow after Nonna's example.

Right now, she felt joy just getting to help Cole, and she didn't let herself think about what he would do with the house when it was done. This house was meant for a family, and Cole was decidedly single. Would he really stay in this big old house on his own?

Her heart sank. Either he would finish it and sell it, or he would marry and bring some lucky woman here to start a family. Each scenario was pure heartache for Cora. She couldn't have him, but she couldn't watch him live out his happily ever after with someone else either. Would she be relegated to the old maid neighbor they took pity on, the one that watched their kids so they could have a date night?

She quickly turned on some music and started dancing. That was her sure-fire trick for distracting herself. She could hear the sound of a saw outside, knew Cole was building beautiful cabinetry for the kitchen. As she swayed to the beat of Ed Sheeran's *Shivers*, she lost herself to the beauty of the moment, this old house, and her friend outside.

The days passed quickly, spring arriving little by little. Cora made her way through each bedroom over the course of a few weeks, now tackling the bathroom tile. Spring break was coming up in a couple of weeks, and she was happy to imagine spending whole days here. The workers that came in during the day when she was at school were flying through their projects, the warmer weather and more light giving them more time to work.

Every day it seemed to Cora that the house was coming back to life, a true glow-up from top to bottom. The win-dows could now be open during the day, and the sound of birdsong was like its own music. Crocus gave way to daffodils which gave way to tulips. Her own garden was largely untended due to her work at Cole's house, but she didn't care. For this one season, she was determined to devote herself to this project, knowing it was rare and special, both the house and the man.

One day in late March, she was in a bathroom with a window that looked out onto the side of the house, the driveway ending right beneath. Cole often set up his workstation out there due to its close proximity to the kitchen door. There was a slight overhang that provided some protection from the elements as well. The window was open, and she was just about to call down a hello to him when she heard him speaking.

"Damn it. This is not a good time. I need to be here. Just handle it, and I'll come in a few weeks." He was kicking up gravel as he walked and talked, clearly agitated. "Of course, the company is important to me."

He listened again, his mouth turned down in a grimace. "Fine. I'll be there as soon as I can." And then, "No, not tomorrow. I have things I need to tend to here first."

He hung up and spent a few moments just pacing and cursing. Cora ducked her head back in the room, not wanting him to know she'd heard his conversation. She sat down on the bottom rung of the ladder. Her heart sank. She didn't often think of his life in Texas. He was so present here, she'd all but forgotten he had another life.

She knew he must take care of that business during the day while she was at school, but she just didn't think of it. That wasn't her Cole, wasn't someone she knew. To think of him returning there, of him not being here hurt more than it should. Unconsciously, she rubbed the spot over her heart.

She must have been lost in thought because she jolted when she heard his voice, realizing he was right in front of her.

"You okay?" he asked, and he reached out to touch the hand that was over her heart. "Something hurting you?"

"No," she said, shaking off her faraway thoughts. "I was just taking a rest and thinking. I was miles away. Sorry." She pasted a too-bright smile on her sad face and hoped he would let it pass without comment.

"That isn't a real smile or a real answer, Cora."

"Just some school stuff," and to quickly move the conversation along she added, "What are you up to?"

"I wanted to talk to you. Bill, my right-hand man in the business, just called. He needs me back there for a few weeks to handle some issues with a new development project. I'm not leaving immediately, probably a week or so," he explained, looking miserable at the thought.

"I'm sorry. What can I do to help while you're gone?"

"Nothing. You should take a break. I know you need to work in your garden, get a handle on your reservations for the bungalow, all the things you aren't doing since you're working so hard here. We can regroup when I get back. Plus, you have spring break in a couple weeks, right?" he asked.

"Actually, I'd rather keep working, Cole. Even if you don't want the workers still coming while you're gone, I can keep up my work. Please," she begged, knowing full well he couldn't resist her pleading voice.

She could tell he was just about to agree when they both heard the sound of a car pulling into the driveway.

"We'll revisit this conversation after I see who's here," he said.

She followed him down the stairs and outside. She was surprised to hear Eliza's voice.

"Hello! I can't ever reach you, so I thought I'd come find you, get a look at the house and the man," said her friend, beaming a smile so bright it could power a small town.

Cora was genuinely terrified. Eliza didn't have one ounce of decorum in her. There was no telling what she would say in front of Cole. This was a disaster. She looked over at Cole and found he was grinning from ear to ear.

"You must be Eliza," he said, clearly thrilled by the impromptu visit.

"Well, she wasn't ever going to invite me, so I just took matters into my own hands. She's told me so much about you, and I wanted to meet you myself," Eliza said, clearly sizing Cole up as she talked.

"Not that much. I haven't told you that much about him," Cora said.

If this little meet up lasted another minute, Eliza was going to confess all Cora's secrets.

"Why don't I give her the tour, and you can get back to work?" she asked Cole, hoping to deflect attention away from the man and onto the house.

"I'm done for the day. I'll go with you on the tour. And then maybe we can all grab some dinner?" he suggested.

Eliza mouthed *yes* with excited eyes while Cora shook her head at Eliza, both to silence her and to beg her to say no to dinner. Her friend was not having it.

"We'd love to," she said eagerly. "This is our usual girls' night out, and we're going to go eat and then go line dancing at The Lone Star. My hubby is on ballet school duty with our girls tonight, so I'm free as a bird."

"Wonderful. I can't wait to hear all about Cora. I'm sure you have all the good stories about our girl," Cole said, like joining their girls' night was the best invitation he'd ever had.

He was entirely too excited about this, and what in the world did he mean by *our girl*?

"Maybe we could just grab dinner together. I'm sure Cole isn't interested in line dancing. Not really his scene," she said, hopefully.

"Nonsense. I'm from Texas. That's totally my scene."

Was that a twinkle in his eyes? Was he just doing this to push her buttons?

"Great. Then it's settled. Take me through this old beauty, and then we'll hit the town," Eliza said, clearly pleased with her plan.

Nothing good could come from this, Cora thought. Absolutely nothing. Cora knew she was well and truly screwed. Inevitably, she would drink too much to overcome this crippling anxiety, and as a result of the drinking, she would spill too many of her own secrets. And then, after all that, she was expected to line dance in front of him. What could possibly go wrong? Her mind taunted her with several embarrassing scenarios as Cole and Eliza carried on walking and talking. Suddenly, she saw Cole's hand in front of her face.

"Earth to Cora," he said with a grin.

"Sorry, I was thinking about something," she said with a tight smile that in no way fooled him.

He narrowed his eyes at her but thankfully didn't press.

"I was just telling Eliza about some of your ideas for the kitchen," he said.

"Oh yes, of course, the kitchen. It's going to be just beautiful when Cole is done with it," Cora offered, trying to get back on track with the conversation.

"You mean when *we* are done with it," Cole interjected. "It's your vision. I'm just the lowly laborer on your behalf."

"Not true. I'm the wallpaper stripper and tile remover,

hardly visionary," she said quickly. "Let's go look at the living room."

She led the way, eager to get this whole evening behind her. The rest of the tour passed quickly. Cora couldn't stay silent about the house restoration for long. Before she knew it, she was talking excitedly, giving Eliza the general goal for each room. She could see Cole visibly relax as she began to talk easily.

They began an easy exchange, finishing each other's sentences, as if they'd been working together for years. Eliza, who hated all things DIY and home projects in general, asked more questions than usual. Cora suspected she just wanted to keep them talking. If Eliza's wide smile was any indication, she'd already married them in her mind. Soon they were back in the front hall, making plans for dinner.

"I need to change and check on Atty, so I'll meet you there," Cora said.

"Mexican, as usual?" Eliza asked.

Cora thought of the volume of margaritas it was going to take to make it through the meal and the dancing and merely nodded in response. She glanced at her watch.

"I'll meet you there in an hour," she said.

"I need to shower and change, as well. I'll drive us, Cora," Cole said firmly.

"I can drive myself," she said.

"Waste of gas. We live on the same road and are going to the same place. Plus, you might want to drink a little. Just let me drive."

"Fine."

She wasn't going to give Eliza the satisfaction of watching them banter back and forth while Cole smirked at her and egged her on. She'd never hear the end of that.

"This was fun," Eliza said, clearly thrilled with what she'd seen. "I'll see you two in a bit. Thanks for the tour, Cole."

She waved at Cole and winked at Cora, and then she was gone. Cora just rolled her eyes and stretched her neck. She moved toward the door herself, and Cole stopped her with a hand on her arm.

"If you don't want me to go, I won't. I can tell you're uncomfortable with the whole idea."

Cora looked up to find him staring down at her with apparent concern and a hint of sadness. She couldn't stand the thought of hurting his feelings no matter her own discomfort.

"No, of course, I want you to go. It's just a case of worlds colliding, and Eliza is bound to embarrass me."

"Are you sure?" he asked.

"Yes. I'll see you in an hour," she said and set off on her walk home, considerably less perky than she'd been on the walk up earlier. This time there was no singing or dancing, just a solemn, steady march back to her house.

Later, she heard Cole drive up a full ten minutes early as she stared at herself too long in the floor length mirror in the dressing room. She'd fretted over what to wear like a teenage girl with a crush, and still, she didn't particularly feel good about her choice.

After dilly-dallying over what felt like twenty outfits, she finally got mad at herself and went with her usual line dancing attire—jeans, cowboy boots, and a white button down, partially tucked on one side. Her hair was a mess, so she quickly braided it, added some lip gloss, and a hint of blush, and was going to call it good. If not good, then at least an admirable try.

She was surprised to hear Cole knock instead of just

letting himself in as he usually did these days. Atty, of course, was making a mad rush to the door. She followed behind him at a regular pace and opened the door. Atticus stood beside her, tail wagging in excitement at the sight of Cole. Dogs were so open and honest with their affection. She wished being a human was as simple.

"Hi, I'm just about ready. Come in while I grab my jacket and make sure Atty has what he needs."

She was nervous and unusually fidgety. This whole dinner and dancing night with Eliza had thrown her for a loop. The truth was she liked keeping Cole to herself. She liked not sharing this new part of her life. She didn't want this collision of worlds, not yet, and maybe not ever. Cole meeting Eliza was a link to Jeff and a reminder of her vow, one she didn't want.

"You okay?" he asked as he stepped in the door and reached down to give Atty some attention.

"Fine," she said, and she heard the shortness in her tone. "Just tired, I guess," she added to take away the sting of her reply.

"Want to cancel and just order a pizza?"

"As nice as that sounds, I can't hurt Eliza's feelings. She's a good friend, and we already told her we were coming."

"We could skip the dancing, just eat some good Mexican food, and call it a night. How about that?"

"That might be an option. Let's just see how it goes." She put on her jacket and grabbed her bag after busying herself filling Atty's water bowl and giving him his dinner. "I'm all set. You ready?"

The ride to the restaurant was silent. Cora was pensive, looking out the window and twisting the handle of her purse in her hands.

"You're mighty fidgety over there, Cora," he said, reaching over to lay a hand over hers.

Her hands stilled under the weight and warmth of his bigger one.

"I don't know. I guess I liked the bubble of our friendship, and I'm not sure I want real life to intrude," she admitted.

He squeezed her hand. "That's nice, but I'm happy to meet your best friend, and I promise I won't beg her to share all your secrets. I'll be on my best behavior."

She knew what was going to happen. Eliza had seen them together, and she would now plot and plan to keep them together. She'd never agreed with Cora's vow, never even agreed that Jeff himself would approve the vow. To Eliza, Cole would be the answer to every hope she had for Cora. And as soon as that happened, Cora knew she would have to give him up.

Alone, she could imagine that it was possible for her and Cole to be this close forever. Once it became public, it would all collapse like the house of cards it was. She was a smart woman, and she knew they skirted the edges of something much deeper than friendship. Just like moments before, when Cole put a hand over hers to reassure her or the many times he brushed her hair out of her face when they worked, their interactions spoke of intimacy and affection. She could gloss over that fact in private, but once it was public, she would have to put an end to it. Anything else was a betrayal of her vow.

Cole didn't move his hand until they reached the restaurant parking lot.

"It's going to be alright, Cora," he said, as they exited the truck.

They found Eliza inside, waving to them from the back of the restaurant.

"Hi there, you two. I ordered margaritas for us, but Cole, I didn't know what you might want," Eliza said as they approached.

Eliza was all dolled up in her western finest for line dancing and clearly excited for this dinner. She was all but rubbing her hands together in glee. Further, she'd positioned herself in the middle of her side of the booth, making it impossible to sit comfortably beside her, forcing Cole and Cora to share the other side.

"I've also got us some queso and guac coming for these chips. It seemed like a night for more than salsa."

"Sure. Sounds good," Cora said, taking a big gulp of her margarita, with little thought to the lack of food in her stomach.

The waitress appeared and gave Cole the most obvious once over ever, clearly happy with the view.

"Hey handsome. What can I get you?" she practically cooed at him and then actually winked.

Worse, he grinned back at her. See, Cora thought. This is why she didn't want to come out into the world with him. She didn't need to see this.

"I'll have a Corona with lime," Cole said.

"Anything else you need, just give a shout," said the flirty waitress.

Cora picked up her margarita and downed a third of it in one big gulp.

"Easy there. That smoothie was a long time ago. The alcohol is going to hit you like a ton of bricks," Cole said.

Cora narrowed her eyes, and Eliza all but swooned in her seat.

"I'm a big girl, Cole. I can manage alcohol just fine. Eliza and I eat here every week and always start the same way."

"Alright. Have at it," he said, throwing up his hands in surrender.

"You two are just too cute," Eliza said.

Cora shot daggers of doom straight at her friend's perky little face. Where was her best friend, her confidante, the one who knew her trepidation about this man and this friendship? Gone, apparently. Cora felt her blood pressure rising and her ire increasing. A different server brought their queso and guac out, and they grabbed chips and dug in.

"So good," Eliza said in between bites.

Cora actually moaned as the taste hit her tongue, the alcohol already going to her head, fueling a sense of freedom.

"Always so good," she said after the first bite.

She noticed Eliza staring at Cole, so she looked up at him as well. He, it appeared, was staring at her with a heated intensity that moved through her much like the margarita, loosening her inhibitions. She stared back.

"What?" she asked when he said nothing and just kept staring.

"You have a little drop of guac right there," he said, pointing to her lip.

She reached up to get it, but he stopped her, catching the bit with his own finger. Her stomach clenched when he licked his finger. She gulped, as loud as a scream in the silent moment. He kept staring, now focused on the movement of her throat as she swallowed. It was Eliza's throat clearing that broke the moment.

"Are you ready to order, or should we just stare at one another some more?" she asked with a grin.

Cora blushed once again. She seemed to be forever blushing when it came to Cole, and now Eliza could witness it firsthand. She would never hear the end of it.

"Sure," Cole said, his voice a bit strained, as if he, too, was still affected by the moment.

Eliza signaled the waitress, who was all too happy to saunter right over, once again focused on Cole.

"What can I get you?" she asked him, as if he was all alone at the table.

"Ladies, what would you like?" he asked.

Cora had to acknowledge that he wasn't giving the waitress a bit of attention in return, deflecting her focus at every opportunity. Right now, his focus was lasered on Cora, turned away from the other women completely. Cora took a gulp of her nearly empty margarita and nodded to Eliza to go first.

"Could I have the burrito supreme, no sour cream?" Eliza said quickly.

Cora had hoped for a reprieve, a moment to think, but Eliza went with her usual order. Now Cora needed to speak, but her brain felt foggy. The alcohol on a mostly empty stomach was coursing through her, slowing her thoughts and making her fuzzy headed. She blinked a couple of times as she looked at the menu, but it didn't help.

"Cora, do you know what you want?" Cole asked.

She shook her head no, feeling lost and a bit confused. He smiled at her with such affection she thought she might faint from the pleasure and sweetness of it.

"Do you want me to choose something, or maybe Eliza knows what you want?" he asked, leaning in close to her.

He was so close she could feel the heat of his breath hit her lips, and without thinking she leaned even closer, but she was unsteady and leaned too far.

"Whoa there," he said, putting a hand on her back, the warmth of which did nothing to clear the fog from her brain.

Then he turned to Eliza. "Maybe you could order one of Cora's usual favorites."

Cora looked at Eliza and found her friend's face a combination of absolute glee at their chemistry and a little bit of concern at Cora's unusual loss of control. She could tell that Eliza was torn between wanting to scoop her up and keep her safe and wanting to see more of Cora and Cole together. *Yes, please*, Cora thought. *Be my friend and not my matchmaker.*

"Of course," Eliza said, smiling gently at Cora. "How about an order of fish tacos? You love those. Right, sweetie?"

Cora smiled and nodded. She felt Cole rub his warm hand up and down her back.

"And another margarita, please," she said in a small, somewhat slurred voice.

The waitress simply looked at her, taking the three of them in as if they were a painting at a museum, and Cora thought of how this must look. The tipsy, little widow sitting beside the gorgeous man who rubbed her back, while the excited and intrigued friend looked on. She really needed that drink.

"Make that a water," Cole said.

"No, a margarita," Cora countered in her teacher voice, but the slipping of her words as if they were falling down a slide took away its power.

"Cora, let's eat before you have another. You want to dance later. Remember?"

His voice had a sing song quality as if he were talking to a small, petulant child. She hit the table with the flat of her hand.

"A margarita, the big one, please," she demanded.

"Fine," the waitress said, clearly not happy to be ignored by Cole.

For a few moments the table was silent, none of them quite sure what to say. Eliza just stared at Cora with slightly alarmed eyes. *Now you get it, Cora thought. Now you see why I'm in such a state, why I told you this was not a good idea. Now you want to be my friend. Well, you planned this so you can deal with it.* She heard Cole let out a strained laugh and saw Eliza's eyes grow even wider.

"Did I say that out loud?" Cora asked in horror, realizing she had.

"Eliza, Cora mentioned you have kids," Cole said, changing the subject. "How old are they?"

And with that, Cora was granted the reprieve she desperately needed. Like most moms, Eliza could hold court on the topic of her children for hours on end. Before she knew it, Eliza was scrolling through photos on her phone, proudly showing off her family. Cora took a deep breath and tried to collect herself.

CHAPTER 17

COLE

Cole was having a hard time focusing on what Eliza was saying. Beside him, he could feel waves of discomfort coming from Cora. He'd removed his hand from her back a few minutes ago, but he was still sitting close enough that he could feel the tension in her body as she sat next to him. His sassy little schoolteacher was a lot of things, but drunk and loose-lipped weren't two that came to mind.

She was off kilter tonight, clearly more bothered than he understood at this unplanned evening with her best friend. He didn't know whether to be hurt that she'd clearly never meant for him to become a part of her real life, or just worried at what had spooked her.

He felt the bench seat of the booth shake and looked down to find her foot tapping a rapid staccato beat on the floor. He slid his thigh over to touch hers, to give her a little of his warmth and strength. Her foot stilled immediately, and she looked up at him with glazed eyes. He smiled at her warmly, hoping to calm and comfort her.

Cole watched enough movies and read enough books to have heard about what love felt like. He'd often wondered at the concept of wanting someone else's happiness above his own. It seemed like mushy nonsense to him. Certainly, his own life hadn't afforded him much of an example.

Right now though, he felt Cora's misery like his own. His desire to comfort her, to fix whatever was hurting her, was overwhelming. He wanted to wrap her up in his arms, hold her tightly until the shaking stopped, make sure she understood there was no end to what he would do to make her happy.

However, even if Cora was open to all that emotion, she certainly wasn't open to it here in front of Eliza, who was somehow the catalyst of this surfeit of shaky feelings. Cole watched as Cora took another big gulp of her second margarita. He needed to keep Eliza talking about her kids in order to give Cora some space to settle down a bit. Eliza, for her part, was happy to keep talking. If anything, Cole sensed that she, too, was worried about Cora.

However much Eliza had pushed for this dinner or how delighted she still might be by what she saw between them, she now seemed to take a mental step back. Clearly she saw how uncomfortable her friend truly was. As if some unspoken message passed between them, Cole felt the two of them bond over their desperate desire to ease Cora's mind.

The food came quickly, and he was pleased and relieved to see Cora dig in with gusto. He'd been concerned she was too nervous to eat, and she desperately needed the food to dilute the alcohol. As she finished the second drink and devoured the first of her three fish tacos, her whole body relaxed all at once.

She went from worried and edgy to chatty and free within a few minutes, and Cole recognized, with a smirk, that she was well more than tipsy now. She was drunk and hungry. He'd never seen Cora drunk, hadn't really seen her drink more than a glass of wine with dinner, but he was realizing that his girl was a silly, giggly drunk, a little boneless, and a lot happy.

"These are so good," she said, her voice happy, the words falling out of her mouth like slow caramel. "I'm so hungry." She said this as she pushed another huge bite of taco into her mouth, shook her head, and reiterated, "So hungry." And then, "Has this room always been yellow?"

She was now staring intently at the yellow-painted wall beside her.

"Yes, Cora, it's been yellow for as long as we've been coming here," Eliza said, still working on her first margarita, no hint of tipsy in her voice. "Always yellow."

"Are you sure?" Cora said. "I feel like the yellow is new." But before Eliza could answer, she turned to Cole and said, "Can I have a bite of yours?"

Without waiting for an answer, she reached over with her fork to spear a bite of his enchilada.

"Of course," he said with a grin. "Go right ahead."

"So good. Food is so good. Don't you think?"

"Yes. Food is good. Here, why don't you take a drink of water?" He said as he handed her the water glass which she took and quickly downed half.

"Water is so good too," she said, wiping her mouth with the back of her hand.

Eliza laughed, and he joined in as he handed Cora the napkin off her lap.

"Use this," he said. "Less messy."

"Great idea," she said, as if she was praising one of her students.

Cole just nodded. The rest of the meal was spent looking after Cora and chatting with both women, the conversation taking interesting turns as Cora continually interjected with questions about the décor of the room, which seemed entirely new to her. She gestured wildly as she talked, often fork in hand, which made it necessary for Cole to watch out for the safety of his face and his clothes.

"Cora, maybe you could put the fork down when you talk. I'm afraid you're going to poke Cole in the eye," Eliza said in her best mom voice.

Cora simply nodded and went on talking. Cole thought she was hilarious and adorable, this unfiltered Cora.

"You are so handsome," she said at one point, turning to look right at him. "It's too much. It hurts me to look at all that handsomeness. Just stop." She put her small hand on his cheek and repeated, "Just stop."

He patted her hand on his cheek and said, "Thank you."

"Stop with the voice too. No more gruff and gravelly. No more. Do you hear me?"

He recognized she was attempting her teacher voice. He put his hands up in surrender.

"How should I talk then?"

"Different," she said as if he was asking the dumbest of questions, going so far as to roll her eyes at him.

"Cora," Eliza interjected. "Drink a little more water."

"I don't want to. I want to talk to Cole about being too much." She looked at Cole. "You know what else you need to work on?" Before he could answer, she gestured like the host on a game show displaying the prizes. "All of this. All of this muscle is too much."

"And the tattoos," she said as if she'd suddenly had a new thought. "No, just no. I'm not a fan of tattoos. Never liked them. Never. And then you show up with all these tattoos which I haven't even really seen, and now I'm interested in them. I think you should take off your shirt."

"Pardon?" he asked in surprise.

"Come on. It's just an open button down over a t-shirt. It's not like you're stripping. Let me see the tattoo on your arm, the one that's sneaking out right here," she said, pointing to the spot on his wrist where the ink swirled out of his sleeve.

"This isn't really the place, Cora," he said, trying to sound firm even though the feel of her small hand on his wrist was doing things to him that made his head spin.

"Please," she said, and he couldn't resist her.

Quickly, he shed the shirt to reveal the tattoo. The phoenix rising from the ashes was not that original, maybe even a little cliched, but it absolutely depicted his own life perfectly. Basically thrown away as a kid, he'd risen from that despair and poverty to become the man he was today.

"Wow," she said in a hushed, almost reverent voice and began rubbing it with her fingers. "It's beautiful, and it suits you."

Of course, she got it, he thought. Wasn't that the kicker here? This prim little schoolteacher, so completely different from him, was the single human being he'd ever met other than Joe who seemed to understand him down to his bones. The combination of that understanding and the touch of her hand was too much. He quickly shrugged his shirt back on and stuffed a big bite of food into his mouth eager to move on from this moment.

"You're changing everything. You have to stop it," Cora said, oblivious to his discomfort.

She was poking her finger at his bicep to emphasize each word. Cole didn't know what to do. Part of him wanted to grab that pointing finger, tug her to him, and kiss the breath out of her. Her rant about all he needed to change about himself was really a list of everything she liked about him, everything that was tampering with her peace of mind, causing her to question her vow. Drunk or sober, Cora Lane was the answer to every question he'd ever had. The gentler part of him wanted to hold her, to ease her worry, to let her know that they could figure it all out.

"Do you hear me, Cole?" she asked.

"I hear you."

"Maybe we should get the check now," Eliza said, signaling the waitress. "Cora, I think we should just call it a night. I'm tired, and you're a little tipsy. Let's just skip the dancing for tonight."

Cora frowned, the kind of comically overdramatic frown of a sad three- year-old, lips pursed, eyes full of despair.

"I want to, though. I'm not that tipsy. I'll drink water," she said, even as she picked up her full water glass and chugged it. "See," she said, pleading. "Come on, El, pretty please. I'll keep the girls overnight any time you choose."

Cole could see from Eliza's face that Cora had come in with a strong bargaining chip in that childcare offer, but Eliza just shook her head firmly. Clearly, as the mom of two young children, she had a greater immunity to Cora's childlike pleas than he did.

"Two nights, an entire weekend away, and they can stay at my house instead of yours so yours can stay sparkly clean. You could even have a staycation at your own clean, quiet house, wild monkey sex and everything. What do you say?"

Cole's face turned sharply toward Cora at her mention of sex, monkey or any other kind. She had never, in the short time they'd known one another, ever mentioned the word *sex*. Clearly with Eliza, this was a topic that came up because other than glancing at Cole with a hint of a blush, Eliza seemed unfazed by Cora's comment.

"Good grief, Cole. You can't look like that and be a puritan. They're married for heaven's sake. What else are they going to do on a weekend to themselves besides sleep and have sex?"

She literally rolled her eyes at him. He couldn't think of any reply at all, his head swimming with thoughts of sex and Cora, a combo he tried to avoid on a daily basis. With her suggestion to Eliza, she'd flung wide the lid of this particular Pandora's box. She gave him a particularly harsh stare and then looked away as if forgetting about him entirely.

"That's a hard deal to pass up, Cora," Eliza said. "I can't believe you came at me with that."

Cora stuck out her hand like they were making a true business deal.

"Shake on it?" she asked.

"It's on you if you fall on your tush," Eliza said as they shook hands across the table. "I wash my hands of it."

Cora grinned like she'd won the lottery. They settled the bill and headed to their cars. Cora was oddly silent for the short ride to The Lone Star, mostly staring out her window, and Cole felt it best to just let her be. He'd helped her into the car and found her surprisingly steady on her feet and her words a bit less slurred. Perhaps the meal and the glass of water had indeed helped. The ride to The Lone Star took about fifteen minutes. Inside, the music was loud, and the dance floor was packed.

"Let's grab a table, and I can hold down the fort while you two enjoy yourselves on the dance floor. Sound good?" he asked.

He'd done a bit of line dancing in his younger days when

he'd wanted to catch the eye of a woman, but he had no intention of dancing tonight. He was happy to sip on a beer and take it all in. Even with the crowd, it was a big enough space that they found a good table, near enough to the dancing that Cole could see them but far enough away to give them some breathing room.

"Feel free to get out there. I'm just going to get a beer, but other than that, I'll be right here."

"I need the ladies' room first. How about you, Cora?" Eliza asked.

Cora agreed, and they left. Cole watched them as they walked away, noting that Cora stopped at nearly every table to greet and be greeted by people who lit up as she approached. Most were couples, and Cole figured they were regulars at line dancing, just as Cora was. A few were men whose eyes lingered too long and whose hugs were just a shade too friendly. He felt tension building in his shoulders, and he cracked his neck to ease it.

Of course, the vet was here, the one who'd been all too eager to help Cora with Atty, the one she admitted often asked her out to dinner which she always declined. In fact, right now it was that fact alone that kept Cole from marching over there to remove the vet's arm from around Cora's waist where it lingered long after the hug ended. Just when he thought he was going to lose it, he saw Cora squirm, a slight shrug of her shoulders as if trying to shake him off. The vet didn't take the hint, and this time Cole saw Cora visibly move away from him and was pleased to see his arm fall to his side.

Cole got comfortable in his chair, ordered a beer, and checked his phone. The waitress returned with a bowl of pretzels and his beer along with some waters he'd requested for Cora and Eliza when they returned to the table. He got lost in a few work emails that came in during dinner and didn't notice when Cora and Eliza joined the other dancers. When he finally looked up, he could see the two of them dancing in the center of the group, clearly at home in the crowd.

He wasn't surprised that Cora was a good dancer, but he was stunned to see that she was one of the best. Her feet flew through the steps, song after song, and she didn't make any missteps that Cole could see. More, she was truly happy doing it.

Two of the hallmarks of line dancing were the inevitable tags and restarts that came in almost every song. A tag was a series of new steps that could occur in a song at an unexpected spot in the music, but a restart was when the dancers suddenly started all over again at different points in the song. It was a sign of a really good line dancer when they didn't miss those cues, dancing seamlessly through every tag and every restart. Cora was that dancer.

Cora really cut loose out there, often laughing, always smiling, and it had nothing to do with being tipsy. He could see that. He settled in to watch, delighted to see this new side of her. Though she and Eliza danced side by side, if someone asked him what kind of dancer Eliza was, he wouldn't have an answer. His eyes were on Cora alone.

Song after song, he found himself grinning as he watched her. Occasionally, she would glance his way, their eyes meeting for a moment. He swore he could feel the heat of it from across the room. Then she would look away, and the moment would be lost.

He was on his second beer with no sign that the ladies would be stopping any time soon when he saw a handsome man step onto the dance floor and stand right beside Cora. He felt himself tense as he looked to see how Cora would respond, and to his astonishment, she beamed a high wattage smile at the guy and stepped closer to him as they danced. *What the hell?*

He told himself it was just a line dance. They weren't holding each other. There wasn't even a reason to touch. Then it happened. This dance had a moment in it when the dancers raised a hand up and clapped the hand of the dancer beside them. Instead of clapping Eliza's hand, Cora reached out to the man next to her, and he reached out to her. Rather than just smacking high five and letting go, the man caught Cora's small hand in his and brought it to his mouth for a kiss.

Without thought or plan, Cole stood up so fast his barstool teetered, moving to the dance floor. He caught Cora's eyes as he made his way toward her, and the look on his face had her eyes widening. Without any effort, he made a place for himself in between Cora and the other man.

The unknown man looked like he was going to say something, but Cole gave him a death stare that had the man moving over further into the crowd of dancers. A new song started to play, and thankfully, it was one he knew. He fell into the dance fairly easily, a few missteps but otherwise able to keep up, and Cora kept her eyes determinedly fixed in front of her, never looking at him.

When the song finished, the DJ said, "This next one is a couples' slow dance to celebrate Tom and Anne's fortieth anniversary. If you want, grab a partner and let's all dance in their honor."

Everyone clapped, and Cora looked over at him.

"They never do this," she said and started to leave the dance floor.

CHAPTER 18

CORA

CORA TURNED TO walk back to the table. Why on earth were they doing a slow dance? She knew the couple, Tom and Anne, were long time dancers here and beloved, but she didn't see why they couldn't just line dance to their favorite song. Why a slow dance, and on the one night Cole was here? Even a partner dance would be better than the intimacy of a slow dance.

"Wait," she heard Cole say and turned to him. "Stay, Cora."

He held out his hand, that big, warm hand that both comforted her and set her senses on fire. She simply stared at it. But how could she resist? It was a dimly lit dance floor. She was a little tipsy. He was so handsome. What harm could one dance do? When would it ever come up again? Didn't she deserve just one dance in a lifetime of loneliness?

And so, in a moment of spontaneity and desperate desire, she put her hand in his. He surprised her by twirling her into him, her body colliding into his as a zing of energy passed right through her like a shock. He was so much taller than her. To reach his lips, she would have to stand on her tiptoes, she thought.

He was staring at her with that intensity that she often saw in his eyes, one hand holding hers and the other a searing heat on her back, applying a bit of pressure to bring her closer to him. The air between felt charged, and she found she couldn't look away from his stare, couldn't fight the pull of his body. It was as if she was being controlled by a magnetic force.

They shuffled back and forth, caught in each other's gaze, both aware of the fleeting nature of the moment. At one point, he twirled her again, bringing her back to him with a tug that felt like ownership. She gulped and never broke eye contact.

Later, Cora couldn't have told anyone who asked what song it was, how close they were to any other dancers, nothing. All she saw or felt was Cole. When the song was over, they broke apart piece by piece as if unwilling to part, their eyes still locked on one another. She took a deep breath and broke the stare, only to notice Cole flexing his hands, as if burned.

"I think I'll sit for a moment," she said. "Thanks for the dance."

"I'm going to step outside for a moment. It's a little stuffy in here," Cole responded.

At the table, Eliza said, "Cora Lane, this place could have burned to the ground from the sparks you two were generating. That man has it bad for you."

"El, I can't talk about it. Okay? I need to go home now. Let's go home," Cora said.

She knew that Eliza meant well, knew it had just been the first time she'd danced like that with anyone other than her husband. It was all too much, and as always when she overindulged in alcohol, her drunken joy gave way to sorrow.

She felt the tears welling up, and she longed for her cottage and Atty with a fierceness that had her moving quickly to the door where she ran right into Cole who was coming back inside.

"Whoa there," he said as he caught her arms. "I was just coming in to suggest we call it a night. I think I'm ready to head home. How about you?"

Cora felt a rush of gratitude like a tidal wave.

"We're ready, too. Let's go," Eliza said before Cora could say a word.

Cole led them to their cars where they saw Eliza off safely. They were silent as they drove home. The air was saturated with all that was unsaid between them, but neither made any attempt at conversation. With each minute in the truck, Cora felt the gulf between them grow wider, but she just wanted the safety and solitude of her own home. When they arrived at her house, Cole moved to open his door, but Cora stopped him.

"No need to get out. I left the front porch light on, and I can see myself to the door. Thanks for tonight, Cole."

She opened the door quickly, stepping out before he could respond. She waved at him as she rounded the front of the truck and headed to her house. He merely nodded at her and watched as she unlocked the door and went inside. Cora shut the door and rested her back against it as she took several deep breaths. Atty came to her with his usual wiggly, lavish greeting, and she gave him his due attention but with a heavy heart. As she knelt to greet him, he tried as always, to lick her face.

"Oh Atty, what have I done?"

She went through the motions of shutting down the house, taking Atty out, and getting ready for bed. Thankfully, she'd taken care of the animals before she left. Only half an hour later, she and Atty were settled under the covers. Atticus fell asleep quickly, always most relaxed when Cora was safe and sound with him. But Cora was wide awake. She replayed the evening over and over again in her mind, each time looking at it in a new light.

On the one hand, it was romantic to remember all the ways that Cole gave her his undivided attention, all the ways he looked after her. She could feel the intensity of that stare even in memory. She felt attractive, even sexy, for the first time in more than five years, maybe for the first time in her entire life.

Her relationship with Jeff had been built on mutual affection, deep love, and friendship. Romance was there, but sex had not been the driving force in their relationship. They'd been in love, affectionate, cuddly like two puppies but not always consumed with desire. Looking back, she realized that Jeff's heart condition had affected their lives more than she usually admitted.

Everything with Cole was different. She wasn't comparing, simply trying to figure out what was going on with Cole by looking through the lens of the only romantic relationship she'd ever had. She was a thinker, and it befuddled her that she couldn't figure Cole out or understand the way he made her feel. With Jeff she'd shared her life with her very best friend. It was like one long sleepover.

Cole roused other feelings in her, an attraction that shocked her and made her feel out of control. She recognized that while she was always safe with him in practical terms, in other ways, he felt a bit dangerous. Both the passion and the challenge of their relationship were new to her, but she'd begun to crave them. It was like she was coming alive again.

When Jeff was in the hospital that last time, his heart giving out one slow beat at a time, she remembered so clearly holding his hand and promising him that she would always love him, that she would stay true to him for the rest of her life. He'd been groggy, weak, barely awake so he didn't respond except to give her hand the slightest squeeze. She'd taken that as a sign that he heard her and appreciated her words.

That was their last communication. Three hours later, he was gone. Cora, overwhelmed with grief, had determined that those words she'd said to him, the last words she would ever say to him, had the ring of a vow. That squeeze of her hand, however light, had been his acceptance of that vow. For Cora, it was sacred, their last intimate communication as husband and wife. She wasn't going to break it, not for anything.

She'd never been a boy-crazy teenager, had only ever dated Jeff. She loved romantic books and movies, but she didn't relate them to her real life. In fact, she'd fallen into widowhood grief-stricken but capable just like her grandmother. She was built for solitude and quiet. She was competent, hard-working, and more than able to take care of herself.

Along with Dr. Brenner, a few male teachers and random guys she met out and about had showed interest. She'd been invited on dates plenty of times, but it was always easy to say no. She never even contemplated saying yes. She felt flattered, smiled, and declined each and every time. Ironically, Cole hadn't ever asked her out at all.

They'd become friends, but she needed to remember that he'd never made a move to make their relationship any more than that. No kisses, no overtures for anything more physical ever happened. Granted, she saw the desire in his eyes, but if he really wanted her, wouldn't he act on that desire? Or, was he conscious of her vow and too considerate to push for more? Maybe he, too, was afraid of bursting their bubble.

She turned over on her back and threw her arm over her head. She figured Cole was fast asleep, probably not the least bit fazed by the evening. And here she was wide awake going over every moment of it again in her mind. She scooped up her pillow, flipped it over, and mashed it right in the center before letting out a huffy breath and settling back down. Eventually, she must have fallen asleep. Her alarm woke her at half past five as always, and she fumbled out of the covers to grab her phone and turn it off.

She was groggy and regretful, and altogether miserable as she slunk off to the shower to wash away the dregs of sleep and the pounding headache that smacked of a hangover. As the hot water sluiced over her, she gave herself a pep talk about putting a smile on her face and winning the day. She was going to forget last night and let go of all her ridiculous angst.

As she wiped the fog off the mirror with her towel, she stared hard at herself. The face staring back at her was pale, her green eyes too big for her face, the bags under them equally large. It was hard to see that woman surviving the day, let alone winning it.

"It's not about how you look, Cora Leigh Lane. It's about what you do and who you are," she said.

She took her time getting ready, partly because she felt like crap and partly because she thought she would be more likely to own the day if she looked a bit better. Instead of her usual messy bun, hair clip, or ponytail, she dried her hair and left it down in natural waves. She chose a simple dress that she paired with a light wash denim jacket since the weather was going to be mild. It was still too early to wear sandals on her always cold feet, so she chose a favorite pair of beige ankle boots. She finished the look off with her favorite dangly, feather earrings and a stack of bangles she'd collected at secondhand shops.

Not bad, she thought, as she looked in the full mirror. The shoes would go on once her morning chores were complete. She'd learned the hard way that cute shoes were no longer cute once covered in chicken poop or goat slobber. Atty slept through her shower as usual and met her downstairs. She let him out back to take care of his morning business and set to work making her favorite lemon ricotta pancakes, a sure fire cure for what ailed her this morning. Without conscious thought, she doubled the recipe to make enough for Cole too.

Soon the kitchen was redolent with the smell of lemon, pancake batter, and coffee. She prepared a bowl of fresh berries for each of them, put some syrup for Cole in a small plastic container, and let Atty in for his own morning meal. She set her spot at the table and settled in to eat, sighing as the first bite hit her taste buds. Soon her headache was easing, and she was feeling quite a bit better.

When the breakfast dishes were washed, she looked at the clock and found she was right on time. She packed Cole's breakfast up in a container that would keep the pancakes warm, tugged on her rubber chore boots, and headed out the door to tend to her little brood. Cole was walking up just as she stepped outside, and she took a moment to steel herself against the potent pull she always felt in his presence.

"Good morning," he said with a sweet smile.

"Good morning."

She didn't let herself focus on that smile, his clean, woodsy smell, the way his dark hair was pulled back, still damp, the way his t-shirt pulled taut across his broad shoulders, or the way the muscles in his arms moved. None of that. She just started the descent down to the barn. She could hear him stepping quickly to catch up with her.

"I half expected to do this by myself this morning. You were pretty out of it last night," he commented in a light-hearted, teasing way, but Cora didn't respond that way.

"I've been taking care of these animals by myself for years. I don't miss my chores just because I had a few too many margaritas. And for your information, I wasn't the least bit out of it when we got home last night."

She heard the primness in her tone. He ignored what she said, just stepped in front of her and stopped her in her tracks.

"I meant no offense."

She noticed he looked her up and down, taking in the dress and her hair. To her surprise, he reached out to touch a strand. She liked both the look and the touch all too much. She stepped around him and continued down to the barn. The minute Cora saw her little flock of chickens and heard the happy feet of her goats rushing toward her, she felt a sense of calm wash over her. Any time spent with her animals always had the power to soothe her ragged edges and calm her heart.

"Good morning, my loves," she said cheerfully as she greeted them, scattering feed for the chickens.

Cole went straight to the goats as had become his habit in recent weeks. They loved him and were eager for food and affection. Cora took care of her donkey and was finishing up her tasks when she saw that Cole had let the goats out into their daytime enclosure. They worked in tandem but without talking to one another, channeling all their sweet talk and affection to the animals.

The uphill climb back to the house was always a good workout, and Cora focused her energy on the beautiful, sunny morning and the sound of birdsong. She didn't realize how lost she was in her thoughts until she felt Cole's hand reach out to steady her as she stumbled on a stone that was sticking out of the ground.

"Steady there," he said, and she turned to look at him, finding those beautiful eyes trained on her with such a look of affection, she felt her pulse quicken.

"Thanks," she replied, "I was lost in thought."

She noticed he didn't let go of her arm, his thumb now stroking a warm spot near her wrist. *No*, she thought, *not good,* and she moved away, causing him to lose his grip on her arm.

"What's not good?"

"Huh?" she said, looking up at him.

"You mumbled *not good.*"

"Oh, yes, I was just planning my day and realized a part of my lesson plan wouldn't work. I didn't realize I said it out loud."

She rubbed the spot on her arm where he'd held her and smiled at him, trying to make the lie believable.

"Your lesson plan," he said, staring at the spot she was rubbing. "Right."

He seemed so nonchalant, touching her, always showing up to help her. He was so damn good at being her friend. For Cora, who'd never had this kind of friendship with any man other than Jeff, it was confusing. She felt his desire for her, but he never pushed for more.

Cora understood the hypocrisy in wanting his attention, longing for a reciprocated attraction when she knew good and well she would never break her deathbed promise to Jeff.

She wanted Cole to fall for her, but she didn't ever intend to take it any further. That wasn't fair to this man who was so good to her. Feeling guilty that she was playing games with him, punishing him for things he wasn't even aware of, she blew out a breath and put a smile on her face.

"I have your breakfast packed up and ready. I just need to grab it when we get to the house."

"Thank you. What are we having today?" he asked.

"I was craving lemon ricotta pancakes this morning, so I have yours in a warming dish. They are my favorite thing I make. I hope you like them."

He put his hand at the small of her back as they made their way around a tricky bit of path on the way to her house.

"I'm sure I'll love them and inhale them as I always do anything you make."

She felt his warm hand press gently into her back, and she shivered involuntarily.

"You alright?" he asked. "Are you cold? You're shivering a little."

"Yes," she said, a hitch in her voice. "It's still a little chilly this morning, but it's supposed to warm up later."

They reached her front door, and she quickly went in to grab his breakfast.

"Here you go," she said, handing the containers to him. "I hope you enjoy it."

In a new move for him, he leaned down gently and kissed her on the cheek.

"Thank you so much. You have a good day."

Then he started walking to his truck. She turned to the door to collect Atty and her school things when she heard him call her name.

"Yes?" she responded, fully aware of the breathless rasp of her own voice.

"In case I didn't mention it, you look gorgeous."

And then he climbed in the truck. She stood at the door, a dreamy look on her face as she let his compliment wash through her, breaking through every wall she tried to keep between them. She watched him as he drove off, waving like a schoolgirl as he turned toward his house.

"Get it together, Cora," she said out loud.

But much later as she read aloud to her class, as she watched over them at recess, as she checked their math and put Band-Aids on skinned knees, she let those sweet words wash over her again and again.

CHAPTER 19

COLE

Cole was in a fog all morning. The taste of those pancakes lingered in his mouth. The sight of Cora in that dress, her hair loose and free, stuck in his mind. The sound of the breathless catch in her voice when he touched her or complimented her played in his ears like a song he couldn't forget.

He'd worried that she would pull away this morning. Cora often retreated whenever they got too close, and that dance last night had been more than close. It was the stuff of dreams. Cole had imagined how it would feel to hold her in his arms, but the reality had been worlds better; her gaze locked on him, her small hand in his, the scent of her surrounding him. It had made him a little dizzy, as if it was he who had one too many drinks and not her.

Right now, working on the kitchen cabinetry, he let his thoughts wander to the night before, replaying it in his mind as he sanded the wood. Even as he'd enjoyed every beat with her in his arms, he'd known in the back of his mind that she would run when it was over. Try as he might, he couldn't steel himself for that rejection.

Right there on that dance floor, they'd been engaged in a sacred moment, a connection so strong that it refused to be squelched by deathbed promises or different backgrounds. When the music ended and she let go, he remembered flexing his hand, both at the loss of her touch and at the fire she spiked in his veins. To his surprise, he was as eager to run as she apparently was, heading for the door as fast as he could make it through the crowd.

The first rush of the cool night air of early spring hit him in the face, and he gave himself over to it, needing the bite to clear his mind and put out the fire in his body. He'd taken a deep breath and walked along the long front porch of the bar where benches lined the wall. The area was not packed, but quite a few other dancers and drinkers were lingering close to the door. Cole wandered further down until he found a relatively lonely spot.

"You're a lucky man," he heard a voice speak from the darkness near him.

He looked up to find the vet emerging from the shadows of the porch.

"How's that?" he asked, not the least bit interested.

"You got Cora Lane to dance with you and on your first time here. I've been trying for that for close to five years."

There was a world of emotions in the man's voice, longing, sadness, and a bit of anger. Cole looked at him closer. The day he'd found Cora standing outside Brenner's office, he'd been too focused on getting her away. He hadn't really noticed very much about the other man. Now he realized he was tall and lean with a handsome face and wavy blonde hair cut short and tidy. His clothes looked expensive, and he smelled like cologne.

He knew he disliked him just for the way he looked at Cora. Somehow hearing Brenner talk about her so easily outside this bar, as if she was a conquest, made him dislike him even more. Anything he said in response would make him the same as Brenner, as if he, too, felt Cora was a prize to be won, a favorite toy to fight over. He wouldn't do that, so he remained silent standing there against the wall.

"Enjoy it while it lasts," Brenner said after a moment. "Cora will only ever settle down with someone like Jeff. It won't be someone like you."

Cole reckoned he outweighed Brenner by seventy pounds of pure muscle. He was taller than him, and perhaps more importantly, he was accustomed to a fight. He'd thrown enough punches in his life to know exactly how to hit the other man to make him feel it a week later. A thousand savage answers played in his mind and a few well-aimed punches, but Cole only cracked his neck and stared hard at the vet.

"You have a good evening," he said and walked back into the bar.

Brenner just disappeared into the parking lot. Much to Cole's relief, he'd met up with Cora and Eliza as he walked through the door. They were as ready to leave as he was. He'd expected the silent ride home, and to be honest, he needed it. His mind was playing both the dance and Brenner's words in a loop as he drove.

Cora leapt out of the car like it was on fire and made a mad dash to let herself in her cottage, eager to get away from him. So, he'd been left with his thoughts and an empty old house for the rest of the night. Sleep had been a struggle, and when it happened, it was in the chair in his makeshift office.

He awoke in the same chair, neck stiff and back aching. A hot shower soothed some of the soreness away and cleared his mind. He pulled his dark, damp hair into a low knot, pulled on some jeans and a faded flannel shirt, and finished by tugging on his old leather work boots. He tied a blue bandana around his wrist as was his habit and headed out to help Cora with the chores.

He was relieved when he checked his phone to see no message from her. He'd half-believed she would text him that he shouldn't come over this morning or that she wasn't going to be at his house to work this afternoon. Knowing she'd run was different than understanding just how far. Apparently, this morning she wasn't running far at all.

The moment he'd seen her in that dress, he gulped. He could see a glimpse of bare leg as the dress flowed around her, making him gulp again and crack his neck to the side, always a tell-tale sign of his tension. The only incongruent part of her outfit was the dirty rubber ankle boots on her feet. It was perfectly Cora, always gorgeous but also genuine.

While she looked like an angelic vision, the look on her face was tense, and other than greeting him, she'd remained silent. His attempts to goad her into conversation failed, causing her to go all prim schoolteacher on him. So, he let the silence grow between them and concentrated on the morning chores.

Later, as they'd climbed back up the hill and he reached out to stop her fall, he felt again that fierce chemistry that kindled so easily when they touched, but she didn't let it go further. She seemed resolved today, different somehow, and he didn't feel like it was a move in his favor.

Another man might have thought she'd dressed so carefully for him, that she'd made her favorite indulgent breakfast as a result of a romantic evening. Cole knew better. Cora had spent the long night building walls. The dress was armor. The pancakes were armor. She had determined to deny him and what was building between them.

She was unreachable, untouchable, resolute. That much

was clear. His compliment as he left had been meant to make a crack in that wall, but though her eyes went dreamy, he wasn't sure he'd made any difference at all.

He spent the day just praying she wouldn't be a no-show at his house in the afternoon. No text or call came through, and Cora was the most responsible, reliable person he knew. So, when he heard her steps along with Atty's crunching on the gravel, he wasn't surprised, but he let the sheer joy of her presence flood him, nonetheless. He knew she'd brought her beloved pup as a buffer, as a distraction, and he was fine with that. It only mattered to him that she'd come.

Gone was the dress, but in its place was something even better. She was dressed in gray yoga pants and a pink work-out tank with a light jacket on against the early spring chill. It wasn't her usual renovation attire, and the shape of her in that form-fitting outfit had his thoughts muddled and his tongue tied. In one hand she held Atty's leather leash, and in the other, she had a bag.

"Hi," she said. "I can work for a little while, but I have a class at the gym this evening. I've been skipping for a few weeks to be here, and I miss it."

Another wall, he thought.

"Of course. I don't want you to miss anything you enjoy, especially not so you can pop tiles here," he replied. "How was your day?"

"It was good. The kids have spring fever, so it's good there's a break soon. How about you?"

"It was fine. I got some work done on the cabinets and arranged for the guys to start painting outside as soon as all the water damage is fixed. You hungry?"

"I grabbed a snack at home, so I'm just going to go upstairs and get started since my time is short. This," and she held up the shopping bag in her hand, "is your dinner. I'm afraid I won't be home to serve it there."

And another wall, he thought again. He just nodded. He wanted to beg her to stay with him a little while, to snack and chat as had become their habit, but he knew pushing the issue would only make her retreat further. So, he let her go without a word other than his usual, "Just call out if you need me."

He kept sawing and sanding the custom cabinets he was building for the kitchen, but all the while he was intensely aware of Cora upstairs. He could hear her talk to Atty occasionally, and he was embarrassed to find he was jealous of a dog. All too soon, she came back down the stairs, clearly ready to leave for the day.

"We're going to head out. I need to get Atty settled at home before my class. Enjoy your dinner. I'll see you in the morning."

He gave Atty a quick scratch on the head as she passed him, and then she was gone.

CHAPTER 20

COLE

THEY KEPT THE same routine they'd had for weeks, but it was also completely different. There was no banter, no flirting, no joking while they ate their meals. Cora was polite and helpful but utterly unreachable. Cole felt like a light bulb had blown, and he had no way of replacing it.

He missed her. Oh, how he missed her, but he consoled himself with the knowledge that being with her like this was still better than not being with her at all. That dinner with Eliza and that damn dance, the one that tormented his dreams and apparently filled Cora with regret, stood between them like a stone wall. He longed to say the right words to make it disappear, but he was afraid of scaring her off entirely.

It all came to a head one afternoon when he received a text from Cora saying she wouldn't be coming after school. It was April, and while the light lasted longer each day, an approaching storm was stealing the light early. Cole tried to keep working, but the thought of Cora out in what promised to be a bad storm made him restless and edgy. He kept an eye on her driveway from his upstairs window, knowing he'd at least feel better when she was safely at home.

By six o'clock, he'd run out of patience. All at once a loud crack of thunder jolted him into action. He picked up the phone and called Eliza, grateful to have added her number to his contacts when she visited weeks ago.

"Hi Cole. How are you?" she said as she answered.

"Not too good, Eliza. Do you know where Cora is? It's late, and the weather's getting bad. She's not home yet."

As he said this, the first drops of hard rain began to hit the roof. The storm began in earnest. Strong winds were causing the trees to bend precariously low to the ground, and the drops of rain quickly became a torrent.

"Well," she said in a hesitant voice that told him she knew something and didn't want to share.

"Eliza, please. She could be in danger if she's out in this weather. Where the hell is she?"

He was praying she was at a school function, a meeting, anything that meant she was inside safe and sound.

"Okay, fine" she said blowing out a sharp breath. "Today is the day that Jeff went into the hospital for the last time. It was the beginning of the end. It's a hard time for her. She's probably," she said, letting out a gasp.

"What? What's wrong?" he said.

"She always goes to their special lookout spot on this day, always. That's where she is, Cole. She's at the second lookout on the Sky Point trail. There's a picnic table, and she sits there and has a drink and toasts their life together."

Cole had no words. As he looked outside at the horrific storm, branches already broken and strewn across his property, he let out what could only be called a growl.

"Where is this trail?"

"Right off Route 32 just past the Elmbrook Road exit. There's a dirt parking lot. Please find her, Cole. I hadn't even thought of it until you called. You have to find her," she said, her voice now as desperate as he felt.

"I will," he vowed and hung up.

He grabbed the blanket off his bed, a flashlight, and his rain jacket. In moments he was in the truck. It took him longer than he wanted to finally pull into the trail parking lot. The rain was coming down in sheets, making it impossible to see even with the wipers on full power.

A sensible man might have stayed off the road, but he'd long ago lost his sense when it came to Cora Lane. Leaving everything but the flashlight in the car, he zipped up his jacket and headed to the trailhead. He willed his heart and breath to slow. Being in a panic wouldn't do either of them any good.

He was soaked instantly. The howling of the wind and the sound of the rain made hearing anything else impossible. He squinted, wiping water from his eyes in a nearly constant motion while shining the flashlight all around the path, taking in every side as he walked at a glacial pace. Even though it was spring, the rain was cold, causing even his big body to shiver.

He couldn't let himself think about Cora being cold, lost, or hurt in this weather. It made him frantic all over again. He hiked for almost half an hour before a break in the wind and thunder allowed him to hear a faint voice from up ahead. He began to walk faster, the mud sucking at his feet, making a slurping sound as he walked.

"Cora," he shouted. "Cora, where are you?"

He kept calling as he walked as fast as the mud and rain would allow. Then he saw her up ahead. She was hunched over rubbing something over her shin and talking to herself.

"Cora," he shouted again, and she looked up instantly.

"Cole! Cole!" she shouted back as she began moving, trying to get to him quickly.

"Stay put. I'm coming to you."

When he reached her, he wrapped her up in his arms, the relief so powerful it nearly took him to his knees. For long moments, they just stood in the rain, holding one another, her grasp, he noted with satisfaction, as firm as his. Feeling her shiver, he pulled her in tighter and looked down at her face, smoothing back her soaked hair.

"Are you trying to kill me? What the hell are you doing up here in this weather?" His words were harsh, but his voice was tender. "Don't answer that. Let's just get you to the truck. Okay?"

So far, she'd said nothing, just stared at him with wide, grateful eyes. She was a mess, a beautiful mess, but every inch of her was wet, muddy, and shivering.

"Are you hurt?"

"I cut my leg," she said. "It's not deep, but it's bleeding a lot."

He looked down and saw that her pants, a pair of thin, black athletic leggings, were torn down her shin and a nasty cut was oozing blood. There was mud and gravel caked in the wound. He bent to pick her up.

"No, I can walk. It'll be too hard for you to walk in this mess and carry me too. I can walk," she protested, but he ignored her, simply scooping her up and trudging forward.

It was hard, but he was determined, and the woman in his arms was the most precious cargo he could imagine. Far more careful than he'd been when he was searching for her, he took his time walking back, but soon enough they reached the truck. No words were said, but he was intensely aware of her shivering body and the puffs of warm breath against his neck.

He settled her in the truck carefully, on the back seat where she could stretch out. He wanted to get a look at her leg and any other injuries before they left in case she needed a trip to the ER before going home. Cole tore the rest of the legging, leaving her leg bare from the knee down. The cut was ugly and dirty, but it didn't look too deep. He knew he could take care of it for her.

Grabbing the first aid kit he kept in the backseat, he warned her, "I'm going to clean this up, Cora. It might sting."

He swiped the alcohol pad across the wound and heard a hiss from Cora. He looked up at her. Her eyes were closed, and a grimace was on her sweet face, but she didn't complain. It took a few pads and a few more hisses before he had all the dirt removed. Then he applied some antibacterial ointment and a large bandage.

"There you go. All set." She opened her eyes and looked at the bandage, taking a deep breath. "Any other scratches or cuts? Did you hit your head?"

"No, I just slipped and fell on my leg. No other injuries. Can we go home now, Cole?"

Her voice was low and exhausted. She still shivered.

"As long as there are no other injuries and you didn't hit your head, we can go home. You want to move to the front seat?"

"Can I stay back here?" she asked, her eyes closed and her voice sleepy.

"Yes, but you have to buckle up."

He helped her sit up and buckled her in himself, and because he was so damn relieved she was alive and safe, he placed a sweet kiss on her forehead. The rain was still coming down as hard as before as Cole climbed in the truck. He turned the heat all the way up to warm Cora up as quickly as possible.

"Can you feel the heat?"

"A little," she said weakly.

He reached up and behind him to feel around for the vent located above Cora's seat. When he found it, he flipped it toward her.

"That better?"

"Yes," she said, and he could hear the relief in her voice.

"It's going to be a slow ride. It's damn near impossible to see, and I need to keep us safe."

He'd torn out of their road earlier like a man on a mission, but now that she was with him, there was no way he was taking any chances. He'd risked himself earlier, but he would never risk her. It took twice as long as usual, but finally they were pulling into her driveway.

Cole was out of the truck as quickly as possible, afraid she would try to get out all by herself. His worry was for nothing. When he opened her door, he found her fast asleep. She was contorted awkwardly, trying to lie down while staying buckled in the seat belt. He carefully unclipped the belt and scooped her up.

"Cole?" she whispered.

It made him happy that his was the name to come first to her lips. He always wanted to be someone she trusted to keep her safe, the one to take care of her.

"Who else?" he asked, placing another kiss on her forehead. "Let's get you inside, okay? Where are your keys?"

"Pocket," she said, snuggling deeper into his arms.

Cora might have been pulling away from him these last weeks, but asleep and in his arms, she clearly had no problems getting close. When they reached her front door, he stopped long enough to find the key in her front jacket pocket. Quickly, he unlocked the big wooden door and let them in. Atty was already barking madly.

"She's home, big guy," Cole reassured him. "I've got her."

Aware that they were both filthy and wet, he put Cora down on the bench in the entryway and began taking off their muddy boots. He set them aside to clean up later. He removed their coats as well, leaving them in a heap on the floor. Right now, his only goal was to get her dry and warm and to double check her for injuries. He'd take care of the mess later.

"I think you need to take a hot shower, wash off this mud, and get warm. Can you do that? I'll wait right outside the door."

Her eyes were closed, but she nodded. He lifted her again to take her upstairs straight to the bathroom where he put her down on the toilet seat.

"Cora, I need you to open your eyes and let me know you're able to take a shower."

To his relief, she did and gave him a weak smile.

"I can do it. I promise."

He busied himself getting the shower running, grabbing her a towel to place within reach, and taking her socks off. Reluctantly, he left the room and closed the door not quite shut.

"I'm going to leave it open a crack. I promise I won't look, but I'm scared you'll fall. Just call out if you need me. I'll be right here."

He heard a mumbled okay and then the sounds of her pulling off her wet clothes. Moments later he heard the shower door close. He'd grabbed a towel for himself while he was setting things up for Cora, and now he began drying off as much as he could. He would have to wait for clean clothes when he got to his own house. Soon enough, he heard the shower turn off and Cora's movement around the bathroom.

"You alright?"

"I'm fine," she said as she opened the door all the way.

She looked so small in the fluffy robe. Her face was pink from the heat of the small bathroom, but her eyes were tired, rimmed in dark circles. Clearly, the night had taken a toll. He noticed she didn't let go of the door, her small frame swaying a bit from exhaustion. Her hair was a wild nest of tangles, no longer dripping but not combed out yet.

"I need to sit a minute before I take care of my hair. My leg is hurting, and I'm so tired."

Cole understood the exhaustion. He'd been out in the brutal rain for far less time than she had, and he felt like he could sleep for a week. Hiking against the wind and rain had been hard enough on his big body. That coupled with the fear and adrenaline that had coursed through his body was draining him now that they were safe. He could only imagine how hard it had been for her, especially injured.

He led her to the cozy chaise right in the dressing room. While he didn't have the first idea of how to help a woman with her hair, he figured it had to be similar to combing out his own after a shower. She couldn't go to sleep with it like that, and she was in no shape to handle it herself.

"You sit right here, and I'll comb your hair out. We need to tend to your leg better now that you're clean and dry."

Touching Cora was always a pleasure, however rare it was. The joy of combing her tangled mass of hair while she fought to stay awake was no different. He found the repetitive movement of the brush soothing, a comfort after the hours spent worrying over her. Here she was safe and sound, letting him tend to her like he wished. He was careful, not wanting to pull, but she never complained.

The room was silent, and the mood easy until he knelt down to tend to the cut that ran down her shin. It was clean now, but already a bruise bloomed around the wound, which was still seeping a bit of blood now and again. He felt anger rise in him.

The image of her bloody and bruised on that isolated trail was too much. All the *what ifs* flooded his mind. The other endings this night could have had coursed through him like poison. It was an anger born of fear. He'd known enough loss in his life, and he wasn't about to lose her.

"Cora," he said, holding her ankle in his hand.

She was dozing off and didn't rouse at the sound of her name. This time the word had a bite to it.

"Cora."

She blinked her eyes open suddenly and looked at him.

"I need you to listen. You hear me?"

She nodded, her eyes wide and a bit frightened. He didn't care. She needed to hear what he was going to say. She needed to know how scared he was.

"I don't care where you're going or what you're doing. You always tell someone where you're going to be. Always. Do you hear me?"

Again, she just nodded.

"You could've been seriously hurt or even killed out there tonight. That's the hardest rain I've ever felt in my life. The wind is bad. Anything could have happened. What if you'd slipped on that rock and gone over the guard rail? What if you'd gotten lost?"

He was fired up now, letting all the poison out as he listed his fears one by one. A glint came into her otherwise tired eyes.

"I've gone on that trail a hundred times, Cole," she said. "I was fine. And besides that, Eliza knew where I was. I go on this day every year, every single year."

Her words started stronger than before, but as she spoke, each word was said slightly softer as if her energy was running out like the sand in an hourglass. He kept hold of her ankle and leaned closer to her face.

"If you are in trouble, if you need help, you call me. Me, Cora."

Each word was said with the force of a bullet.

"Eliza knew."

"What in the hell was Eliza going to do? Leave her babies and her husband and go out to search for you? I don't think so. Call the cops and have them search? On a night like tonight, they had plenty to do already. No. You call me. I will always come. Anytime, anywhere, right away. You need help. You call me. Understand?"

She just stared at him.

"Do you understand, Cora?" he repeated.

She didn't flinch, didn't budge even an inch, just kept staring at him.

"Cora Lane, you are going to drive me mad. Maybe you already have."

"You won't always be here," she finally said. "I've lived here for years and always been perfectly fine."

"Well, you weren't perfectly fine tonight. And I'm here now."

They were nose to nose, both breathing heavily, both fired up. Cora was weak as water, but she wasn't backing down, and damn if that didn't fire him up even more. Even spitting angry at her, he was so in love he couldn't see straight. He wanted to kiss her, wondered what she would do if he just planted his lips on hers. It would take the barest hint of movement to bring them together, but he was already pressing his luck tonight, so he held himself in check.

Neither of them broke the stare, both unwilling to lose the argument. She tried to shake her leg free of his hold, but the movement must have caused her pain because she winced. That caused both of them to look away at the same time, him to tend her wound and her to look at it. When they finally spoke, it was at exactly the same moment.

"Just say you'll," he said as she said, "Fine, I'll."

Neither saw the need to finish their sentence, both certain of what the other was trying to say. He bent his head low to press a kiss to the newly bandaged cut on her leg. Then he stuck out his hand.

"Do we have a deal?"

She took his hand to seal the deal but still argued.

"I can take care of myself."

"Don't I know it? But give a man a break. I could've had a heart attack."

She smiled at him, a weak but breathtaking smile, and put her hand on his cheek.

"Thank you, Cole. Truly. Thank you for finding me."

"I'll always find you," he replied and then stood to his feet before he did something that would ruin this fragile peace. "Let's get you settled in bed."

In a matter of minutes, he had her tucked in.

"Do you want something to eat or drink? You need a little food before I give you some painkillers."

"Maybe some toast with peanut butter and a cup of tea," she suggested.

"You got it. Just rest here. I'm going to see to Atty and the animals down at the barn, and then I'll bring it right to you."

"The animals are fine. Only Atty needs to go out, and then he's all set," she replied, her eyes closing as she snuggled deeper under the covers.

Cole said nothing, just left her to rest and went to take care of things downstairs. His first stop was to take Atty out, for which the big dog seemed very grateful. The rain was still hard but a bit less intense, and Atty was quick. After drying them both off, Cole cleaned their shoes and hung the jackets up to dry in the laundry room.

He gave Atty a treat while Cora's bread was in the toaster and the kettle boiled. He helped himself to several of the oatmeal cookies in the cookie jar. When the kettle dinged, he made them both a cup of tea. He spread a generous helping of peanut butter on her toast and carried it all up on a tray. Atty followed behind him, eager to get to bed himself. Cora was dozing, but she opened her eyes as he came down the small wooden stairs into the room. She sat up and propped her pillow behind her when he put the tray on her lap.

"Yum," she said, with her mouth full of food.

He laughed. He sat beside her on the edge of the bed, sipping his tea.

"I think I should stay here tonight. I'll sleep on the couch, but I don't feel comfortable leaving you alone. I just need to run up to my house for some dry clothes, and I'll be right back."

"Just in case, Cora," he said when it looked like she would protest. "Give me a break here."

"Okay," was all she said.

She ate every crumb of toast, even licking peanut butter off her fingers which seemed like a good sign to Cole. She didn't argue about taking the painkillers, and she promised she'd call out if she needed him.

"Don't get up in the night by yourself. Even if it's just to go to the bathroom, you call me. Those stairs are impossible in the dark, and you have a sore leg."

"I go up and down those stairs every night in the dark, Cole. I think I can get to the bathroom by myself," she said with a lot more sass now that she had food in her stomach and a soft bed in which to relax.

Cole was torn between relief that she was clearly okay and frustration that she was so stubborn. He figured that would always be true. He gave her what he hoped was a stern look, and to his relief she just rolled her eyes, shook her head, and mumbled, "Fine."

"I'll be back in fifteen minutes."

He moved as fast as the rain would allow. Luckily, it had slowed to a more normal pace, and he was able to drive up the hill to his house with no trouble. He could see water rushing down the ditches on either side of the road, and there were scattered limbs everywhere but nothing he couldn't maneuver around. It was hard to believe they still had power after such a storm, but he was grateful. He imagined the morning would tell a clearer story of the damage the area had sustained, but for now, they had electricity and hot water which was enough.

At home, he took a quick look around to make sure all was well, no trees fallen on his house, no water pooling in the basement. He was grateful for the work he'd done on the drainage around his house as well as his new roof. He shed his soaked clothing and grabbed clean gray sweatpants, a t-shirt, and a favorite old hoodie. The rain had chilled him to the bone, and he'd been in those soaked clothes for what felt like hours. He wasn't ashamed to admit he was freezing.

He longed for a hot shower, but he didn't want to leave Cora for that long. Already, he was antsy to get back to her.

For one thing, he didn't trust she wouldn't get up and try hobbling around on her own. It was also true that he missed her, genuinely missed being in the same place that she was. It was ridiculous but true. He didn't live with her, wasn't sharing all the parts of her life, was quite accustomed to sleeping up here at his house while she slept in her cottage. Yet, the thought of having an excuse to be near her all night made him move faster. He didn't want to waste a moment of that time.

He stuffed his book, toothbrush, and some other essentials into his old backpack and headed to the truck. When he arrived back at Cora's, Atty was waiting at the door for him but thankfully not barking. Clearly, the smart dog had learned what the sound of his truck on the gravel sounded like and could distinguish it from others. He gave Atticus extra love for that fact.

He locked up and shut everything down for the night before climbing the stairs to check on Cora. Glancing down into her room, he saw she was out like a light. He could make out only the top of her head, the rest of her buried under the covers. Even Atty's disappearance to go check on Cole hadn't woken her. He pressed two fingers to his lips and then held them out in the air toward her, a makeshift goodnight kiss.

He made his bed on the couch and settled in, thinking he'd read a while, but his eyes wouldn't stay open. The long, stressful night acted on him like a drug. Hours later, morning came to him in pale slivers of light as he began to awaken. There were no curtains on the many windows in Cora's upstairs living room, but there were enough tall trees to give it the feel of a treehouse.

As he opened his eyes a little at a time, he realized that it was quite early, but already a weak sun was struggling to shine. He heard the sound of water running downstairs and the low voices of the TV news. Cora had clearly started her day, and he'd been sleeping too soundly to notice. He hadn't even heard her feet walking across the creaky, wooden floorboards.

CHAPTER 21

CORA

CORA WAS SURPRISED at how deeply Cole was sleeping on the couch. He was pure temptation for her as she passed through the living room on her way downstairs to the kitchen. He was lying on his side. His hair, usually held back in a band, was loose, and she was surprised to note how wavy it was. Her fingers itched to brush it back from his face. She'd seen it damp after a shower, disheveled from a day of work, but never completely free, and it was a detail she saved in her memory like treasure.

His face was peaceful, his body relaxed, and he appeared almost vulnerable lying there like that with his big, rough hands curled under his face against the pillow. She wanted to hug him to her, to crawl under the blanket with him, and steal some of his warmth for herself. She wanted to tend to him as he so often tended to her.

She shook off those wishful notions and forced herself to leave him there. The cut on her shin was sore and bruised, but she was able to walk with no trouble. A good night's sleep had done her a world of good, and she felt like herself this morning. Thank goodness it was Saturday.

Yesterday was brutal. It was always a hard day for her.

The anniversary of the day Jeff went into the hospital for the last time, never to return to their home was, in many ways, more painful than his actual death. She supposed it was the surprise of it. He'd been in the hospital before and always came home. That last time it was apparent immediately that things were different and dire.

All the markers were hard. Their anniversary, his birthday, the date of his death were all difficult days. For each of those milestones, she climbed up to their favorite lookout point to mark the occasion. There was also a bench and a tree in his memory down near the barn, tucked away in a private little glade. She went there often to talk to him. While she knew he wasn't there, it still helped her get clarity and collect her thoughts when life got tough.

But the lookout was special. They'd found it the first weekend they lived in the cottage. Tired of unpacking boxes and overwhelmed at the amount of work ahead of them, Jeff had suggested they get out of the house and go explore the area. It was Cora who'd picked the trail, liking that it was close to their home. Along with Atty, they'd hiked the whole way up to the top, enjoying the respite from the move. On the way down, Jeff coaxed her to sit with him on the picnic table that was at a lower lookout point on the trail.

"We need to get home. Those boxes won't unpack themselves," she remembered saying to him.

He'd grabbed her hand and twirled her as if they were dancing. She'd giggled and given in, climbing up to the top of the picnic table to sit cuddled up next to him.

"They won't unpack themselves, but they also don't have to be unpacked this very minute. Give me ten minutes, just ten minutes to sit here with you in this beautiful spot and soak up this lovely sunshine. Okay?"

They actually stayed about an hour, Atty resting in a sunny spot on the ground below them. It had been heavenly to sit there enjoying the day, content in the moment together. Jeff had produced an apple and a protein bar from his backpack.

"Sorry. It's not much, but we haven't been to the grocery store yet. So, we have to share."

He broke the bar in half and cut the apple into sections with his pocket knife. It was the kind of perfect romantic moment that can't be planned. Over the years, they returned to the spot again and again, sometimes with just a protein bar and an apple to honor that first time, but other times they packed a full picnic. On some visits, they talked and planned their future. Other times they simply enjoyed the silence. It became their special spot. That was why Cora returned there to mark some of their saddest days as well as the happiest.

Yesterday she watched the dark clouds gathering, but she was determined and stubborn. She'd packed her hiking clothes and changed right after school. When she saw the rain coming, she'd made the last-minute decision to have Carrie, a fellow teacher who babysat Atticus if Cora ever had to be away, take Atty back to the cottage instead of taking him on the hike with her.

As she parked in the trail lot, she remembered to send Cole a text that she wouldn't be at his house that afternoon. She'd thought of it earlier in the day, but Cora knew that if Cole had enough notice, he would start asking questions she didn't want to answer, and so she left it until the afternoon when it was too late for him to change her mind.

The beginning of the hike had been fine, a bit gloomy and blustery but nothing more serious. She'd made it to the lookout, sat down on top of the table without incident. She thought she would have plenty of time to get back to the car before the bottom dropped out. Then suddenly, it began to rain, not just a shower but sheets of water so cold and hard, it hurt when they hit her skin. She scrambled from the picnic table and started walking as fast as she could back toward the car.

It quickly became as dark as night with thunder clouds thick overhead, and she found she couldn't see a foot in front of her. She slowed her pace, but the ground became slick with mud in a matter of minutes. Her shoe slipped on a stone, and she fell hard, smashing her shin against another craggy stone, a large rip tearing in her black leggings. It was so painful, and immediately tears started to fall. She'd struggled to her feet and kept hobbling along at a snail's pace.

For what felt like an endless amount of time, Cora fought her way back down the trail, always praying that the next curve in the path would lead to the parking lot. She was so tired, and the gravel in her shin was causing it to sting as she walked. More than once she considered just sitting down against a tree until the rain stopped.

Then she heard his voice calling her. It was frantic, so unlike Cole's usual gruff tone that she doubted what she'd heard, imagined that she was becoming delusional in her desperation. But the voice kept calling, and then he was there, close enough that she could see him through the rain. Her relief was palpable. She felt so safe in his arms, so sure that he would take care of her that she let herself relax, let the weight of exhaustion overtake her. She wasn't entirely sure of all that took place from the time he found her to when she felt the soothing comfort of her bed.

She had a brief recollection of showering, and she remembered trying in vain to argue with him that she could take care of herself. She also remembered his wild eyes as he looked at her, still so clearly afraid of what could have happened to her. But mostly, she recalled with absolute clarity the singular feeling of safety, of knowing that she could let go, of being certain that it was okay to be vulnerable with him. Even her attempts at insisting she could take care of herself held less of their usual fire, and it wasn't entirely due to her exhaustion. Some of it was simply the overwhelming rightness of him being there. One memory was clear.

"You need help? You call me. Understand?" she remembered him saying.

She balked because she had to. It was what she did. Deep inside, though, she simply thought one word over and over again—*Yes, yes, yes.* It was those words she was thinking as she fell asleep, and it was the peace they brought that was still with her when she awoke.

Later, as she set about taking care of Atty, starting a load of laundry to wash, putting the coffee on, and getting ready to cook breakfast, she thought over what he'd said last night. Would he stay? His words had the ring of a promise. If she was supposed to call him when she needed help, then didn't that mean he would actually be there to help her? She'd counted his eventual departure as yet another reason why they couldn't be more than friends, but if he planned to stay, that reason was no longer valid.

She hadn't bothered to dress for the day, simply thrown on her robe and put her hair in a clip. With her first coffee of the day in hand, she put on her rubber boots and set out with Atty to see how her little flock was doing. That was where Cole found her about a half hour later when he came rushing into the chicken run.

"Cora Lane, what in the name of all that's holy are you doing down here?"

"I'm doing what I do every single morning."

By the look on his face, she knew her answer only served to wind him up further.

"Is that right? So, you could have died last night, have a cut the size of Texas on your leg, and you thought this was a good time to trek down a wet hill to see to some farm animals? Do I have that right?" he asked hotly.

"Well, I didn't die, thanks to you. It's just a cut which is clean and bandaged. Again, thanks to you. I took the hill slowly, and these are not just *some* farm animals. This is my family, Cole. Understand?"

"I'm only trying to take care of you. But no, no, you have to fight me tooth and nail. You'd test the patience of a saint, woman. You hear me? A saint," he repeated for emphasis.

Yet, even though he was clearly angry with her, he didn't stomp off. He just got right on with finishing the morning chores. He stayed close to her, occasionally reaching out a hand to steady her or putting his palm on the small of her back. Cora let him do it. It seemed to her that they were playing roles, acting on the outside as they felt they were supposed to while their deepest hearts tended to one another without a word.

As if struck by lightning, Cora realized this was love. She let that truth work its way through her and found that she felt equal parts fear and joy. It wasn't lost on her that Cole had rescued her on the same trail where she'd gone to mourn Jeff. From the moment they'd met, he'd been pulling her out of the cocoon of her grief. Now she needed to decide what to do about it. How could she keep her vow and have Cole's love too?

Cole hovered all of Saturday and flatly refused to let her work at the house. He even opted to stay with her and watch movies rather than working himself. She made a big breakfast and at least one other pot of coffee, and they watched movies, read, and chilled all day. At one point, she dozed off and woke to find her head resting against his shoulder, her body curled up close to him. Neither said a word. Cora felt her body was letting go of her vow even as her mind fought to keep it. By nightfall she convinced him she would be fine on her own, and he'd reluctantly gone home.

The following week, two weeks before spring break, was not a good one. Her students were restless and edgy, eager to have a break. Several projects at Cole's house hit snags. She should've been done popping off old tile, but one particular bathroom was giving her fits. Whenever she got fed up with it, she would busy herself painting the bedroom walls for a while.

When she'd originally thought of the week off from school, she imagined she would spend it at Cole's house, getting lots done with full days to work. However, he hit her with some news on Tuesday that made her rethink everything. As soon as she arrived at his house for their afternoon work, she knew something was wrong. He was on the phone when she arrived, but she could tell he was surly and spoiling for a fight just based on the one side of the conversation she heard.

She merely waved as she made her way up the stairs to the bathroom that had become her Waterloo. The eggplant-colored tile in that bathroom was going to be the death of her. It was held so firmly to the wall she thought it must have been stuck on with a magic spell. It was truly unbelievable that tile could survive not just the ravages of time, but also all her attempts to break it, smash it, and literally dig it off the wall.

She guessed she'd been working for about half an hour when she heard Cole's boots stomping up the stairs. She had only two tiles and a bleeding knuckle to show for her effort. The minute he came into the small space, the energy shifted. He was bristling with agitation, shifting restlessly from foot to foot. She smiled, hoping to soothe him a bit.

"What have you done to your hand?"

"The corner of this tile," she said, indicating the one right beside her, "tried to bite me."

She was trying to add a little levity to the tense atmosphere.

"You're going to tear your hands up. I'm going to tend to that knuckle, and then you are on paint duty for the foreseeable future."

He moved to help her up. She batted his hand away.

"You can just ratchet that anger way back, and the bossiness can go with it. A busted knuckle is nothing. I'm not some frail little woman who needs you to tend to her. And there is not a single chance that I'm going to stop working on this tile. I've been working on it forever, and I'm not giving up now. This is where I take my stand. Right here in this heinous bathroom."

"Don't be difficult just to be difficult," he said.

"Excuse me. Who are you, and what did you do with my friend?" she asked.

It was like him to be over-protective, to be gruff, even to be bossy. It wasn't like him to be this angry or sound so mean. Usually, her attempts to put him in his place would make him smile. He seemed to like her sass, but today his frown stayed firmly in place. She was concerned.

"Cole, what's wrong?"

She watched as he tried to hold onto his anger, his emotions clearly written on his face. Then he sat down suddenly on a heavy sigh.

"I have to go back to Texas for a while."

She knew the trip was on the horizon, but she'd put it at the back of her mind. He never mentioned it again after that first time, and so, she let herself believe it might not even happen. Hearing him say it now, she felt the words like daggers.

"Why?"

"A development we're building has hit some major problems, and they need me. To be honest, I haven't kept up there like I should. I've left my team to fend for themselves for months, and now they're all looking to mutiny. You remember when I mentioned I needed to go back a few weeks ago?" he asked.

She nodded.

"Well, I nearly left it too late. I'm leaving in the morning out of Newark, and I'll be gone a few weeks."

"I'm sorry. It won't be the same here without you, but I can keep working, and I'll do anything else you need. I'm happy to arrange workers, coordinate jobs, you name it." When he frowned, she said, "Seriously, let me help."

"No way. You have enough on your plate with school and your own home. Plus, it will be spring break the week after next. No. We'll just stop it all, put this place on hold, and get back to it when I can come back."

Cora didn't like the sound of that. It had the ring of finality, like he might be gone much longer than a few weeks. She imagined him diving back into his life in Texas and forgetting all about this house, all about her. It hurt her heart.

"We're making such progress, and you know I love the work. Please, Cole. You've been such a good friend to me. Let me do this for you."

Some of the anger seemed to dissipate, and he reached his hand out to grab hers.

"You're a good friend to me, too. But I can't ask you to keep working like this when I'm gone. And I don't want you to be alone here. You could get hurt, and no one would even know."

"If you say no, I'm still going to come. And if you lock up and don't give me a key, I'll just bust out one of your new windows."

She tried to sound tough, but honestly, she didn't think she could break a window, especially not one he'd just bought brand new.

"Okay, tough girl," he said, throwing his hands up in surrender. "I'll let you work, but there's a condition." She nodded at him, already agreeing. "Please FaceTime me every night."

She grimaced.

"What?" he asked. "I worry."

"I know, but do you have to make it sound like you're my dad checking in on me? And why can't we FaceTime just because that's what friends do? Huh? Why does it have to be like a wellness check? You sure know how to make a girl feel good."

"So, you'll miss me?" he asked, smirking. "Is that what I'm hearing?"

"Don't be an ass," she said, smacking him lightly on the arm.

"Cora Leigh Lane, did you just call me an ass?" he asked, feigning shock. "I never thought I'd see the day."

He was laughing now. Her heart was glad, but her pride kept her fighting.

"Number one," she said, holding up her finger which he promptly batted away playfully. "I'm not some Puritan. That's not even a bad word."

This time she held up two fingers, and he swatted at them too.

"Number two, you've done this to me. You've driven me to it. You've only yourself to blame, you bossy, pigheaded Neanderthal."

She was fired up now, and it felt good. Before she could think of more to say, he silenced her by brushing his hand down her cheek.

"Alright, little fighter, I get the point. And for the record, I'll miss you too."

She let herself lean into his touch for a moment, but no more was said. The next day he was gone before she was up. She found a note on her door that said, *I tended our little flock this morning. I'll be back soon. FaceTime at 7.* Her stupid, traitorous heart held the note close and read it three or four more times. It felt like a note from a lover, not just a friend. *Our little flock.* That word *our* hit her in the heart like an arrow.

It was the truth. While she'd been worrying over her vow, they'd been building something together. She thought she was helping him restore his house, but he was silently restoring her heart. Even as she sighed at the sweetness of that thought, her faithful, vow-keeping brain reminded her that the space would do her good. She saved the note under her pillow anyway.

For the rest of the week, she stuck to her usual schedule. Chores, school, work at Cole's house, eat, sleep, repeat. She took Atty with her each day for company as she was keenly aware of Cole's absence. It was an ache that wouldn't subside. She found herself staying late at the house, just to be surrounded by his things, searching for an old work shirt in the hamper that might still carry his scent. He called every night at seven sharp, and she was always ready.

His smile when he saw her face on the screen hit her like a spark of electricity every time. His whole face would light up as if he'd just seen the best thing he could imagine. Cora knew she must look the same. They would chat while she showed him her progress. He would ask her if she was eating enough, sleeping enough, working too hard, and then ask about the animals.

She would ask about his work and how it was going, but he didn't seem to care for that topic as much as listening to her talk about her days. One thing she didn't share was just how late she was staying at his house every night. She knew he would fuss, so she kept that to herself. For ten days she kept that schedule, and she had to admit it took a toll.

Before Cole, she'd cooked for herself every day. Now, she found that she didn't feel like going to the trouble without him around. So, she ate what she could grab while she worked or what she could scarf down at the kitchen counter before going to bed. It wasn't much. She found she didn't sleep as well as usual, tossing and turning, only to wake up feeling worse than when she went to bed. This made no sense. One morning while getting ready for school, she gave herself a lecture in the mirror:

You lost Jeff and kept going. You lost the love of your life and didn't let it take you down. You grieved, yes. But you got up every day and took care of yourself. Get it together, Cora. Cole's gone to Texas to work for a few weeks. It's not like he died. It's not like you won't ever see him again. Stop acting like a lovesick fool and get over it. He isn't yours. He will never be yours. You made a promise, a vow. Act like it.

But her pale face in the mirror didn't seem to get the

message, so she pinched her cheeks to bring up the color. Her clothes were loose from skipping too many meals, and worst of all, her eyes were dull. There was no spark. It made her angry, this notion that she was grieving for a man who wasn't her husband. It was disrespectful to grieve for a living man when her husband was gone forever. It made her feel guilty.

A few people asked her if she was okay, parents dropping off their children in her classroom each morning, the teacher across the hall. Even Cole told her she looked like she was about to drop when he called the night before. She avoided talking about it by distracting him with a funny story about the goats. However, she met her match the minute Eliza saw her walking into the restaurant that week for their usual girls' night out.

"Cora Lane, are you coming down with something? You look awful." As usual, Eliza didn't beat around the bush. "Seriously, I've been living in the land of the sick all week with my girls, and you look as bad as them."

"No, I'm just tired. I've been working at Cole's house late while he's gone and just haven't been taking care of myself. That's all."

Cora could see the concern in Eliza's eyes, and even though her friend's words were often blunt, she saw the love and fear behind them. Eliza had seen her through such terribly hard times, and she was very protective as a result.

"You look like you've lost weight too. Are you eating?" Eliza asked.

"Not like I should. I just got caught up in all the work and let it slip. Seriously," she said reaching out to pat the back of Eliza's hand, "I'm fine. I love you for caring, but I'm fine."

"Cora, that's not like you. You cook for an army even

when it's just you. It's your go-to stress reliever. You miss him, don't you?" Eliza's voice was soft and tender.

"It's not that. I mean I do miss him, but that's normal because we've been working so closely on the house."

She saw she was twisting her hands on the table and sounded a bit frantic, so she simply gave up and said no more.

"It's okay to miss him, sweetie. It's okay to need him, to love him. It's all okay. You know that," Eliza said, putting her hand on top of Cora's fidgety ones.

"No, it's not. I took a vow, Eliza. It's okay for me to love Cole as a friend, but it's not okay to need him or want him or be desperate without him. I don't want to feel this way. I don't want any of this. I was doing fine, absolutely fine until he showed up. Now he's gone and look at me. It's pathetic. I'm pathetic." Cora heard the tears in her own voice.

"You made a vow to an unconscious, dying man, a vow he likely never heard and certainly didn't get a chance to support. I've told you a million times that the Jeff I knew and loved like a brother would never want this for you. That's not who he was. That's not who you are."

This was familiar territory for Eliza, a speech she gave often. Cora always chose to ignore it, thinking it was just her friend's way of letting her off the hook. She did the same now, though her wayward heart latched onto those words for dear life.

"Enough," Cora said. "Let's binge on chips and salsa. You said yourself I've lost weight. So, help me put it back on, and tell me all about those sweet little girls who've been sick."

They dug into their food with gusto and laughed their way through a few baskets of chips and a margarita each.

"I have an idea," Eliza said as they got ready to leave the restaurant. "Don't say a word until you hear me out."

Cora nodded.

"Brent's mom and dad can't join us for our annual spring break trip to Florida next week. They canceled just yesterday because his dad's brother fell and broke his hip and is in the hospital. So, we have an extra room that will just sit empty, already paid for. Come with us, Cora. All you need is a plane ticket and running money."

Cora was about to say no when Eliza held up her hand.

"I'm not finished. It's a resort, everything in one place. You can veg by the ocean or at the pool, have movie nights with us, sleep in, get some sun, eat yummy food. Please, Cora. Please. It will be so much fun."

Cora was going to say no. She really was, but instead she found herself saying she'd think about it. There was a ton of work to do at her own house, the rest of the school year to plan, not to mention her promise to work at Cole's house. She didn't like to leave Atty or any of her flock. In fact, in five years she'd never taken a single vacation, never dipped her toes in the ocean or been on an adventure. The furthest she'd traveled was to see her parents or her siblings, and the stress of those trips canceled out any kind of vacation potential.

She'd become almost afraid to leave her small corner of the world. It felt like it might disappear, might only be a figment of her childhood imagination, a lifetime of longing made visible. She understood now that her childhood, though abundant in every material thing, had been a study in poverty when it came to emotional safety and affection. Finding Jeff and their home together had been like coming upon an ocean in the desert. The fact of his passing made her cling to their life harder.

She always said that she needed no vacation from her life. It was simple but abundant, sometimes sad or lonely, but never unfulfilling. The world beyond her was scary. Who knew what might ruin her peace, what might bring her right back to the unkindness of her youth? However, for the first time ever, she was tempted. Every year Eliza invited her to go away with them. Cora always used money as an excuse, and it wasn't a complete lie. She could swing the extra expense, but it would cost her a project at the cottage.

Eliza's offer this year was different though. She didn't have to pay for anything but a plane ticket and incidentals. She could manage that and still have enough for her summer projects. According to Eliza, direct flights to Florida from their small regional airport were affordable and abundant, and there were still seats left on the same flight that Eliza and Brent had booked. She knew Carrie would gladly look after Atty, and Dr. Brenner would be happy to check on the barn animals. Everything she had planned could wait. Didn't she deserve a break?

She was going to dig out her bikinis and her sun hat and go to Florida. She was going to get some sun and rest, drink a few fruity cocktails filled with rum and little umbrellas, and read books that weren't about restoration or education. When she came back, she would be clear-headed, refreshed, and ready to think of Cole as the good friend he was and nothing more. She didn't need more time to think about it. She said yes to Eliza while they were still at the table.

CHAPTER 22

COLE

Cole was exhausted right down to his bones. He'd always been a hard worker, but the pace he set on his trip back to Dallas took it to a whole new level. All he thought of was Cora and getting back to her. He worked like he was a character in a movie trying to deactivate a bomb, the timer clicking down the seconds until the explosion.

His team was building a new gated community in the most affluent part of town. They'd spent months clearing and leveling lots and planning the overall design of the development. Now that the lots were sold, they were building custom homes for each buyer. It was exactly the kind of work they did all the time, but this one kept hitting road blocks.

He had a reputation as the premier builder in the area, and the people who paid for his team to build their homes expected Cole himself to be on site regularly. His impulsive move to New York left some of them disgruntled. Every day since he'd gotten back, he spent hours reassuring his customers, battling the city over a few tricky permits, and trying to sort out problems with various utilities.

It was almost ten when he finally made it back to the modern high rise apartment he called home in downtown

Dallas. His view from the top of the steel and glass structure always made him feel miles away from his pitiful childhood, made him feel like he'd truly risen above it all. The sleek, minimalist style was soothing, devoid of clutter, fresh and clean.

More than anything, the lack of noise was a reprieve from the madness of the world. Sure, he could stand on the balcony and see the cars zooming past, hear the pedestrians on the street below, but it was as if he was watching a movie, the volume set low. Always prizing his freedom and solitude above all else, this apartment had been his favorite place until now.

He found himself lonely in this tower in the sky. He felt a yearning for the mess and clutter of his renovation, the bark of Atticus, the sound of Cora's singing as she peeled away layers of paint and wallpaper. For a moment, he let himself imagine her here. She wouldn't like it. It wasn't her taste at all. Cora loved anything cozy and warm. The older an item, the more she loved it, always talking about how many stories that mantel could tell or how much life that broom had swept away.

While she might not like the apartment, she would love the view. He could envision the two of them standing on the balcony, arms wrapped around each other as they took it in. He could see Atticus settled on his own bed, watching the stars. It was a sweet dream.

He was restless tonight, exhausted in body, but awake in his mind. He was accustomed to their nightly chats. He relied on that connection. However, he wasn't going to bother her while she was in Florida. According to Eliza, Cora hadn't taken a vacation since Jeff passed and few even before, as they were always working on the house. She was in dire need of a break.

He liked the image of her soaking up the sun, reading a book as she lounged by the pool or at the beach. Today Eliza, who had become his friend as well, had sent him a photo of Cora doing just that. She was wearing a pink bikini, her skin tan and glowing, her hair wet from the pool, a sun hat hanging off her chair. She was engrossed in a book, miles away in her mind, and the peaceful look on her face caught his breath and made his heart ache with longing. That photo was now his lock screen, at least until there was a chance Cora would see it.

She'd called him a couple of times on her trip, but their timing was off, him working late and her on beach time. So, their conversations were short, no FaceTime. Tonight, he guessed he was in Cora withdrawals. He tried reading. He tried a shot of whiskey and then another. He tried looking at the stars from a lounge chair on the balcony. Nothing worked. Now he was pacing. If he could build houses in the dark, he would have a hammer in his hand right now.

Then his phone started buzzing. When he scooped it off the glass and chrome coffee table, he saw Cora's name. She'd chosen FaceTime, and he nearly dropped the phone trying to accept the call. When her face appeared, he swallowed hard. She was wearing something coral-colored with thin straps that were tied in bows on her tan shoulders. Her hair was piled on her head, tendrils hanging down, begging to be touched. She was clearly outside, the night sky in the background.

"Hi there, pretty girl," he said without thinking.

"Don't you *hi there, pretty girl,* me, Cole Houston. I've had it with you."

Cole might have worried he was in real trouble had it not been for the glazed look in her beautiful eyes and the slight slur of her words. If he wasn't mistaken, she was a bit tipsy.

"Cora, are you drunk?"

"I am not. All I've had is a few of these fruity drinks," she said, waving one such drink in the air, spilling a little as she swayed and nearly fell off her chair.

"What kind of fruity drink is that? Do you remember the name?"

"Of course, I re- re- bemember. It's a storm, I think, or maybe a tornado, something with rain," she said as she held the drink up as if to examine it.

Yep, he thought, definitely drunk.

"Maybe a hurricane?"

She slapped what must have been a table in front of her that he couldn't see.

"Ding, Ding. You win. It's a hurricane," she said, laughing so hard she nearly fell off her chair again.

"Careful there, Cora. Are you by yourself?" He was beginning to question the notion that Eliza and her family were the right people to take Cora on vacation. "Where are Brent and Eliza?"

"They needed a family night. I don't want to get in my way," she giggled. "I mean their way. I was in their way, so I came to the pool area and got these delicious drinks."

She waved said drink again. Then she whipped the phone around so fast he nearly became dizzy.

"See the ocean back there, Cole. I can see it. Can you see it?"

The phone moved as if it was actually in the ocean.

"Cora, can you turn the phone back to your face, please?" To his relief, she did. "I think you might want to go inside now. Go find Eliza. No more fruity drinks for you tonight. Can you do that for me?"

Cole felt like his heart now lived outside his body and

moved around instead with Cora. The thought of her drunk and alone at some resort patio bar was making him crazy.

"No, I won't. You are not the boss of me."

This was said with all the indignation of a toddler.

"Don't I know it?" he muttered.

"I have some things to say to you, and you're going to listen. That's why I called. Got it?"

"Got it," he said.

"You have confused me enough. Do you hear me? Enough," she said, hands gesturing wildly, drink still in hand. She took a sip, and when he opened his mouth to speak said, "No, I talk. You listen."

He merely nodded.

"Because of you I have confusion and sparkles and flutters all over the place, and it's driving me crazy." Her hands made swirling motions, the little bit of drink left in the glass sloshing over the side. "See what you made me do. Now I'm all out of drink, and I'm sticky. You are bad, Cole Houston."

"Confusion, sparkles, and flutters, you say?" he asked.

"Stop talking. I talk. You listen. Bemember?"

He thought it best not to correct her.

"I *bemember*."

She smiled and nodded like he was the best student in her class.

"Every day I think: what would Cole think of this, would Cole like my bikini, would Cole want to swim in the sea with me? Cole, Cole, Cole, all the time. And never Jeff, never. It's not right to mess with a woman who made a vow. You should be ashamed. Here I am trying to be noble and faithful and good, and instead I'm wondering what you look like in your swim trunks. I bet you have killer abs. See. It's ridiculous, shameful, and it's all your fault."

By the end of this tirade, she was pointing her finger at him. Well, she was pointing her finger, but it was more at something vaguely in front of her. Clearly, the rum had messed with her spatial awareness. He felt it best not to mention it.

"May I say something now?" he asked after a long, quiet moment.

"Maybe. Say it and then I'll tell you if it's okay."

He laughed. It was madness how much he loved her. His heart was so full from her words, but he was certain she wouldn't *bemember* a thing in the morning. Still, it felt good to know she was feeling the same chaotic emotions that he was.

"Well, for starters, I'll answer your questions. I would think the world of anything that involved being with you. I can guarantee that you look amazing in your bikini, and I most definitely would swim in any sea with you."

She beamed a smile that had the wattage to light up an entire house.

"Really?" she asked.

"For sure. As for the abs, you'll have to be the judge of that. Maybe I'll show them to you when you get back home."

She beamed again, but it quickly became a frown.

"No, no, no. You're doing it again. Confusion, sparkles, and flutters. Bad, Cole, very bad. I'm a woman with a vow."

And now, it seemed she might cry. Cole panicked.

"No, I'm not doing anything. I'm sorry if I made you upset. You are a wonderful woman, and you're noble and faithful. There isn't a bad bone in your body."

He wasn't even sure what he was saying, just mumbling nonsense to soothe her. He was relieved to see she looked a little calmer.

"I don't know why this is happening. I've never felt this ever in my life. I meet men all the time and nothing. Not a flutter, not a sparkle, no confusion. My vow has always been super easy, and now you've spoiled it. I look at you and I feel fluttery and sparkly, like my insides might fly away."

She was back to the wild gesturing again. He needed to get her to Eliza quickly. He wanted to revel in what she was saying, but her safety was more important. Her eyes were now closed, and she was humming.

"Cora, can you hear me?"

She just nodded.

"I need you to use the words. Say *Cole, I can hear you.*"

He heard her mutter "Bossy, impossible man" and then, "I can hear you."

He smiled and said, "I need you to get up now before you fall asleep and go back to your room. I'll text Eliza to come and meet you. Okay? Say okay if you hear me."

She nodded her head quickly and then kept nodding, which made her giggle.

"Say the words, Cora Lane," he said again, this time a bit harsher.

She narrowed her eyes and leaned closer to her phone.

"Okay, bossy pants."

But she moved to stand up, and Cole felt relief flood him. He sent Eliza a quick text to come down to meet Cora. As he hit send, he heard a retching sound from the phone. Cora was sick. When her face came back into view, she was wiping her mouth with a napkin, and he could hear a male voice speaking softly to her.

"Cora, are you okay? Who is that with you?" he asked urgently.

"This nice man named? Hold on a minute," she said,

and then she turned away. He heard her ask, "What is your name, nice man?"

The deep voice said, "Tom."

She turned back to the phone beaming, "This nice man named Tom helped me. I got sick, Cole."

"Cora, can you hand the phone to Tom, please?"

Cole tried to keep his voice calm. Cora did as he asked. Soon, a handsome face came into view.

"Hi, Tom," he said in a friendly voice. "I'm Cole. Thank you for helping my girl, but her friend is about to come down and get her, so you can move along. Got it?"

"I'll just sit here with her until her friend shows up," Tom had the nerve to say. "She shouldn't be wandering around by herself in this condition. Or, I could escort her to her room."

"Cora," Tom asked, turning to Cora who was out of sight. "Would you like me to walk you to your room?"

Cole chimed in before Cora could speak.

"No, she is fine right where she is. Her friend Eliza will walk her to her room."

Cora took the phone right out of Tom's hands and glared hard at Cole through the screen.

"I can take care of myself, bossy pants."

Cole cracked his neck and rubbed at the scruff on his chin so hard he nearly scratched himself. He was about to speak when she leaned in so close that he could nearly see up her nose.

"No worries, Cole. No confusion, sparkles, or flutters happening with Tom. Only you. I'll just wait right here for Eliza," she whispered.

Cole felt a rush of love move through him like a tidal wave.

"That's good. No confusion, sparkles, or flutters allowed for anyone but me. Okay?"

She beamed again, nodded, and tried to wink, but it was more of a mad blinking like a gnat flew in her eye. He beamed right back at her.

"Goodbye Tom," he heard her say.

For a moment, they just stared at one another, the connection so alive it fairly crackled across their phones. Tomorrow it would all be different. Either Cora would forget the whole conversation, or she would remember and be mortified. Either way, the sweetness of this moment had to be savored. Soon enough, he saw her eyes move and smile at someone in the distance. Clearly, Eliza had arrived.

"Eliza's here," she said softly. "Goodnight, Cole."

Cole took a chance she was too drunk and sleepy to ever remember this moment clearly and said, "Goodnight, my love."

The call ended, and he leaned against the balcony railing with a big smile on his face. His girl might never remember tonight, but at least he knew he wasn't in this alone. Cora would likely fight her feelings forever, but in this moment, it was enough just to know she was filled with confusion, sparkles, and flutters. Cole laughed again at her words. Only Cora would describe love quite that way.

The next day Cole finally made it through all the work that had piled up, tied up loose ends, and made his plans to fly back to New York. The only disappointing part of the day was that he didn't hear from Cora. He expected a text, a call, anything to acknowledge the night before, even if she didn't quite remember it all, but the phone was silent.

Right before he left his makeshift office in the onsite trailer, he gave up and sent her a quick text. *Hope you're feeling better. Still smiling from our little talk.* He even added an emoji of a smiley face with heart eyes. He knew he was a goner for the woman if he was using emojis.

The text quickly showed *read,* but no reply came. Three dots danced and stopped and danced again as if she was composing and deleting endless versions of a reply. That made him laugh. Cora would not be feeling too good today, likely hungover. Nothing about the call had been remotely like the always appropriate Cora he knew. Finally, a text came through. *A gentleman wouldn't mention it. I'm wearing dark sunglasses under a large umbrella, sipping ginger ale and hoping a hole in the ground opens to swallow me up.* She included the emoji of a woman smacking the side of her head. He laughed out loud.

He replied: *I couldn't resist. You were just too adorable.*

She simply gave him the thumbs down on that one.

He gave up resisting and called her. The little minx let it ring five times before she answered.

"Hello, Mr. Houston," she said with a snippy bite. "What can I do for you?"

"Cora Lane, you had me laughing so hard last night and again with those texts that I had to hear your voice. How are you really? I was a little worried when you vomited in front of a strange man who wanted to walk you to your room."

"Don't remind me," she groaned. "That is why I don't drink like that often. It never ends well. I'm too much of a lightweight. That poor man."

"Poor man, my ass. He wanted to walk you to your room and walk right on in. I just about snapped my phone in half until I had that little chat with him."

"Honestly, I don't remember all the details, just needing to call you, then throwing up, and then Eliza. It's all a bit blurry. There's no telling what I said or did. I'm not fit for the public."

Her voice had lost its snippy bite and was now pure misery.

"It was fine. You were just talking to me. I'm your friend, and so is Eliza. Sure, I'd like you to be more careful, but other than that, you made my evening with your call," he said and then asked, "How do you really feel?"

"Like a marching band took up residence in my brain and someone stole all the moisture from my mouth and swapped it with cotton balls. My stomach is rolling, and the sun is extra bright." He was just about to reply when she added in a small, sad voice, "I feel like hell, Cole."

The whispered voice immediately put them in a bubble, just the two of them, as if she was sharing a secret.

"I know. Are you drinking water? Have you had some painkillers?"

"Yes, I'm drinking water and ginger ale to help my stomach, and yes to the painkillers, but it's late afternoon, and it just won't stop."

"Cora, why aren't you in your room taking a nap in the dark? Why are you at the pool in the sun with all those people? That's not helping."

"I didn't want to miss a day of this glorious weather. Only two more days and I'll fly back home where it will still be a chilly spring for a few more weeks."

"Do you trust me?" he asked.

He was ridiculously pleased when she said yes without missing a beat.

"Okay, then. Pack up your stuff and go to your room. Take a hot shower and put on something comfy. And for goodness sake, close those curtains. I know you have them wide open to let in the light. Today is not the day for all that sunlight. Can you do that?"

"Yes, that might be a good idea."

She sounded so tired.

"What is your room number?"

"Why do you need to know that?" she asked, suspiciously.

"Room number, Cora."

He used his harsh voice, the one that made her eyes go wide.

"625," she muttered.

"By the time you get up there and get showered and changed, someone will be delivering something to you. Check the peephole to be sure, but answer the door, or you won't get your surprise."

"What surprise? Cole, what are you up to?"

"Go up to your room, and you'll find out."

"Cole," she began.

"Pack up and get your ass moving, Cora. I'll speak with you later."

As soon as he hung up, he looked up the number for the hotel and called the concierge. He made arrangements for crackers, peanut butter, and banana slices to be delivered to Cora with her favorite lemon lime soda and plenty of water.

He also arranged for a delivery of wildflowers and a stuffed dog that looked as much like Atty as possible. He even sent the concierge a photo. When she balked a little at his request, he simply offered her an enormous tip and promised to speak with her supervisor to give her a glowing recommendation. He used his strongest Texas drawl and all the honeyed words it took to get what he wanted delivered to Cora as quickly as possible.

When he was done, he left the site for the day, stopped

for his favorite steak dinner, and imagined his girl eating her favorite comfort food with flowers on the table beside her, and a stuffed pup to keep her company. He might be new to this love business, but it felt damn good.

CHAPTER 23

CORA

CORA MADE IT to her room in a haze. Her head was throbbing worse than she'd let on with Cole. She quickly pulled the curtains closed against the bright sun and slipped out of her swimsuit. In the bathroom, she turned the hot water on all the way and waited for it to heat up. The minute she stepped under the spray she nearly wept in relief, simply standing there for a moment to let it pour over her. She took her time washing her hair and body and stepped out. Throwing on an oversized t-shirt and underwear with nothing else, she dried her hair, and took some more pain relief tablets.

A knock at the door startled her. Checking the peephole, it looked like one of the bellboys from the lobby. She opened the door but only part way.

"Hello," she said.

"I have a delivery for Cora Lane," he said, gesturing to a cart in front of him.

"Thank you. Please just leave it right here in the entrance. I'll be right back."

She was a bit uncomfortable standing there in just the shirt, but it did come all the way to midthigh. She grabbed some cash from her wallet and walked back to the door.

"No, thank you," he said when he saw the money in her

hand. "The tip is taken care of." He turned to leave, closing the door behind him.

Cora turned her attention to the cart. There was a huge bouquet of flowers, not roses or carnations or any other hothouse flower, but rather daisies and other wildflowers. She inhaled their scent, not the odor of a funeral, but the heady perfume of nature and sun. Spying the stuffed dog, she grabbed it immediately, holding it to her.

"Like Atty," she mumbled, stroking its ears.

There was a silver domed dish alongside a six pack of her favorite soda in the little cans she preferred. Under the dome, she found a platter of crackers smeared with peanut butter and topped with banana slices. Her heart did a thump in her chest, and her whole body sighed. This was perfect.

Just as she was about to scoop up a cracker, she noticed a card under the napkin. She picked it up and read: *A few of your favorite comforts to make it all better. Now take your snack and your pup and crawl under the covers to munch and then nap. Your friend, Cole.*

In a rare show of absolute compliance, Cora did exactly as he requested. She picked up the tray of snacks along with a can of soda and settled in her bed. She took small bites and tiny sips until her stomach stopped rolling and her headache subsided. Then she cuddled the Atticus lookalike and fell into a deep sleep.

She awoke the next morning feeling much better. Apparently, Cole's cure-all helped. Before she could over-think it, she picked up her phone to send Cole a thank you text. He'd beaten her to the punch with a message of his own: *Good morning. I hope you slept well and feel better. I'll leave you alone for your last couple of days at the beach. Working day and night to get back to NY when you do. Have a good day.* She couldn't help but smile.

CHAPTER 24

COLE

COLE WASN'T LYING. He was working all hours to make it back to New York by the time Cora got home. The truth was he knew he was going to leave whether he was done with work or not. At this point, the whole development could go up in flames, and he would walk away without so much as a backwards glance. He knew now that his life was wherever she was, even if she was never his to love.

During his stay in Dallas, he spent a couple of evenings chatting with Joe, the man who'd taken him in all those years ago. Aside from giving him a home and then a job, Joe also became a sounding board for Cole. He suspected that it was Joe's patient silence and steady presence that made him so trustworthy. The older man never pushed for information, never asked many questions. Somehow that lack of pressure made Cole open up. This time was no different. He told him all about Cora, and as always, Joe offered good perspective.

"Love doesn't come just because we want it, doesn't care if it makes sense or is convenient, and is no respecter of persons, my boy. Maybe you never believed in it before, but this little gal has you all knotted up with longing. I wouldn't

255

give that up if I were you, not for a bunch of houses on a golf course or even a fat payday," Joe told him.

Those unguarded moments with Cora on the phone had given him so much hope, but he still had doubts. Did she feel as strongly for him as he did for her? Would she ever be willing to give them a chance? He knew they had a powerful chemistry that neither could control, but Cora fought it with the determination of steel.

By Saturday morning he was boarding a plane back to her. He was equal parts nervous and excited. He wasn't foolish enough to think that she was suddenly going to jump into his arms, but he missed her so much he was willing to take a cool, remote Cora over no Cora at all.

He'd chatted with Eliza to get their flight details. It meant a connection in Philly instead of a direct flight and a change of airport from Newark to the smaller regional airport near their home. But he was willing to pay whatever the charge to see her face right after he landed instead of waiting hours for them to both get back home separately.

His flights were both smooth with no delays and little turbulence. He found himself antsy as he waited for the plane to come to a stop and the cabin door to open. He'd always been such a laidback guy, but Cora changed all that. Now, he just wanted off this plane so he could sprint to baggage claim where Eliza said he could find them. He had no checked bag, but that's where she would be, so that's where he would go. He jogged down the escalator and scanned the area for her.

He didn't need a description of her outfit or any other help in spotting her. She would stand out in any crowd for him, and so he wasn't surprised when his eyes found her immediately. She was standing off to the side of a nearby baggage carousel. He was all but running once his feet hit the ground at the bottom of the escalator.

She was staring at her phone while Eliza and her family were waiting nearer to the carousel for their bags. She was a sight for sore eyes, all tan, sun-kissed skin and natural beauty, even after a day of flying across the country. She looked rested and relaxed and so intent on her phone screen that she didn't look up even once as he crossed to her.

"Hey," he said when he got close enough that she could hear him.

She got the strangest expression on her face and shook her head as if trying to shake off some odd thought. He repeated the greeting, this time even closer to her, and her head snapped up immediately, staring at him in surprised wonder.

"Cole? What are you doing here? I was texting you."

She looked so excited to see him, and he couldn't help but grin at her happiness. Of course, he was also more than a little thrilled to know that her preoccupation with her phone had been because she was trying to contact him. That did wonders for his heart.

"Eliza helped me plan to meet up with you here."

"But you were flying in and out of Newark," she said, confused.

"I wanted to see you."

At that, Cora smiled and rubbed the spot over her heart. Cole didn't think she realized all her tells, all the little ways she gave him encouragement even as her words often made him despair. She might be a woman set on keeping a promise she'd made to a dying man, but she was also a woman who felt something for him, no matter how much it confused her.

"Is your chest hurting?" he asked, pointing to the hand she held over her heart.

"No," she said. "Why?"

He pointed again. She looked down at her hand over her heart, her eyes growing wide.

"I'm just tired. I guess," she said, letting her hand drop to her side.

He simply nodded at her.

"You look great, so tan and gorgeous."

She blushed, and he felt his heart rate spike. That was pretty typical for any interaction with Cora, and damn if he hadn't missed it these last few weeks.

"Thanks. It was a good trip."

"I'm so glad. You deserve good things."

Soon Eliza and her crew joined them.

"Hi Cole. Brent, this is Cole. He's Cora's friend."

Cole shook hands with Brent and then knelt down to greet the girls.

The littlest one said, "Are you Auntie Cora's boyfriend?"

"Claire, my goodness, what a question," Cora said.

Cole simply said, "Well, I am a boy, and I am her friend, so that might be true."

The little girl just giggled.

"Cora, are you going to ride with Cole?" Eliza asked, and he wanted to hug her for helping him out.

"It makes sense, Cora. We're going to the same street after all," Cole added.

It was in fact such a practical solution that Cole knew Cora couldn't refuse. It was either ask her friends to make an extra, out of the way stop on their way home from a long trip with little kids, or simply ride with Cole who was heading to the exact same place. More, he didn't really think Cora wanted to refuse.

"For sure," she said.

They walked with Eliza and her family all the way to the parking garage where they finally split up to go to their separate cars.

"Wait a minute. If you parked at Newark, how is your truck here?" she asked.

"I paid a couple of the guys working on the house to move it for me."

"So, not only did you pay to park for weeks at Newark, but then you paid someone to drive to get your car and park it here?" she asked. "That's nuts."

She wasn't wrong, but she wasn't entirely right either. Cole liked the peace of mind he got from paying for premium parking at an airport, the knowledge that he wasn't at the mercy of public transportation or a car service after a long flight. He wanted the power to get in and drive, the ease of heading home immediately.

He figured everyone had their little quirks, the things they were willing to shell out money for that others might find odd. Even more true was the fact that he would have paid any amount of money to be heading home with Cora next to him in his truck. It was that simple. They found the truck easily, and Cole loaded their bags while Cora climbed in the passenger seat. He saw her shiver a bit as she settled into her seat.

"Quite the temperature change, isn't it? I think we both got used to that warm air down south." He cranked up the heat as well as turning on her seat heater. "It'll warm up soon."

"This is typical New York spring weather, always cool

even into May. It's good for the garden, but not always for the gardeners."

While they drove, Cole peppered her with questions about the trip. They hadn't spoken for a couple of days, and he was eager for the sound of her voice. She asked him about his work and if it all got finished. He nodded and smiled, unwilling to reveal just how little sleep he'd gotten these last few days, working so desperately to make it back for just this moment.

"You look tired, Cole."

He glanced at her to find she was staring intently at him.

"I am tired. I had a lot of fires to put out in a short time, and I really wanted to get back here."

"You need to drop me off and then go have a nap. Do you hear me?"

She sounded concerned, and it warmed his heart.

"Is that right, little schoolteacher?"

"You can tease me. It doesn't change the fact that you need a hot shower and a long nap, tough guy."

"And then what?" he asked, as they pulled into her driveway.

Once he stopped the car, he turned to look at her.

"Then maybe I'll make you some dinner, and you can come over and eat with me."

"Deal," he said. "Let me help you get your bag inside and make sure everything's okay."

"Nope. I've carted this bag all by myself the whole trip. I can get it into my own house, and of course, everything is alright inside. Go home, Cole. Get started on that shower and nap assignment I gave you." She was insistent but still smiling. "Besides, I'm going to text Carrie to bring Atty over and see what my little flock needs."

"No can do. If you're going to be down here working, there's no way I'm going to be napping."

"Cole, I just spent the week lounging by the pool or at the beach. I even slept on the plane. I'm all good. I'm in the mood to jump right in. Plus, that dinner isn't going to cook itself. I probably need to run to the store. Go," she repeated. "I mean it. If you don't leave, then dinner is off."

He could see she'd dug her heels in, and he was also feeling the effects of exhaustion.

"You drive a hard bargain, but I can admit when I'm defeated. I'll go."

"Thanks for surprising me at the airport and for the ride," she said as she climbed out and grabbed her bag. Then she walked around to his window and shocked him by reaching in to kiss his cheek. "I'm glad we're back."

It was those words he was thinking of on repeat as he drove home a moment later, all through his shower, and as he drifted off to sleep. *I'm glad we're back.* Me, too, he thought. Me too.

For the next few weeks, they slipped easily back into their daily routines. Cole was amazed at how much she'd accomplished in his absence and how much she'd overseen for him. The house was coming together, less a construction site and more a home every day. Cora had even begun drawing up plans for the garden as well as marking areas that needed clearing and trees that needed cutting or pruning. The weather finally turned toward spring for good, bringing sunny skies and warmer temperatures.

He was delighted when he got the news that the fixtures and appliances for the kitchen were all in and ready for delivery. He was keeping the kitchen a secret from Cora. She could see the custom cabinets he was building, but he didn't let her see them once he painted them, and he banned her from the kitchen once everything was ready to be put into place. Large plastic sheets blocked the entrance to the kitchen at all entry points so that she couldn't get even the smallest glance. He wanted it to be a total surprise. It was as close to a declaration of love and intent as he felt he could make at the moment.

He was tired of holding back, tired of keeping his love a secret. He wanted to shout it out loud, hold her hand as they walked, kiss her whenever he wanted. He knew it was risky. Cora still walked a fine line. Her eyes might tell a story of longing and affection, but her words never strayed from their intent to keep her promise to Jeff. He thought she might be happy to live in that limbo forever, two friends spending every day together always frozen in place.

While nothing was worth losing her over, it was also true that he couldn't lose a chance he wasn't willing to take. If he never pushed her at all, he would never know what was truly possible. And if she refused? If she saw the kitchen and just ignored it, or worse, ran, what then? These were the thoughts that circled his mind at night. He was torn between the excitement of what might be and the fear of losing her all in one bittersweet moment.

Regardless, the kitchen was going to be finished, and she was going to see it. He couldn't put it off indefinitely. So, with fear in his heart, he scheduled all the deliveries and last-minute jobs. When all of it was completed, he sent Cora a text that today was the day she could see the kitchen.

CHAPTER 25

CORA

Cora made a mad rush to Cole's house right after school, not even stopping to drop Atty off at home. Today was the day the kitchen cabinets, countertops, and appliances were installed. She'd given Cole several suggestions for each item, but she couldn't wait to see how it all came together.

During the renovation he always asked for her favorite choices, but she made sure to let him know that all the options she gave him were good. In fact, when they'd been picking out items, she hadn't even added her favorites to the various lists of choices for lighting, flooring, paint colors, fixtures, and appliances. While they talked about all of it, she never pressured him to select any particular thing.

She tried not to let her eyes linger too long on the retro turquoise Smeg refrigerator, a dream of hers. Not only was it expensive, but it wouldn't fit in the small, confined space she had for a full size fridge. She didn't let her gaze stray to the Aga cookers or the beautiful cabinets she would have selected. She loved the idea of beige cabinets with glass doors, creamy quartz countertops with the appliances giving the room pops of color and added warmth.

For Cole's house, she suggested a more modern aesthetic.

She knew he disliked old things, always thinking back to the hand me downs of his childhood. So, she added sleek, sophisticated options to the lists she made for him. She was always reminding herself that this wasn't her house, wasn't meant to be her dream.

The kitchen would be the first time that an entire room was complete. She'd been distracted all day at the thought of seeing it. Cole had done a first rate job of keeping it a secret. When she finally arrived at the house, she and Atticus were out of the car and flying to the door in moments. Cole met her there, smiling at her eagerness.

"Well hello, you two. In a hurry?" he asked when he saw them.

He gave her a quick kiss on the cheek, a habit they'd developed since returning from spring break. It made Cora's heart flutter, but she told herself it was just a friendly greeting, no different than hugging Eliza or patting a student on the back.

"Out of the way, Mister. I need to see this kitchen. It's all I've thought about all day."

"Have at it."

Cora rushed through the side entry and stopped short at what she saw. She turned to take it all in. It couldn't be. As she looked around, she realized that Cole hadn't picked a single thing off the lists she'd given him. Rather, everything in the room was from her dream, one she hadn't even shared. She turned to look at him, finding him leaning in the doorway.

"How?" she stuttered. "I don't understand. I can't—." She couldn't seem to find the right words. "I never told you."

"You didn't have to. I saw your face when you saw what

you loved. I know your style from your house. I know you," he replied.

"But why?"

"I like what you like. I knew it would make you happy," he said easily.

"But it's not my kitchen. Why does it matter?"

Her heart was beating a fast rhythm of dread and panic and a kind of foolish hopefulness. She wasn't ready for this. She couldn't be. She had to think of Jeff, of her vow. *No, no, no* was the steady refrain in her head.

"Cora, surely you know the answer to that."

"Say it. Tell me why," she demanded.

"You aren't ready. Don't push me. Not today. Just enjoy your beautiful work."

"Say it," she said in a voice tight with anxiety.

"No."

"Say it," she said again louder.

She couldn't stop pushing him, suddenly full of panic and fury. This kitchen was tangible proof that she'd let it all go too far. She'd been pretending that her vow was still intact, that she was merely helping a friend, but this room was a testament to the fact that the vow was well and truly broken. Every detail of this room was all for her, clearly a labor of love. Here in the bright light of day was everything they'd never said but felt. She wanted to cry in anguish. Instead, she took heartache, turned it into anger, and focused every bit of it on Cole.

"Say it," she bit out one final time.

"Because I'm madly in love with you. Because I want this kitchen to be yours. Because I want you to be mine. There, is that what you wanted?"

She was shaking her head no before he even finished, tears running down her face.

"I can't. I'm not—It's not," she stammered. "I have to go. Come, Atticus."

"Nice. You push me to say what you already know, what you must feel from me, and then you run. Nice, Cora. I was just trying to please you. Just let it be a kitchen. It doesn't have to be more than that."

He sounded mad and desperate and miserable.

"I have to go now," she said, and she was out the door as fast as she entered.

She sped to her car, Atticus running to keep up with her. She fled that kitchen and that house and that man like she was fleeing the scene of a crime. The last thing she saw as she looked back was Cole standing in the driveway, his hands in his hair, despair on his face. Though it broke her heart, she gunned the gas and flew home, her real home.

Once there, Cora went through her chores as if on autopilot, just trying to keep her tears at bay. And when the animals were fed, and Atty was taken care of for the evening, she disappeared to her room to grieve in the dark. She didn't want food. She didn't want to reach out to Eliza. She didn't want anything that her regular comforts could provide. Fully dressed, she toed off her shoes and climbed straight under the covers. Even though it was late spring, she was chilled to the bone, turning the electric blanket on high to chase away the cold that pervaded every part of her. Only then, surrounded by a cocoon of blankets in the dark did she let go and let the tears fall.

She thought of Cole's words. He was madly in love with her, said with a scowl and enough anger to make a woman think he hated the whole idea. That was so like him, so familiar to her now that she knew him so well. She *had* forced it out of him. He knew that, but she pushed him anyway.

Now, she let herself think about that kitchen. Not once had she hinted at what she would choose. Certainly, he could have a clue from her own house. She and Jeff had certainly tried to make the dream a reality on their budget. Her own cabinets were a similar color, but she painted them herself and installed the glass doors, all from Angelo's store. The overall aesthetic was similar, a country kitchen with a French feel. There was a neutral pallet, a bright, inviting space with touches of her favorite mossy green and slate blue, a hint of yellow here and there, everything with a patina of age, a nod to another time.

However, Cole's kitchen was her dream made real in every way and with no worry about expense. The Aga, the Smeg refrigerator, the high-end cabinets that were exactly what she'd wanted for her own. It was uncanny, like he'd read her mind. She made modern choices for him to match his sleek, minimalist style. Yet, none of his choices were on the list of options she'd given him. None of them were selections he made with himself in mind. They were all for her. It was the grandest gesture anyone had ever made for her.

Everything, from the pot rack hanging from the ceiling just waiting for gleaming copper pans to the extra faucet over the Aga to use for filling large pots to put on the stove, was plucked straight from her wildest dreams. There was even a marble slab on the new island for baking. How did he know? He could have guessed the colors from her own kitchen, could have seen her looking at the refrigerator or Aga, but he put all of it together in such a perfect way. To be seen and known like that made her feel naked and vulnerable but also loved.

And that was the problem. She had been unfaithful to Jeff and their life together. She cried all over again for that. Cora reminded herself that no marriage would ever compare to the one she shared with Jeff. She reminded herself of the loneliness of her childhood and the complete eradication of that by Jeff's love and care. She listed all the things that made her life full and whole, busy and vibrant. To open her heart that way again, especially with a man so different, that was the perfect recipe for heartache. Maybe Cole was enamored with her, but it wouldn't last.

Deep in her heart she didn't believe anyone would stay enamored with her for very long, a vestige of childhood pain. Her parents found her lacking so wouldn't everyone else? That was what had made Jeff's love so special. It had staying power. It was caring, devoted, and kind. It didn't push her or challenge her. Everything with Jeff had been as easy as breathing, all except for the part where he died and left her forever.

But Cole—he was altogether different. He was often harsh. He didn't care what others thought. He challenged her vow. He made her think. He wasn't easy. What she saw in his eyes when he looked at her scared her and excited her. It seemed impossible that a man like that could be hers.

But that kitchen spoke of devotion and attention. A kitchen he wanted to be hers hinted at a shared life. That wasn't a brief affair, a trampled heart. Was she wrong? He seemed so desperate for her to let it go, to simply accept that he liked what she liked. There had been panic in his eyes when she pushed him and fear when he made his confession of love, almost like he expected her to run. He'd even said she wasn't ready. If anything, he seemed as vulnerable and overwhelmed as her in that moment.

All night Cora tossed and turned. Sleep never found her. The next morning, she went through her routine again on autopilot. She checked her phone every few minutes, hoping for a text from Cole, wanting to text him herself. She looked up the hill as she left for school, hoping to see his truck, some glimpse of him. But there was nothing, and so, she carried on.

She taught lessons. She fed animals. She went to meetings. She cooked. She cleaned. And she did it all again. On the fourth day, she finally sent a text, but she got no reply other than the confirmation it had been read. Worse, she hadn't seen his truck in all the days since they'd parted.

In the nearly five months she'd known Cole, they hadn't gone a day without seeing one another, except for her spring break trip and his return to Texas. Even then, they texted and called. Now he was gone. It seemed to her that he disappeared, not just from her life, but from the place altogether. On day five, she let herself drive up to his house and found no truck and the house in darkness. That evening she met Eliza for pizza. The minute she saw her friend sitting in their corner booth at Prima, she broke.

"Oh honey, what is it? Is it your family? A student? Atticus? What happened?"

All of this was asked before she even opened her mouth. That's how bad she looked, how apparent her sadness was.

"Well, there goes my plan for not talking about it."

"Why would you ever plan not to talk to me about something? What is the point of having a best friend then? Spill it now before I panic," Eliza replied.

There over their favorite pizza and red wine, Cora let it all out. It was a teary mess of words, but she said everything that was in her heart.

"Honey, I love you dearly. You know that. And I know firsthand what you felt for Jeff. I was here for all of it. You can't betray a dead husband by finding another love. You know that, right? Your vows were for life, not death. And more than that, your sweet, wonderful Jeff would never have wanted that or asked that of you. Your happiness made him happy." Eliza laid her hand over Cora's on the table. "Your vow is about your fear. It's your way of protecting yourself from any more loss or ever experiencing rejection again like you felt as a child."

Cora wanted to protest, even opened her mouth to do so but stopped.

"Is that true?" she asked instead, and Eliza nodded.

"Do you really want to live the rest of your life without Cole?"

Just the thought made Cora shudder. But what had she thought would happen? Had she planned for them to only be friends forever? Had she truly imagined he would be satisfied hanging out with her with no promise of more? How would she handle watching him date and fall in love with someone else? If that happened, he would be lost to her forever. She realized that she hadn't let herself think it all out, hadn't wanted to entertain life without him. Yet, she was too fearful to grab hold of a life with him.

"I'm so afraid, Eliza."

"I know, honey. I know. But the man who built that kitchen for you, who took care of you when you were sick, who has shown over and over again that he adores you, he's a safe place to land, Cora. You can trust him."

"How can you be sure? How can you know all this when I didn't?" she asked.

"It's so easy to see from the outside. I've seen how he

looks at you, how you look at him, how he speaks to you and about you. I know what adoration and devotion look like. And so do you. You just haven't been willing to see it."

"It's too late. He's gone. He won't answer my texts. He isn't at his house. I've lost him," Cora said through fresh tears.

"He'll come back. Trust me. He either got called away for something he can't control, or he went away to lick his wounds. But a man that looks at a woman like he looks at you will always come back. You just need to make sure you're ready when he does. You can't reject him a second time."

"I don't understand how this happened. I've been fine on my own, just fine," Cora said.

"No, you haven't, sweetie. You've been stuck. I want you to think about something. Okay?" Eliza asked, and Cora nodded. "When we line dance, what do you always say is the hardest part of any dance?"

Cora was puzzled by the question but answered anyway. The restarts," she said.

"Exactly," said Eliza with a sweet smile. "You always say that it's so hard to remember when to restart. In fact, someone always tends to call them out to us because we forget. Life is like that, too, Cora. You've been dancing the same dance for years, and now it's time to restart. Don't miss it."

Cora drove home with a heavy heart. She was finally ready to accept that she was in love with Cole, which was a relief, but now she was afraid she'd left it too late. In her driveway, she glanced up toward his house. In recent months, it had loomed large with bright, welcoming lights. Tonight she saw only darkness.

She checked her phone again for a reply to her text. Nothing. She sent a brief message: *Hope you're okay. Thinking of you.* It was bland and generic, but at least she was reaching out. She wasn't going to bare her heart and soul in a text. Once again, it was read without a reply. So, she screwed up her courage and called only to have it go straight to voicemail. He was definitely done with her.

How many times could one heart break? She went to bed crying and woke up the same way. And so it went on for six more endless days. She didn't call again or text. She'd messed up, rejected him, and now, she would pay the price.

CHAPTER 26

COLE

COLE READ AND re-read Cora's brief texts, hoping he'd missed some hidden declaration of care, some hint of regret, but there was nothing. Clearly, Cora was merely checking on him. Her big, tender heart was probably sorry he was hurt, even if she didn't want him. It was typical Cora. She showed care for everything and everyone. He didn't want pity or regret. He wanted her heart, and it was clear it wasn't ever going to be available to him.

He refused to let himself text back. If he told her why he left, told her that Joe was dead, that he'd left everything he had in the world to Cole, she would seek to comfort him, to help him, and they would be right back where they started. He needed her. Good grief, the longing was ridiculous. He, who'd been alone for his entire life, suddenly needed one woman to comfort him, to hold him, and to love him. And she would. That was her nature, the essence of her heart. But it wouldn't be what he really wanted. It wouldn't be because she was as desperately in love with him as he was with her. It would be out of friendship, loyalty, and kindness.

His whole life felt like a mess. Cole prided himself on keeping everything neat and orderly. He ran a tight ship on his construction sites, was a minimalist when it came to possessions, and didn't let fickle emotions guide his decisions. Yet, in the space of a few months, he'd fallen in love with someone who would perpetually belong to a dead man and then lost the one other person who'd ever been true family to him. The neat compartments of his life were no match for the power of love and loss.

He had Cora to thank for the fact that he'd finally told Joe he loved him. In opening his heart to her, he'd apparently opened it in every way. In the weeks since his conversation with Joe about his feelings for Cora, he'd called him more often. One night as they said goodbye, he felt compelled to tell him how he felt.

"Joe," he said softly. "Thank you."

"For what? For talking to you on the phone?" the older man asked.

"For all you've done for me. For taking me in. For saving my life," Cole said, uncommon tears springing into his eyes.

"It was my pleasure, Cole. I love you, son. And for the record, you saved me too. You gave me a new purpose, made life new again."

Cole took a moment to let those words sink in, a lone tear streaking down his cheek.

"I love you, too, Joe. I really do."

They'd spoken nearly every day after that, and while they never again mentioned that tender conversation, it did create a new connection between them. When his foreman called him the morning after his disastrous kitchen reveal, he'd sobbed at the news that Joe was dead after suffering a massive heart attack. It was a huge loss, and coming on the heels of his fight with Cora, it nearly broke him. The one peaceful thought he had was gratitude that he'd finally told Joe he loved him.

Now on top of his grief, there was also the endless legal rigamarole with the inheritance. He'd already bought Joe out of the construction company years ago, but that man had a finger in a bunch of pies and a house and land to boot. It made Cole smile to think that Joe, who drove an old beat up truck covered in dust from a work site and enjoyed nothing more than a burger from a fast food joint, had actually been a very wealthy man. Most people didn't see beyond the hard hat. Joe never cared for fine things. He used his money to help people.

Cole would be selling most of what Joe left behind, but it would be months before it was all done. He'd already made himself a wealthy man in his own right, already bought himself the security his childhood lacked. Now Joe made him even richer. The funny thing was he'd felt richer when he had Joe alive and well in his life. The money left him cold.

That's why he found himself sitting at the end of the bar in an old familiar Texas honky tonk. It was a week after he left Cora and a typical lively Saturday night at The Rooster. The bar was packed. Every table was occupied, and anyone not sitting and drinking was line dancing. It should have felt like comfort. After all, it's where he'd spent many other Saturday nights. But now, it just felt like loss. It made him long for Cora even more.

He wanted to line dance with her, to watch her spin and step and laugh. He wanted to buy her a drink and watch her get tipsy on just a few sips of something with a ridiculous name. He wanted to drink her in and collect all that joy and beauty for himself.

But instead, he was nursing a beer and trying not to make

eye contact with the blonde at the other end of the bar who was staring his way. He didn't recognize her, but he knew the deal, knew what could happen when two lonely, single people started making eyes at a bar. He'd been there, done that, and now he just wanted the one woman he didn't think he could ever have.

Why had she pushed him? He warned her. He told her to let it be. He knew she wasn't ready, wasn't even close to being ready to hear his declaration. But she just kept pushing. To be honest, it had all happened accidentally at first. He was ordering the light fixtures when he saw her looking at the brochures of vintage appliances. She'd already chosen a few high end stainless steel models for him to look at. Yet, the whole time he was talking to Bill at the service desk, Cora had been pouring over the Aga stoves and the Smeg fridges.

Her eyes lit up, and her fingers kept sweeping across the glossy photographs. Time and again her hands lingered over the colors she liked. As naturally as if he'd done it forever, Cole logged those choices in his mind. When it came time to order, he chose the things that Cora would choose for herself. Then it just became habit; to watch her when she wasn't looking, to see what she lingered over when he was busy elsewhere.

Late at night, as he drifted off to sleep, he imagined her in that kitchen, cooking their meals. He imagined moving up behind her as she stirred a pot on the stove, pushing her hair aside to kiss her neck. He could see himself twirling her around in a dance as they cleaned up together or lifting her onto the counter for an altogether different activity. He wanted those things more than he wanted to breathe. However, the moment he voiced that to her, that desire for it to be her kitchen, she bolted, and the look on her face had broken him in two.

It was abject fear, complete bewilderment. Had she really not been anywhere close to being on the same page as him? Sure, he knew she was still mourning, still dedicated to Jeff, but he'd sensed a shift in her over the months of working together. He'd felt affection and care. He'd imagined that she was moving at her own steady pace to the same spot as him. But she hadn't been doing that at all. It wasn't just that they were on different pages. It seemed now it hadn't even been the same book.

For a moment, he let himself imagine selling the house as it was, just making a phone call and having a realtor handle it. He could leave his things behind. He didn't care about them anyway. He could come back to Texas and go back to doing what he did best, building fancy new houses on golf courses and picking up women like the blonde across the bar.

Right this minute, he could give her a wink and go home with her, and it would put an end to any possibility of anything with Cora. It would force him to let her go because he knew he would tell her. He didn't have it in him to keep that secret. What he felt for her was pure love, and to touch another woman would be a betrayal. Cora would never put up with an unfaithful man. Hell, she was still faithful to a man who'd been gone for five years. If he cheated now, it would be over forever before it ever started.

The thought made his gut churn. He didn't want the blonde across the bar or any other woman. He wanted Cora. He would always want only Cora. The thought of not seeing her, of never hearing her laugh again made him feel dead inside. Right then and there, he decided. He would finish up here as fast as he could and head back to New York. A lifetime of friendship with Cora was better than even one more day without her.

CHAPTER 27

CORA

ANOTHER STRING OF endless days passed with no word from Cole. Cora felt she might be slowly going insane. She, who was usually so excited to be with her students, her animals, so content in her routines, was just numb, just passing time. She hadn't felt this lost since Jeff died, and the strangest part was that this seemed just a little harder because she knew it was her fault.

When Jeff died, she knew she'd done everything she could for him. No one could have loved him more or better. She hadn't left anything unsaid, had no regrets. The end was a clean cut with a sharp knife. It left her sliced and bloody, but it wasn't a jagged wound. This with Cole was something else entirely, an infected cut that wouldn't heal. She left everything unsaid, nothing but regret on the table. She ran away and left the man she loved hurt and rejected. With his disappearance, she was left with no way to repair anything, no way to make things right. There was so much she needed to say to him and nothing but silence into which she could speak.

Oh, how she missed him. She still cooked enough for him, still thought of him when she planned her day. She missed his rare smiles, his sexy swagger, his complete and rapt attention when she spoke. She even missed his gruff harshness when he was worried or scared for her. She missed his care. She knew now that what she really missed was his love. All along he'd been showering her with love, and she'd refused to acknowledge it.

She missed the way he made her heart race, the way he made her think, the way he challenged her. She missed everything they'd done together, the little routines that brightened every corner of her life. This grief was unbearable because it was unnecessary. She caused it, and now that she saw the error of her ways, she was stuck in hell without him. And it showed. She'd lost her appetite and had a gaunt, frail look with too big eyes set in a too thin face. Her usually sunny personality and ready smile all but vanished.

By Friday afternoon after school, she was done. She let Atticus out of the car and left everything else in it. Without stopping at the door, she headed straight down the hill to the bench where she went to talk with Jeff, right beside the blooming pink cherry tree she'd planted in his memory. She knelt down at the foot of the bench in the carpet of pink petals and sobbed. Drained of energy, filled with despair, she cried so hard her body shook.

"I didn't mean for this to happen, Jeff. You know I didn't. I always keep my promises. But Cole just showed up. I tried to deny it. I ignored it. I fought it. But it just kept growing, and now I've ruined it and broken my vow to you all at once."

Before Cole came along, Cora often came to the tree to talk to Jeff. It was where she said aloud anything that was troubling her. The act of saying it all aloud always seemed to calm her and help her find a way forward. Once Cole appeared in her life, she'd quickly shifted to talking to him, and so, she hadn't been to the tree in months. Funny, she hadn't noticed that until now. Oh, how blind she'd been.

"I'm so sorry. I know you didn't ask for any vow. It's not who you were or how you wanted me to live. You would never have wanted me to be alone. I see that now. Eliza made me see that. You know what a straight shooter she is. I've got to let you go. I'll always love you and what we had together. You saved my life in many ways, my love, but I need to let you go now. I love Cole, and I want to build a life with him, or at least that's what I'm going to do if I ever find him."

The thought of never seeing him again had her sobbing all over again. With no worry about being seen or heard, Cora cried until she was nothing but a raw nerve, a human tear. She cried until it hurt, until her eyes were swollen, and her throat was dry. When that storm of emotion passed, she drew a deep breath and looked up. She didn't trust her eyes. There just at the edge of the grassy area where she sat, she saw Cole. But he was turning away as if to walk back up the hill. She knew in her heart it was likely just a mirage born of sorrow, but she called out his name just the same.

CHAPTER 28

COLE

COLE WASTED NO time exiting the airport parking lot. As the busy interstate gave way to the winding country roads of the Hudson Valley, he felt a pressing need to get to Cora immediately. It had been another week of tedious legal dealings before he'd been free of Texas. He hadn't contacted her at all. What he needed to say would be said in person.

He spent the flight rehearsing what he would say, how he would sell her on the idea of them as a couple. He was done just being her buddy, done not holding her hand, not sleeping next to her in bed, not having the right to love her out loud. If she rejected him, he liked to think he was strong enough to walk away, but the truth was he knew he wouldn't leave. He knew it that night at the bar, and he knew it now. He was meant to be wherever she was, and he wouldn't ever stop fighting for more.

When he pulled into her driveway, he was fired up with purpose. He was going to win her heart come hell or high water. He strode right up to the door and knocked. Nothing. He knocked again. Her car was in its spot, so he knew she was here somewhere. He tried the door handle, but it was locked. Was she napping? Was she sick? Beginning to worry, he went to the back gate and quickly surmised she wasn't in her back-yard either. Now running, he made a beeline down the hill to the barn and the animals. That's when he heard her.

It was late afternoon, the sun less aggressive in the sky, the winds light. The day would be classified as fair according to any weather report, but the sound he heard made a lie of that. Somewhere there was a storm. She was crying. No, that was too soft a word. She was sobbing, even wailing, deep cries of anguish. He followed the sound down into the valley to the rushing stream that marked the end of her property. There, in a small alcove of trees he'd never noticed, he found her. She was on the ground, in a little ball of despair, and in front of him he saw something that stopped him cold.

She was crying at the foot of a tree with a bench right under it. The spent pink blossoms of the weeping cherry carpeted the ground, surrounding her. On the bench, there was a plaque that read: *To My Beloved Husband, I'll Meet You Under the Cherry Tree One Day Soon.*

Cole felt his heart fracture at the realization that while he'd been planning how to win her heart, she was weeping over the loss of Jeff, a man he clearly couldn't compete with and a love she obviously still mourned. Her heart was still full of her long dead husband, and it didn't look like there was any room for him there.

These were the cries of someone in agony. She hadn't been home missing him and hoping they could be more. She'd been here awash in the grief that lived right beside her every day. He turned to go, to make the steep climb back up to the truck. There was no place for him here, and he was very glad she hadn't noticed him.

"Cole? Cole?" he heard behind him as he moved away. "Is that you? Please say it's you."

He turned to find her wet eyes staring at him like he was water in a desert.

"Yes, Cora. It's me. I was just coming to tell you I was back. I don't want to intrude."

Then she did the one thing he would never have expected and would always remember. She launched herself off the ground and ran to him, wrapping him in a hug so tight, he stumbled and took both of them to the soft ground cushioned with pink petals. He landed on his knees with her wrapped around him like a koala bear.

"I'm so sorry," she murmured into his neck again and again like a prayer.

He did what came naturally to him. He rubbed her back and stroked her hair. He held her tightly and rocked back and forth trying to soothe her. He murmured soft words to calm her. She was still crying. Her tears wet his neck and spilled onto his shirt.

"It's alright, baby. Whatever it is. It's alright. We'll make it alright."

He said this over and over, the endearment rolling off his tongue automatically. She just kept crying and apologizing. He pulled back and gently lifted her away from him so he could see her face.

"Cora, stop apologizing. What are you sorry for? What's wrong? Let me help."

Moments ago, he'd been a broken mess, but he couldn't handle her sorrow. He had to set his pain aside and help her.

"I should have told you before you left. I should have told you months ago. I was so foolish, so sure it couldn't happen again. But it was fear, I think. Please forgive me."

Her gorgeous watery eyes were staring at him with so much emotion. He didn't trust what he saw. It looked like love. Her fierce hug felt like love, but he wasn't taking anything for granted. She had, after all, been sobbing in anguish at the foot of a bench dedicated to her dead husband.

"What are you talking about?"

She smiled then.

"I love you. I'm in love with you, and I think it happened almost immediately, but you scared me, and I didn't believe I could feel this twice, and I made a vow, and…"

He would never know how she intended to finish that little monologue because he was kissing her with all the passion, love, and longing he'd felt for months. The miracle of it was that she responded in kind. When they finally took a breath, he looked down at her. He cupped her precious face in both his big hands, overwhelmed with wonder and joy that this woman he adored would be his.

"I love you too, baby, so very much. From the moment I first met you, I've been yours."

Because he couldn't resist, he kissed her again.

"Cole, I'm sorry I was so stubborn and scared. I thought I lost you."

"No. I was afraid, so afraid you were never going to love me back, that you'd never be mine. I spoke out of frustration and fear. I wouldn't have been able to leave you, not ever. You're everything to me, Cora."

"But you did leave, and you stayed away without a single word."

There was such agony in her voice. His fierce angel was brought low, and it was all wrong. He continued stroking her face, smoothing her hair, touching her constantly just because he could.

"I told you about Joe. Do you remember?" he asked.

She nodded.

"Well, he passed a few weeks ago. I got the call just after our big fight, and I had to go back to Texas."

"Why didn't you tell me?" Cora asked.

"You were so upset with me about the kitchen."

"Regardless, you had to know I would have cared that you suffered such a loss."

"I was gutted by our fight. When I got the call, I just left. I wasn't thinking clearly. But you did help me even if you didn't know it."

"How?" she asked.

"Joe was so good to me, treated me like a son, and I'm afraid I didn't know how to treat him like a father. I enjoyed spending time with him, but I always kept him at a distance. Without you, I don't think I would have ever realized I loved him. Before you, I didn't know what love felt like. Thanks to you, I told him I loved him and how much he changed my life."

"I'm so sorry you lost him. I wish I could have been with you, and if I'd stopped being stubborn sooner, maybe I would've been. I let you down," she said.

He hugged her fiercely, pressing her face into his neck, his arms a tight band around her.

"No, Cora. No. You had to figure things out. You're entitled to that. I found out about Joe, and I ran away, which is exactly what I accused you of doing."

Cole was stunned to find himself crying, tears running down his face unchecked as he rocked Cora on his lap. She pulled back and looked at him. Cole had the feeling he was being truly seen for the first time in his life. She gently wiped the tears away, kissed him, and put her small hand on his heart.

"Both of us were confused. I didn't think this kind of love

could happen to me again. I didn't trust it. I just wanted to stay in my safe cocoon. Clinging to Jeff, as much as I loved him, kept me at a distance. If I didn't risk my heart, I couldn't be hurt anymore. You broke through that wall I'd put up, and it terrified me. It took me too long to trust you. Because of that, I wasn't with you when you needed me."

"Sweet girl, you're exactly what I need, and you have been from the first time I saw you. I was so scared that I'd pushed you too far that day in the kitchen. I was afraid to talk to you or text you, for fear you'd just tell me to leave you alone. I just wanted to take care of things for Joe and get back to you. But once I got there, I was shocked by my grief. Joe was my family."

He stopped then and let more tears fall. It felt good to acknowledge all that Joe meant to him, to share it with her.

"On top of that, Joe left everything to me so there was estate stuff to handle, and it's not done yet. Finally, I just had to get back to you."

She snuggled deeper into his arms, and the sweetness of that rocked him to his core. This woman he loved was seeking refuge in him.

"But when I realized you were here, you were walking away. Cole, you were leaving again."

Cora's face remained buried in his neck as she said this. He gently pulled her back and looked at her.

"I thought you were crying for Jeff, crying because you wanted him. It broke my heart, and I couldn't stand here and watch that."

"No, sweetheart, no. I was telling Jeff what I'd done, how I'd been too afraid, how I'd let you go. I was crying for *you*."

"Say it again," he said, aware his voice had gone husky at the endearment.

"What?" she said with mischief in her eyes. "You want to hear me say I was crying for you again?"

"Damn it, woman, you know what I want, and it sure as hell isn't about your tears," he all but growled at her. Pulling her close, his lips a breath from hers, he said, "Say it again."

"Okay, sweetheart, I will."

That was all that was said for a while because he was kissing the breath out of her.

CHAPTER 29

CORA

SHE WAS WAITING outside with Atticus in the strong summer sun. Cole would be here any minute. They'd been together for almost six weeks, him still living up at the big house and her still in her cottage. Cole instinctively understood her need to take it slow. While they spent a lot of time together, especially since it was her summer break, they still maintained their own spaces.

She'd been alone a long time, and he'd been alone forever. She felt like they needed to pace themselves so that this fiery love didn't burn out before it had a chance to grow. Most of their days were spent working on his house. They shared meals and often talked or made out like teenagers late into the night. Yet, Cole always stopped it there, going up the road to his lonely bed without her. She wanted more, and she knew he did too, but both of them were protective of what they shared, not wanting to rush it.

Today they were heading up to the lookout that she'd only shared with Jeff. She'd been unsure if this was a good idea. It was a somewhat edgy move given how big a role her relationship with Jeff had played in keeping them apart for so many months. But her gut told her it might be exactly what they needed. They'd spent the last six weeks enjoying each other's company, sharing quiet conversations late into the night, snippets of their childhoods, hopes and dreams, silly stories.

However, they hadn't talked at all about their future, nor had they really spoken of Jeff. It felt like the weight of what they didn't say was taking up more space than the joy of what they shared. It was time to do something about that. She couldn't help but smile as Cole pulled into the driveway. She was rushing to him as he all but leapt out of the big truck to get to her.

"Hey baby," he said in that voice that made the blood in her veins sizzle. "I missed you."

He grabbed her in a tight hug as he always did in the mornings. She let the warmth of him soak into her bones, an entirely different sensation than the heat of the sun on her skin. He held on tight, the hug lasting a long time as he buried his face in her neck. Then he pulled back and kissed her, not just a morning peck but a deep, lush kiss of passion and longing.

"There," he said, "That's better. I needed my Cora Lane fix this morning." Brushing her hair back from her face, he looked at her with so much affection, she felt the truth of it in her bones. How's my girl?"

"I'm so good," she said. "So very good."

"Is that so? And what do you think is causing all this goodness?" he asked, winking at her, and making parts of her flutter that had only recently come back to life.

He was flirting with her, and it was delicious.

"Well," she said, drawing the word out, "There's this sexy man who keeps coming over here and kissing me and holding me and saying things that make me all hot and bothered. I think that might have something to do with it."

He was about to kiss her when she continued, "But also, it's a really nice day out so that might be it. Never can tell."

Cole goosed her in her side causing her to giggle and try to get away. He caught her to him, his arm a steel band around her waist.

"Cora Leigh Lane, love of my life, you better take that back right now," he said as he planted fervent kisses on her cheeks.

"I don't know what you mean. It really is a gorgeous day."

He tickled her again, making her fight to get free.

"Stop," she said in between giggles. "Let me go, you caveman."

"Never," he said in a voice more serious than she expected in the playful moment.

She looked up in surprise and found him staring at her.

"I'll never let you go, baby. Not ever. You're mine, every last inch of you. All mine. You got that?"

The hand that had been tickling her now held the side of her neck, caressing and yet possessive at the same time.

"You promise, Cole Houston?"

He leaned even closer, moving their faces toward one another until their noses were touching, and she could feel the warmth of his breath.

"It's more than a promise. It's my life's work. It's everything," he said fervently before leaning in to kiss her. When they finally broke free, he said, "We better get going, or we're never going to leave."

Soon they were in the truck with Atty settled on the backseat behind them. Cora had packed a picnic basket along with Atty's treats and water bowl. She pulled her sunglasses down from her head and settled her head back against the seat. Cole focused for a few moments on pulling onto the busy highway, and Cora found herself lost in thought.

Their moment in the driveway was intense and passionate, as was always the way with them. One minute they would be snuggling on the couch or laughing about something silly, and then they would be all over each other. She would think: *This is it. This is THE moment.* But Cole reined it in each and every time.

Not only did he not take the physical passion any further, but he rarely let their talks wander into discussions of a shared future. Was he scared it would spook her and cause her to pull back? Or, was he scared for himself, in too deep, and already regretting it? She rubbed her hand over her chest because either answer made her heart ache.

"You okay?" he asked, reaching over and holding her hand.

"I'm fine."

"You don't sound fine. I may be new to this relationship business, but even I know that when a woman says she's fine, she rarely is."

"I was just thinking. That's all."

"About what?" he asked, kissing her hand.

"About us, actually."

"And thinking about us put that look on your face?"

His voice was now laced with worry.

"A few little things worry me. That's all," she said.

This was said as they pulled into the dirt parking lot that led to the start of the hiking trail.

"I don't like the sound of that, Cora," he said, as he cut the engine and turned to face her.

Atty, always attuned to Cora's emotions, stuck his whole

body between their seats and nuzzled Cora. She patted him and said, "I'm okay, buddy."

Then she reached over and put her hand on Cole's thigh, feeling the tense muscles there.

"I love you, Cole Houston. I love you with all that I am. Do you hear me? Having a few worries doesn't change that. We're still new, and I just want to make sure everything goes well."

His face softened as it always did when she told him she loved him, especially when she said it first.

"I love you too, so much. You're everything I think about and dream of. You know that, Cora. Tell me you know that."

She stroked his cheek and smiled at him.

"I know that, Cole. I really do."

Atty was restless, and so she suggested, "Let's hike and talk. How about that?"

He merely nodded, and she mentally kicked herself for making him edgy and unsure. Within minutes they had their backpacks on ready to go. Of course, Cole weighed them in his hand to make sure he got the heaviest bag. Even then, he suggested that he could carry both.

"That's ridiculous, caveman," she said as she wrestled the backpack from him and hoisted it easily onto her back.

"You're a badass, but I'm always going to want to do things for you."

He stroked his finger down her cheek and kissed her gently. With Atty on a long leash and their backpacks loaded, they set off. They walked a few minutes without saying anything.

"So, hit me with it. What worries do you have?" he asked.

"You're holding back with me, being careful, or maybe overwhelmed about getting involved in the first place," she said, just deciding to put it right out there.

He stopped in his tracks.

"Whoa there. Where the hell did that come from? You think *I'm* holding back? You think I regret us? You have to be kidding me."

He was flushed with anger, she thought with shock. She'd hit a sore spot. But before she could think of how to walk it back, she found herself pressed up against a tree, his hand behind her shoulder to prevent her from being scratched by the bark. The other hand cupped her face.

"You listen to me, and you listen good. Got it?" he said in that gruff, growly tone of his.

She nodded.

"I will never have regrets about my love for you. Do you hear me? It's the best thing that's ever happened to me. And I'm damn well not overwhelmed, at least not about our relationship. Am I overwhelmed with what I feel for you? Every day. But it's not because I regret it. It's because it's so big, so intense." She started to speak, and he put a finger over her lips and said, "I'm not done."

"As for holding back," he continued. "Maybe I am. You've felt all this before. You had to take a chance on me, and I'm nothing like Jeff. It took a lot for you to let go of what you had with him, and I'm so grateful you did. But hell yes, I'm going to be careful. I don't want to spook you, don't want you to run, or decide I'm not what you want. I don't want to screw this up."

His words were hissed out, like he was in pain, short and terse and full of emotion. And to her shock, she thought she saw a glimmer of a tear. When he caught her looking, he turned away, staring off into the woods.

"I don't want you to hold back. I want all of you. And for the record, everything about you is perfect for me."

He seemed not to hear her, wasn't even looking at her. So, she reached up and put her hands on his face, directing his gaze back to her.

"Now you listen. Do you hear me?"

His face didn't soften. His gave no hint that he even heard what she said except for the vein pulsing in his temple. He was listening. He was longing. He just didn't want her to see how emotional he was.

"I don't need you to be careful. I'm not going to get spooked. I'm all in. Do you hear me? All in."

She stopped her little rant to place a hard kiss on his frowning lips. That sparked a reaction, his pupils going darker, a hitch in his breath.

"You're a miracle to me, something I didn't even know was possible, a gift I'm not sure I'm worthy of," she said.

He shook his head and looked away from her again, but she moved his face back to hers and said, "Eyes, please."

More heat seemed to darken his eyes at her command.

"I had a good marriage to a good man. And I will always love him because he was the first person who showed me that I was enough. In that way, he saved me. I felt loved and safe. I'll never forget that. And yes, I made a vow, foolish now I see, and utterly unkeepable in the face of you, Cole Houston. I made it to a man on his deathbed, and I let that be my defense against the world, let it keep me and my heart safe. You just punched that wall to rubble and charged right in."

She had his full attention now. His eyes were watery with tears, and the love she saw there threatened to undo her before she could finish what she needed to say.

"As good as that marriage was, I was just a girl then, innocent and naïve. What I feel for you is love, but it's so different than anything I've ever known. I don't understand all the feelings you spark in me. But I know I want to keep feeling this dizzy, buzzy feeling that pulses through my body every time you look at me, every time you kiss me. So, as tough and mean as you seem to think you are, Cole, this prim little schoolteacher thinks every little thing about you is one hundred percent made for me."

Now he grinned.

"I think you're hot for me, baby. Is that what you're saying?" he asked with a devilish twinkle in those still watery eyes.

"Yep, big guy. So hot for you. Can you handle it?"

"Oh, I'm so totally the man for the job."

She let him feel the shiver that his words caused.

"No more holding back. I'm not fragile," she said in all seriousness.

He kissed the tip of her nose and nuzzled her cheek. Atty was growing restless, clearly having explored the area as far as the long leash would allow and now circling their legs like a maniac. They were essentially tied up like captives on a pirate ship.

"We hear you, buddy," Cole said as he unwound the leash and they began walking again.

He grabbed Cora's hand and held tightly.

"I'm not careful because I think you're fragile. You're the strongest person I know. I'm careful because this matters so much. I treat you differently because I'm trying to be the man you deserve."

He was so earnest and sweet in that moment, trying to prove himself to her.

"Do you at least want me like that, though?" she asked.

She could hear the self-doubt in her own voice and hated it. He was more experienced than her, more worldly, and she still worried at times that she was not enough. Those were old fears and hang-ups, and she needed to be honest with him if she was going to put them to rest for good.

"You're kidding, right?" he asked, incredulously. "Tell me you're joking."

She just stared at the dirt path, kicking at a pebble with the toe of her shoe, and said nothing.

Then she mumbled, "You always stop."

"I'm trying to do this right. I'm trying to make sure you want me forever. And you doubt that I want you? That's absolutely unbelievable."

She just stared at the ground some more. All she was doing was making him mad. This was not going how she imagined. Suddenly, she found herself pressed against the trunk of yet another tree, and once again Cole had the presence of mind, even in his frustration, to buffer her shoulder with his hand against the rough bark. He pressed his entire body against hers, allowing her to feel the heat and hardness of him. She took a shaky breath.

"Look at me, baby."

That voice coupled with the feel of him was almost enough to make her swoon. She raised her eyes slowly.

"I want you every minute of the day. I want you when you're painting our future bedrooms in your overalls with your hair piled on your head and when you're wearing those skimpy clothes you wear to yoga. I want you when you're in your pjs asleep in my arms on the couch and when you have magic marker on your fingers and paint on your pants after school. I want you when I'm awake and when I'm sleeping, when I'm with you and when I'm anywhere else. It's as unchangeable and resolute as my love for you."

He stopped to kiss her passionately, running his hands over her body with restless movements.

"And if that's not enough, then hear this. You are the sexiest, most gorgeous creature I've ever seen. I could stare at you all day, touch you all day. But my wanting you isn't about your looks or your hair or what you wear. You breathe, and I get hard. You smile, and my insides light up. We could live in total darkness where I never got the joy of looking at you, and I would still want you with a ferocity that threatened to eat me alive. It's you, baby. It's just you, Cora Lane. And it will always and only be you."

What followed was the kind of kiss that could have made even the trees blush. When they were finally back to the hike, their hands were locked tightly in one another's. For a long time, they didn't say anything, both busy playing and replaying the other's heated words, both awash in the discovery that they were wanted and loved even more than they knew. It felt like something to savor.

CHAPTER 30

COLE

Cole felt like the smile on his face might be more powerful than the sun overhead. As they walked, their linked hands swinging between them, Atty at their side, tail wagging, Cole felt a kind of peace he hadn't known existed. He looked down at Cora and was pleased to note the same wide smile on her face. He'd imagined that getting to love her out loud would change his life. Certainly, loving her even in the most secret part of his heart had already changed him as a man, but the reciprocity of it was powerful.

He was always touching her now, desperate for that connection. It didn't matter if it was just the touch of her hand or the passionate kisses they often shared late at night. The power of her touch was an enigma. How he could be both soothed and excited at the same time was a mystery he thought would never be solved. One mystery he did intend to solve was how on earth she could question how much he wanted her. He thought it was so obvious. Yet, she felt him holding back.

He supposed he was, but only because this love was so new and so precious to him. He'd spoken honestly when he said he wanted to nurture and cherish it, set it apart from every other experience he'd ever had. But he could see it her way. Even though she'd been happily married, she was still so new to the passion that flared so easily between them.

He'd like to be the kind of man who didn't take pride in that, who didn't appreciate there was one thing he had that the sainted Jeff hadn't, but he wasn't. Every single time her pupils dilated, and her breath caught, every time she leaned further into him, grabbing at his hair or his biceps, and especially any rare time she initiated a kiss or a touch, Cole felt a rush of pride. Was it so wrong to want there to be parts of her love that were only for him?

Truthfully, he was happy she'd had such a happy marriage, that there had been someone to love her and take care of her before him. He wouldn't ever begrudge the love of his life her happiness, but he'd be lying if he said he didn't feel a little jealous, a little sad he couldn't have been the first and only man to love her.

Of course, he knew Cora wished the same. She was often a bit preoccupied with these imaginary, perfect women she thought he'd known. While it was true he had been with beautiful women, what would stun Cora, if she could ever fully grasp it, was just how empty those interactions were. Physical release had been the goal. Distraction had been a nice side benefit. Not one of those women ever touched his heart or his mind, much less his soul.

"Cora," he said gently as they walked. "There's nothing better than this right here. Just me and you all alone on this beautiful day."

"I agree. It's pretty perfect."

Soon enough, they reached the spot they were looking for, the picnic table perched at her special lookout.

"Here we are," she said as she shucked off her backpack

and climbed up to sit right on top of the table. "I love it here."

She leaned back, her hands stretched out behind her. Cole copied her motions and sat down right beside her.

"You never told me why you always stopped here," he said.

"Well, we climbed to the top plenty of times, but for some reason we always ended up here every single time. We planned a lot of our life right here."

Cole had to admit he was surprised she wanted to come here today, but he was glad for the break. Most of their days were spent working at his house, but they always ended up at Cora's when the work was done for the day. While he knew it made sense, it still worried him. Of course, Cora wanted to be in her own home, and there were the animals to think of, as well as the simple fact that it was fully furnished. Still, they never spoke of what would happen when his house was done.

Did she think he was planning to live there all alone? Would she ever consider living there with him? Was it even realistic to think she would leave her cottage? The truth was that he was afraid to shake things up, afraid to ask questions for fear that her answers wouldn't match his deepest desires.

"I'm guessing you're pretty confused about why I brought you here. Right? I mean what man wants to visit the special spot his girlfriend shared with another man?"

She grimaced a little as she said it.

"I did wonder," he said, scratching his beard. "But you know me. I'll follow you anywhere."

"Well, I think we may be living with a big elephant in the room," she said.

He sat up at that and turned his big body more fully to hers.

"What elephant?"

"Maybe two elephants," she said.

"That seems like too much elephant for any one room," he said with a frown.

"I agree."

"What, my love, do you propose we do about it?" he asked.

He could see both a playful glint in her eyes and the barest hint of nerves.

"Well, first I think we need to call these two elephants by their names," she said.

He said nothing, just looked at her expectantly. She swallowed hard. The nerves were clearly winning, and the playful glint was disappearing. He wrapped an arm around her and pulled her close, kissing her temple.

When she still didn't speak, he said, "I think you should name them."

"Well, one is Jeff," she said with a sad sigh. "And the other is the fact that in just a few weeks we're going to be done with your house, at least most of the work inside. We haven't really talked about what comes next."

He hated the hesitation in her voice, the hint of fear.

When he didn't respond immediately, she said shakily, "Maybe you aren't ready for what comes next. I shouldn't have brought us here. It was a mistake. I'm being presumptuous. I'm sorry."

Then she dropped her head in her hands. Hell no, he thought.

"Cora," he said, putting his hand under her chin. "Look at me." When she finally raised her eyes to his, he continued," I am one hundred percent ready for whatever comes next with you, always, for the rest of my life. The truth is I don't exactly know what you want *next* to be."

He saw an inkling of hope enter her beautiful eyes at his words, but he still saw doubt.

"I'm in this forever, Cora. You're it for me. The only thing that matters is what you want to come next."

"Well, we've only been together a short time, so I don't want to presume," she said. "I mean it feels like we've been together for a lot longer because we were falling in love from the moment we met, or at least it does to me."

"Me too, since the first moment I saw you, so presume away, baby. You want me to sell my house and live with you? Just say the word. You want to sell your house and live with me? You want to sell them both and move to Tahiti and wear nothing but sunshine and smiles? I'm there for it."

He was trying to lighten the mood, but every option was absolutely true. There was nothing she could ask for, save their being apart, that mattered to him in the least. All he needed was her.

"You'd sell your house?" she asked, clearly stunned at the notion.

"I'd do anything for you. I just want you to be happy and well, happy with me."

"Well, I thought your house made more sense for us. It's bigger, and it's a fresh start. I love my house, but it's a bit small for a family," she stopped mid-thought, eyes wide as she realized what she'd said. "Not that you want a family. I'm sorry. I just…"

He silenced her with a kiss.

When she moved to end the kiss and keep talking, he said, "I'm going to spell a few things out for you so you can stop your fretting. First, I absolutely want you to live with me in my house, our house. Why do you think I've put off furnishing it? I wanted you to do that for us."

He watched her eyes grow round with questions and her mouth open to speak. He silenced her this time with his hand over her mouth.

"Can I trust you to be quiet, or do I need to keep my hand here?"

She nodded, and he moved his hand from her mouth to caress her cheek.

"Next, hell yes, I want a family with you. I want some time alone to love you, a year or two just for us, and then I want however large a family we can have. Let's fill up that big old house."

Once again, she began to speak, and he silenced her this time with just a look. "I'm not done."

He let go of her and stood up from the table to fish in the front pocket of his jeans. When she saw the ring, she gasped. She scooted to the edge of the table to be nearer to where he stood. He knelt in the dirt in front of her.

"Cora Leigh Lane, I don't care how long or short a time we've been together. I've wanted to be your husband almost from the beginning. I've been carrying this ring around in my pocket for weeks, always hoping one day you'd say yes. Please say yes."

He felt the tears welling in his eyes, the thunder of his heart.

"You haven't asked me a question yet, Cole," she said, her attitude sassy but her eyes soft with love.

"Are you ready, Cora? Please don't let me ask if you aren't ready. You say Jeff is an elephant in the room with us, so don't let me ask if you aren't ready to say goodbye to him yet."

He knew he was pleading, heard the desperation in his voice, but he didn't care. He had no pride, no shame with this woman, only love. Tears were running down her face as she reached out to stroke his beard.

"That's why I brought you here today, to tell you that I said goodbye to him weeks ago, to make sure you know that I'm all in, that I'm ready for everything with you. I thought it was a fitting place to let go of the past," she said.

She swiped at her tears and straightened her shoulders as if readying herself.

"Ask me, Cole."

"Cora, baby, will you marry me?"

Before the words were all the way out, she was in his arms.

"Yes, yes, yes!" she squealed with delight.

After a long hug and a longer kiss, he stood up and helped her down from the table. Then, he placed the beautiful emerald cut solitaire on her hand and kissed it.

"It's gorgeous, Cole," she said.

"It has to be to be good enough for you," he said.

"You're too good to me."

"Not possible," he said.

"No, you really are. You've been so patient, so understanding. I don't think I would be the same if our situations were reversed. If you'd loved another woman and were so unwilling to give her up, I'd be crushed. But you just stood by me, kept being my friend, let me set the pace, waited endlessly. I didn't know love like that existed until you, and now I can't imagine ever being without you. I'm so grateful for you."

Cole was moved beyond reason by her words, by the tender tone of her voice. That she could be grateful for him seemed astonishing. *He* was the lucky one. He pulled her to him, burying his face in the crook of her neck, a spot he believed was made just for him. His words were muffled, but judging by the tightness of her grip, she heard just the same.

"I had no choice but to wait for you. It wasn't selflessness. It was need."

They stayed in each other's arms for long moments until Atticus finally announced with a sharp bark that he'd had enough of the mushy stuff. Cora gave him a bone she'd packed and a bowl of fresh water. She and Cole shared a bag of homemade trail mix. They talked of everything and nothing, just happy to bask in the joy of the moment, the promise of a shared future.

At some point, they agreed to a small wedding soon and a long honeymoon somewhere hot and far away. Just before they left, Cora walked closer to the edge of the lookout. Instinctively, Cole reached out for her hand, afraid she might fall.

"I'm fine," she said. "Come stand with me."

He moved closer, tucking her against the shelter of his body.

"It's a beautiful view," he said, looking out at the mountains in the background and the deep green valley below, dotted with farms and houses.

"It is," she said. "But right now, we're saying goodbye. It's time for us to find our own special place."

She blew a kiss into the air and said a soft *goodbye* into the breeze.

Cole surprised himself by speaking aloud. "Thank you. I'll take good care of her. I promise."

The breeze picked up at that moment, fluttering the leaves on the trees and catching whisps of Cora's hair. What seemed like a choir of birds sang out, carried along on that sweet wind. They both felt the weight of the moment, the peace of it, like a heavenly answer to their earthly words.

Neither of them said anything. Cole thought Cora must agree that it was a moment perfect just as it was, without comment. Even Atty sat beside them still and calm, his fur rippling in the breeze. It wasn't until they were in the truck driving away that either of them broke the silence.

Waiting to turn onto the highway, Cole asked, "Where to now, baby?"

She just smiled and said, "Anywhere as long as I'm with you."

He winked at her and turned toward town. He wanted a pizza and a lifetime with Cora. For the first time in his life, he thought he had a good chance of getting everything he ever wanted.

ACKNOWLEDGEMENTS

First and foremost, I want to thank JMK, who must be the number one hype man and dream chaser in the world. From the moment I told you all those years ago that I longed to be a writer, you not only believed in the dream but made sure I pursued it. You're the first reader of everything I write for a reason!

To my parents, I'm grateful to you for introducing me to stories and always saying yes to the giant stacks of books I wanted to check out from the library. In doing so, you introduced me to the wider world and the many wonders to be found there. It's also true that you two are the best book peddlers out there, selling books everywhere you go.

To my children, thank you for taking such an interest, for every time you ask how the writing is going, for showing up at book events, and for believing in the dream too.

To Julia Dahl, words cannot express my gratitude for your skilled editing and guidance. Not only were your suggestions spot on, but your encouragement came at just the right time. Thank you for being a woman who lifts other women up and champions them. And for the record, we both know Cole would not be the character he is without you.

To Samira, a million thanks for the cute and cleverly crafted social media posts that help my books find their readers. Not only do you create the posts and take the photos, but your genuine enthusiasm for my work means the world to me. You are a gift!

This is my first novel, but it is not my first book. *Apricity* only exists because Lulu came first. For that reason, thank you to every parent, child, bookseller, and school who have shown so much love to my little mouse detective.

And finally and always, to Apollo, you keep your part of the deal perfectly. Snoozing while I write and then ready for a long walk in the woods as soon as I shut my computer.

www.ingramcontent.com/pod-product-compliance
Lightning Source LLC
Chambersburg PA
CBHW032345310726
48973CB00007B/1867